AT PRAIRIE'S END

OTHER FIVE STAR WESTERN TITLES BY ROBERT J. HORTON:

AT PRAIRIE'S END

A WESTERN STORY

ROBERT J. HORTON

FIVE STAR

A part of Gale, Cengage Learning

GALE
CENGAGE Learning·

Farmington Hills, Mich • San Francisco • New York • Waterville, Maine
Meriden, Conn • Mason, Ohio • Chicago

GALE
CENGAGE Learning®

LIBRARY OF CONGRESS CATALOGING-IN-PUBLICATION DATA

Horton, Robert J.
    At prairie's end : a western story / by Robert J. Horton. —
First edition.
        pages cm
    "First appeared as a seven-part serial in Street and Smith's
Western story magazine (6/6/31–7/18/31)."
    ISBN 978-1-4328-2769-4 (hardcover) — ISBN 1-4328-2769-3
(hardcover)
    I. Title.
PS3515.O745A83 2014
813'.52—dc23   2014003141

First Edition. First Printing: June 2014
Published in conjunction with Golden West Literary Agency.
Find us on Facebook– https://www.facebook.com/FiveStarCengage
Visit our website– http://www.gale.cengage.com/fivestar/
Contact Five Star™ Publishing at FiveStar@cengage.com

Printed in the United States of America
1 2 3 4 5 6 7 18 17 16 15 14

ADDITIONAL COPYRIGHT INFORMATION

CHAPTER ONE

There was a hitching rail in front of the house by the trail that led from the sweeping lowlands to the deep, green forests that climbed the mounting ridges to the high hills. The golden sunset of an early September evening robbed Nature's paint pots to tint the land with glorious color. Came a scented breeze to laugh in the trees and purr soothingly in the nodding grasses.

The girl ran with the lightness of a nymph to the rail and leaned upon it with her hands, her firm, rounded arms bare, her hair sparkling gold dust and burnished copper in the wind, her supple body weaving as she leaned to look down the trail toward the flowing plain.

"No sign, Mother!" she called over her pretty shoulder in a voice clear and musical and sweet.

"It would be better luck not to look for him," came a voice from the porch. "All these years I've never expected your father until I saw him." The voice was passive, but with no suggestion of weariness. "We better go in to supper, dear."

Hope Campbell looked again into that prairie void, strung with its necklace of pink buttes and girded with its silver ribbon of river. A purple mist seemed to be gathering under the high blue canopy of sky. Hope always had loved this hour, this brief merging of the day with night, when golden youths rode out of the mist on gray chargers and saluted her with kisses flung from laughing lips. Out of the mist someday would come her shining knight, resplendent in purple and gold, with a silver band about his locks, to whisk her away to a lovers' heaven.

She laughed at her fantasy, her full, red lips parting that the pearls behind them might flash in snowy brilliance, then her hazel eyes turned to the mountains in the west, dark and austere against the crimson banners that signaled the end of day.

"Are you coming, Hope?" called her mother from the porch.

"Yes, Mumsey, dear," she answered. And as she reached the steps: "Do you know what I would like to do, Mother, if Bismarck were not still lame, and if Father hadn't forbidden me to ride so late? I'd like to ride . . . up the trail to the timber, and down the trail to where it dips into the plain, and into a cloud, maybe . . . anywhere! Did you ever feel that way, Mother?"

"Once . . . I did," Jane Campbell faltered. "And it ended by my doing it finally, with your father." No bitterness, no irony, just a patient wistfulness—and then the mood was gone. "Don't be silly, Hope. We must have our supper. You cooked it, so I'll put it on the table." She went inside the house while Hope paused, listening to a weird, lonely cry that came from the air above.

At this moment a slight, crab-like man, with arms and legs that crooked, a weasel face, and dark, burning eyes came around the corner of the house and approached her.

"Did you hear them, Miss Hope?" he asked in a querulous voice.

"Did I hear what?" the girl asked, startled at his sudden and silent appearance. "Did I hear what, Vagle?"

The man seemed to shiver and clasped and unclasped his long, slender hands. "The loons, just now," he said softly. "The loons from down at Square Lake."

"Oh, is that what those sounds were?"

"Yes, they were the loons," crooned Vagle. "They have come up quite a way tonight. It ain't often they leave the lake to come this far. This is a long way from the lake, Miss Hope, but they are here."

"Well, they've got to fly around once in a while," said Hope with a trace of annoyance. "Have you had your supper?"

"I know they have to fly once in a while," said the crab man. "But they never fly as far as this, up in the foothills, I mean, unless they come to bring a warning. We must be careful, Miss Hope, for maybe something is wrong."

"Oh, you and your superstitious and wild imagination!" exclaimed the girl impatiently. "You shouldn't have such things in your head. And, why! You've got your gun on again, Vagle." The words came sharply, edged with anger. "Didn't Father tell you not to wear that gun? You know he did, and you must take it off."

"John Campbell knows I wear my gun at night when he's away," said Vagle firmly. "That gun has been fired more than once in John Campbell's cause, Miss Hope. It can be fired again."

"Vagle!" Hope's tone was rather frightened. She had nearly called him "crazy". Her father and mother had cautioned her never to accuse him of being crazy. He wasn't that, but. . . . "How is Bismarck?" she asked gently, turning aside the point.

"He's better. Nawthin' to worry about. You'll be on his back in a day or two, ridin' like a streak."

"Well, you take good care of him and go around for your supper."

"But I can wear the gun, Miss Hope?" he pleaded anxiously.

"Oh, I suppose so," said Hope doubtfully. "But you mustn't shoot it, remember that."

She went thoughtfully into the house. Ordinarily she paid little heed to the hallucinations of Vagle, or to his weird imaginings. He was not quite right in the head at times. No one seemed to know how old he was; it was doubtful if he knew himself. His

9

hair was snow-white and his wizened face was marked with lines and intricate patterns of wrinkles. But he was strong of body and most of the time rational. Occasional comments showed he had led a wild, dangerous life on the open range and in the boisterous cow towns. It was rumored that he had been a formidable gunman. John Campbell had brought him home some years before, and he had charge of the horses and cattle on the place and did other odd jobs. He worshipped Campbell.

Campbell had built his rambling, log structure himself, with such help as he was able to hire. It was neatly whitewashed and had a shingled roof that was painted green. It had a certain appearance of stateliness. It was situated just within the foothills west of the far-reaching plain—the prairie lands of the great, north range. Behind the house were a barn, corrals, and a tidy bit of garden. It was cool and quiet there in summer, and protected from the icy winds of winter by a bulwark of high hills to northward.

"Hope, you look worried about something," said the girl's mother as they sat down to supper. Mrs. Campbell was a slight woman, with large dark eyes, gray hair, and more than mere traces of a former beauty. Her voice was soft and motherly, often passive but never harsh, and she talked the language of the range. "I just gave Vagle his supper in the kitchen and he's wandering in his head again. Something about loons."

"Yes," said Hope. "The loons were flying up from the lake tonight and he said they were a bad omen. When he gets like that, it gives me the shivers."

"You mustn't mind him, sweet. You'll be used to him in no time. You haven't had a chance to get acquainted with his moods, being down to school falls and winters. He's smart in some ways. Somehow I've always felt safe with him around when your father is away."

"I'm glad I'm through with school, Mother," said the girl

impulsively. "I'm glad to be home with you, and it's so comfortable here. Father has made such a nice place."

"Yes," said her mother. "And did you know that we didn't have a title to this place until . . . well, we haven't got it yet."

"What?" Hope stared in surprise. "Doesn't Father own it?"

"He will own it, dear, in December. You see this is government land and it wasn't open to entry until year before last when this part at this end of the range was opened. John filed at once and by paying a dollar and a quarter an acre on our hundred and sixty acres in December we get title."

"But with Father building and doing all this work, and running cattle, I don't see. . . ." Hope stopped speaking with a puzzled frown.

"Very well, you must know all about it," said her mother, "but you must never mention what I tell you to anyone, not even your father. This is a beautiful place, dear. We have water and pasturage and our land runs down into the prairie. They say that someday they'll even grow wheat here." She lowered her tone and nodded her head. "It's the best place of its kind hereabouts. Your father picked a good spot. But we couldn't buy it because it belonged to the government and is what they call homestead land. We've been living here for years as"—her voice became a whisper—"squatters. That isn't a nice word on this or any other range, Hope. But it was the only way we could eventually own it, because by squatting on it and living on it we would have the first right to file on it when the land was opened for homestead entry."

She paused to fill their cups with more tea. Hope was listening intently. After a space she resumed.

"As soon as it was open for entry, your father filed on it. If we were to go on living on it for five years, we would get it free. But we are getting title to it in fourteen months by paying a dollar and a quarter an acre. Then we own it with title direct

11

from the government, which is the best title of all."

"But there's more than this land that can be settled on that way, isn't there, Mother?" asked Hope.

"Most of it has been taken by big stockmen," replied Mrs. Campbell. "They had their 'punchers file on quarter sections and the 'punchers will deed them over to the ranchers. Besides, no outsider would dare to come in here and file. Which is right, because this is stock country and I'm like your father, I don't believe it'll ever be worth anything except for its grass. We have proof of that, so far. Farms need water and this is dry land. Someday, maybe, it'll all be thrown open, but it won't be in my day nor in yours."

"I'm glad Daddy will own it in December," said Hope with a joyous smile. "Father has plenty of money, hasn't he, Mother? Because I would feel awful if I had been to school so long and had taken that trip to Helena and Butte and Salt Lake City this summer if it was. . . ."

Her mother's soft, rippling laugh checked Hope's speech. "We are very well off," said the older woman, with just a hint of a shadow in her eyes. "Your father has always made money, dear."

"Why does he go away and stay for days at a time, Mother?"

"Oh, business," was the reply. "Buying and selling cattle and such. He never knows just when he's coming back, so I never worry. Once he had to go as far as the big market in Chicago, and he's been to Kansas City several times."

It seemed to the girl for a moment that her mother's cheerfulness was a bit forced. But when she smiled, Hope put the thought aside.

"It's beautiful up here, Mother," said the girl soberly. "I'm so glad I'm home for good. There's only one thing. . . ." She stopped speaking with a flush of guilt.

"I know." Her mother nodded sympathetically. "It's lonesome."

"Oh, not with you here, Mother," Hope protested. "And somebody stopping in from the trail almost every day? And Daddy home at least half the time. And with Bismarck to ride? You mustn't say that, Mother."

"It's true enough. You're young, dear, young and beautiful and healthy. You're bubbling over with life. And you've had so much company about you in Great Falls and elsewhere. You want young people, and you should have them. We're going to give a big party up here later on, your father says. And you can go down to Pondera now and then. But you must be careful about the men here, dear. I don't for a minute think that any of the 'punchers or ranchers' sons hereabouts would treat you with anything except respect, but you must look out for the bad ones."

"Why, Mother, I've seen gamblers and supposed-to-be-gunmen, and all kinds of characters down in the Falls, and I can tell a bad egg the second I lay eyes on one." Hope laughed merrily. "And I can take care of myself, too. I can even shoot. You know that."

Her mother seemed to shudder at the word shoot. "Of course," she said. "Well, we might as well do the dishes. And I forgot to tell you, dear, that your father's graduation present will be along any time now."

"Present? Why, you dear!" Hope gave her mother a hug. "I suppose it's a secret."

"That's what I thought it was going to be," said her mother. "But John said it would be so big and you'd see it and know what it was long before it got up to the house and so I should go ahead and tell you. It's a fine piano, dear, and it's coming all the way from Minneapolis."

★ ★ ★ ★ ★

Long after the lights in the house were out, and the wind blew strong under the stars and the moon, Vagle moved silently about the yard, among the trees, and on the trail, his eyes alert to his vigil, his gun ready at his side for an emergency, his ears tuned to first distant echoes of flying hoofs, should they come.

CHAPTER TWO

The afternoon sun was streaming into the main street of Pondera. The air bore the subtle perfume that comes before the Indian summer, and sends the hunters afield for prairie chickens, the grouse of the plains. On a corner—one of the few prominent corners in the town—stood a tall man. In physical appearance he was a tower of rugged strength. His face was lined and seamed and fiercely burned by the hot winds that had swept the prairies in summer. He was dressed in the manner of the range and wore a stockman's model hat. A gun belt was buckled about his waist, and his weapon was snug in its holster on his left with the butt pointing inward. His was a stem face, square-jawed, with prominent cheek bones and steady, gray eyes. He was clean-shaven.

Out of the corner of his eye he was watching the casual approach of another tall man, a thinner man, who wore long mustaches, slightly gray, bushy eyebrows under which a pair of shrewd blue eyes looked keenly, and who walked with a slight limp in his right leg—the result of an injury earlier in life, perhaps a bullet wound. The larger man, to all appearances, was unaware of the other's existence. When the man came up to him he stopped and stood beside him, squirting a thin stream of tobacco juice into the heavy dust of the street. He looked at the sky, at a building across the street, up and down the street, anywhere except at the larger man, before he saw fit to speak.

"Nice weather, John," he said in a commonplace voice.

"Nice enough to make a man want to go hunting," was the answer.

"I reckon you'll wait for deer and elk and bear, Campbell," said the other. "You never was much for going in for small game."

John Campbell looked him squarely in the eyes for the first time. "That can be taken to have two meanings, Sheriff," he observed.

"I reckon I'm meaning the first," said Sheriff Tom Lane. "No need for double meanings now, is there, John?"

"I never had any use for 'em," said Campbell tartly.

"Haven't seen you around in some time," drawled the sheriff.

"What of it?" The question came, sharp and keen-edged. "Do you want to know where I've been for any particular reason?"

"Can't say I do, but I'm hoping for the best, John. 'Course, you know your girl is back from her trip. She says she's home to stay. Mighty fine girl, that Hope. Bright as a dollar and pretty as the devil. You're a lucky man, John, all-fired lucky."

Campbell's eyes had brightened. "Going to be lonesome for her up there at the place," was his comment. "Well, I've done the best I could to start her right. I'm only hoping she won't forget she's range stock."

"No chance of her getting stuck-up," said the sheriff with spirit. "I've talked to her since she came back and she belongs. You know what I mean. This is her favorite stamping ground."

"You were talking to her?" Campbell asked with a frown. "Did you . . . was there any mention of me?"

"Sure. Why not? She's anxious for you to get home. I told her you was away on a cattle deal, but you'd be back as soon as you could, knowing she was home."

"That was all right," said Campbell. "Nothing more, eh?"

"Not from me," said the sheriff firmly. "I'm on your side now."

"You've been pretty square," said Campbell slowly. "We've had some brushes, but nothing very serious."

"Except once," Lane corrected in a firmer voice. "But I'll say this, John, that for a man who can tell his gun what to do, and having it do it, almost without touching it, you've kept a mighty clear head."

"There were times when I had to," observed Campbell.

"There will be more times, now that Hope's home to stay," said Lane soberly. "You've got to protect that girl, Campbell. I mean as to your actions. That's all I've got to say, so don't feel peeved. And while we're talking, is there anything in what's going around to the effect that you're going to sort of look after the range for the stockmen out west there?"

Campbell smiled. "I'll have to wait till I'm asked to answer that one. Where'd you get the idea? There's no rustling around here."

"Oh, I've heard it hinted," said Lane vaguely. "I'm thinking they're going to ask you to keep an eye out over there. You might even have to go on my books as a deputy."

"And get paid both ways," snorted Campbell. "They figure it's a buy-off, eh? Well, they don't have to buy me off for anything and you know it. My slate's clean around here, and everywhere else, so far as you and I are concerned."

"Don't be so touchy," said the vexed sheriff. "Nobody has to buy you off for anything. It would be a good job at good pay, that's all, and I don't think it would hurt you to take it."

"We're saying a lot without saying it out loud, ain't we, Lane? All I ask is a square deal. I haven't got that always, Sheriff. Sometimes I have to make the deal square myself. I'm prepared to do it again if necessary. I'm still able to be up and about."

"Let's go have a drink," Lane suggested soothingly.

"All right," Campbell agreed, "but I'm not keen about it."

They crossed to the Board of Trade saloon. Standing at the

17

head of the bar, John Campbell towered above everyone in the place. His gaze darted here and there until he had noted everyone present. He met the sly glances of many, the bold stare of others—and in no man's eyes was other than respect.

The bartender came on the run and put out a bottle and glasses. "Keep track of 'em, Sheriff," he said. "Here's a pitcher of water."

"There'll only be two," Campbell told him, "and we won't need any water."

Lane poured the first drink, which they took at a gulp.

"John, can I talk to you as a friend and not as an official of Chouteau County?" asked Lane, toying with his glass.

"If it's advice you have to offer, you'll be wasting your breath," replied Campbell. "If there's one thing I don't need, it's advice. I have my own problems and I'll solve them in my own way."

"It isn't advice, John," said the sheriff earnestly, "and I'm going to talk long enough for you to get my drift. You've been away a lot since spring, John, and rumors have seeped into my office. I've never mentioned them to a soul. But I can't forget them. You're the toughest proposition this range ever produced, and you won't deny it. But there's got to be an end to this thing, John, an absolute end. I take it that you've had a good . . . er . . . season. I can tell it by the way you act. Why not let the game go at that and quit?"

"Do you know how far east I've been?" asked Campbell quietly.

"As far as Culbertson, anyway," the official answered promptly.

Campbell looked at him thoughtfully. "You know more than I thought," he said frankly. "I've been thinking along the line you were talking about, Tom, but there's just one thing that bothers me." He frowned deeply and this was not lost on Lane.

"Better tell me about it," prompted the sheriff. "Remember, I'm taking off my star during this little talk."

"It wouldn't make any difference," said Campbell impatiently. "I respect your star, as far as that goes, but there's times when my eyesight's poor and I can't see it shine. It's pretty hard to about-face without seeing somebody, you know."

"Ah, you think maybe some of 'em might drift in here and try to snare you? Not if I have anything to say about it. What you leave behind, John, you leave behind so far's I'm concerned. I've forgotten everything. You haven't done anything around here for years. So far as I know, nobody has anything against you. You're one man in a thousand, outside the cattle ring, who could file on that place up there and get away with it. You'll have your title before the year's out and nobody I know of would dare to call you a homesteader. Not to your face, anyway. You've got all the money you need and you can make a good living here. And now with the girl back, well . . . you know."

Campbell hastily poured the second drink and pushed the bottle away. "I know too well," he said cryptically. "Here's to an open winter."

They drank.

"I'm not going to say any more," Lane announced. "I believe you're thinking about the same way I am, Campbell. Great snakes, you've got brains. Surely I don't have to tell you anything. I wanted to sound you out for one thing, which I've done, and I just wanted to put the bug in your ear that I'm on your side against all comers, for the other. Now I reckon we understand each other to some extent."

"Pretty white of you, Lane," said Campbell. "But I'm not promising anything. I'm just doing a lot of thinking."

"Well, so long, old-timer," said the sheriff cheerfully. "You know how to find me if you should ever want to see me. And give my regards to the wife and girl when you hit back up home."

For some little space after Lane had gone, Campbell stood at the upper end of the bar, his brows knitted in thought. The sheriff had as much as said, in fact he had said, he would back him up in any play that had to do with blotting out the past. Always more or less a man of mystery, Campbell was respected and feared throughout the range. Even now, though the proprietor of the place would have liked to go up to him and extend a hearty greeting, he held back, repulsed by the look in Campbell's eyes. And those eyes again were sweeping the room to hesitate for a moment upon a man who was playing at a gaming table in the rear. He hadn't caught this man's eye, didn't know if the man had seen him. But his own gaze, when it fell upon the gambler, narrowed and grew hard and cold. He pursed his lips, beckoned to the bartender, and bought a cigar. He struck a match on the underside of the bar and lit his smoke. He puffed slowly and held his place, an aloof and sinister figure. And men directed surreptitious glances at him and thought of some of the stories they had heard about him, and looked at the double cartridge belt and the gun, snug on the left side.

It was inevitable that the man about whom he was thinking, at whom he looked repeatedly in that interval, should finally raise his eyes from the cards on the table. When this happened, Campbell caught his glance and held it—held it until he had given a signal by a nod of his head. Then Campbell walked out of the place.

He waited on the sidewalk for some little time to give the gambler an opportunity to cash in his chips and quit the game. When he saw him come out of the saloon, Campbell walked down the street and entered another resort of similar character. The gambler followed him in and he led the way to a little back room in the rear, a private card room, giving an order to the bartender on the way.

"We'll sit down, Pearlman," said Campbell when they were

alone in the room. "How's tricks?" Campbell's tone and manner were amiable, but the keen, cold light still was in his eyes.

Pearlman, a small, dark-faced man, with pockmarks and cruel eyes, seemed ill at ease. He sat gingerly on the edge of his chair and his right hand rested lightly on the edge of the table just above his gun.

"Just so and so," he said in a thin voice. "How're you?"

The bartender brought in a bottle and glasses. "Help yourself," Campbell told his companion. "I've had my allowance for today."

Pearlman poured a stiff drink as Campbell waved the bartender away. He gulped down a glass of water after the drink, and poured another. When he had done this, his eyes brightened and he took out tobacco and papers and rolled a cigarette with steady fingers.

"Is it as bad as all that?" Campbell inquired mildly.

"Bad as all what?" asked Pearlman as he lit his cigarette. His right hand was again on the edge of the table.

"Anybody who ever knew you could see you've been running short of drinks," replied Campbell pleasantly.

"Yeah? Well, maybe there's a reason," said Pearlman in a meaningful tone. "I'm . . . but it doesn't matter now."

Campbell's eyes had snapped once at the man's tone. "No, of course not," he agreed. Then he leaned his elbows on the table. "Long time since we've met up with each other, ain't it, Pearl?"

"Haven't seen you since. . . ." Pearlman appeared to be examining his mind as to when they had last met.

"The Fort Benton affair, wasn't it?" Campbell suggested.

"Yes, I guess that was it," replied Pearlman, lifting his brows.

"Where you been since then?" asked Campbell, relighting his cigar and regarding the man across the table from him quizzically.

"Oh, roaming around," was the evasive answer. "Nothing

good since."

"Pearl, why did you come here?" Campbell's voice was grim.

"Why, I heard the play at the tables up here was good, and I. . . ."

"You're a liar," Campbell interrupted sternly. "Put your right hand in the middle of the table. I don't want you to make a fool of yourself and get it an inch nearer your gun."

Pearlman's jaw snapped shut, but he slowly slid his hand to the center of the table, not once taking his eyes from Campbell's.

"You came here because you had an idea in the back of your head that I might be hereabouts," said Campbell. "You might as well come clean. If you don't, I'll have you ridden out of town on a mule."

"Sure, I thought you might be around," said the other. "Why not?"

"Why, of course, why not?" Campbell nodded. "Now I reckon we understand each other better. If we do, you can put your hand back where it was."

Instead of doing so, Pearlman used it to pour himself another drink. He wiped his lips with the back of his hand and lolled back in his chair. "That's all," he remarked in a tone of satisfaction. "Tell you the honest truth, John, I needed these drinks. I'm much obliged. I'm running on a pretty slim stake and I need every cent I've got to try and bolster it up at stud."

"Sure, I know," said Campbell sympathetically. "So you drifted up this way, thinking you might run up against me and make a touch, eh?" His tone was not such as to make his listener suspicious.

"I thought there was just a chance that you might have something up your sleeve that I might horn in on and make some money," said Pearlman frankly.

Campbell pursed his lips, a characteristic when thinking deeply. He gave Pearlman the impression that he was considering whether to take him in on something or not. It was a situation that pleased the smaller man and gave him confidence. Campbell surely could use him. He was lightning with his gun, a good hand with men.

"Can't say anything yet," said Campbell. "Meanwhile, you can't run around without a piece of heavy change in your pocket, that's sure. How much you got, all told?"

"About a hundred and fifty," said Pearlman wryly. He appeared actually ashamed to mention the amount, and Campbell knew thereby that he was telling the truth. He must have time to decide what to do about this man.

"If you haven't forgotten how to keep your mouth shut, I'll stake you for the time being," he said.

Pearlman grinned. "Lot of good it would do me to talk now, wouldn't it?" he said cheerfully.

Campbell drew a roll of bills from a pocket and shook out several. "There's five hundred, Pearl," he said. "Now go out ahead of me."

Pearlman's eyes glistened as he took the money, counted it, and put it in his inside coat pocket. "So long," he said as he went out the door.

Campbell sat at the table a long time. Then he put a bill under the bottle and left the place by the rear door.

CHAPTER THREE

The twilight lasted long in the prairie town. When it had blended with the night, and the dark velvet sky had drawn its canopy of stars over the vast, brooding land, Pondera came to life. Its resorts filled, men came riding in from nearby ranches, and gamblers and other like characters, who had slept through the day, made their appearance, and the places of refreshment and chance lent themselves to the easy task of making merry. The town was not crowded, for the beef shipments were not over. Later, when the range work for the year had been finished, there would come the big rodeo, with its picturesque throngs, its contests, its great ball, and its quarrels, fights, and shootings. Thus it was not difficult at this season for one acquainted to pick out the strangers in town, of which there were comparatively few.

After he had eaten supper, and night had fallen, John Campbell went out to make a round of quiet visits to the various places where men congregated. He had intended going right home, but the unexpected appearance of the man, Pearlman, had caused him to change his mind. He went here and there, his eyes alert to scan the face of every man he saw. It might be that Pearlman had others with him, and, if so, Campbell wanted to know.

When he had finished his rounds, he paused at the upper end of the main street. He had determined that Pearlman was in town alone. The next thing was to get rid of him and—for good.

He could not forget what the sheriff had told him, and Lane had been thoroughly in earnest. Campbell really was troubled. He needed the backing of a friend. He finally decided to visit Lane, although he was not sure that he would disclose what was in his mind.

The sheriff happened to be in his office and greeted Campbell cordially. After Campbell had taken a chair, Lane leaned forward and looked at him closely. "Something's turned up already," he said convincingly. "John, I'm honestly glad you came to see me. There's something up and you can't deny it. I can see it in your eyes."

Campbell scowled and swore under his breath. He hadn't expected to bring his business there to a head so quickly, if at all. He was angry with himself for coming. And yet. . . . "I don't want to make any fuss here in town," he said, frowning.

"Of course not," Lane agreed. "Maybe we can figure a way out. There's something in that two heads being better than one stuff, John."

Campbell glowered. "First time I've had occasion to think of it for some time," he grunted. "Well, anyway, Pearlman's in town. Ever hear of him?"

"That little rat of a gunfighter and tinhorn gambler? Of course, I've heard of him, but I never heard anything good about him."

"Oh, I wouldn't exactly say he's a tinhorn gambler," drawled Campbell. "I've seen him play square for some pretty high stakes. He's handy with his gun and he's smart in more ways than one."

"I guess you maybe know him better than I do," grumbled Lane.

"I ought to," said Campbell grimly. "He was in with me on that Benton deal some years ago. You remember that, I reckon."

"That was a bad break," said Lane slowly, shaking his head.

"They nearly nailed you for that one."

"Yes, but how many of 'em around here know anything about it, except by gossip?" flared Campbell. "What anybody knows about me here is by rumor. They can't put their finger on a thing. But Pearl knows all about that bank robbery and more in the bargain. I wouldn't want him to start shooting off his mouth. There are rumors I wouldn't want to reach the ears of Hope or the wife. Not that I think for a minute anybody who lives here would open their mouths to them. It wouldn't be exactly healthy. But. . . ." He bit his lip and paused.

"I know." The sheriff nodded soberly. "Pearlman might get on a talking streak. Where'd you see him?"

"He was in the Board of Trade all the time we were there. I caught his eye afterward and gave him the signal. Then I talked to him where we couldn't be overheard in another place."

"What did he say? How'd he happen to come here? He ought to know I won't let him or his kind hang out in this town." Lane was angry and meant what he said.

"Don't you butt in or he'll spill plenty and *pronto,*" said Campbell sharply. "I've got to handle this. Nobody's with him so far's I've been able to make out. He came up here on chance of meeting up with me. He was just the same as broke and said he thought maybe I had something in mind . . . which I haven't . . . and that he could horn in on it. Got frisky after a few drinks. I cooled him down. He wants money, of course. I suppose they're after him from somewhere, and that would make it bad. 'Specially if they found him here."

Lane's brow was wrinkled in thought. "We've got to get rid of him," he said as if to himself. "There's no doubt about that."

"That was understood from the beginning," said Campbell dryly.

"What was the upshot of your talk with him?" asked Lane.

"Well, first I fed him some liquor. He needed it and I saw he hadn't been able to keep up on his drinks and then I knew he was short on a stake. I didn't have much time to think what to do, so I decided it was a good plan to keep him in good spirits till I found out what to do. I gave him five hundred to keep him busy."

"I'd have given him a punch in the jaw, or . . . no, that wouldn't do. You've got him resting easy for the present, but you can't keep on passing money to him, can you? Do you owe him anything?"

Campbell shook his head. "Not . . . money," he said quietly.

Lane started. He rose from the chair behind his desk, walked to the door, closed it, and took to pacing the room. Every now and then he would look at Campbell, and the latter's expression always was the same—a grim, questioning gaze. Lane could read his mind by that look in the steady, gray eyes.

The sheriff stopped in front of his visitor. "If you kept on giving him money, it would never end," he said. "If the amounts were reasonable, you could almost do that, John. But he'd keep hanging around here. I'd have trouble with him sooner or later, because I hear he's treacherous and hot-tempered, and the devil of it is he can't be trusted!"

Campbell nodded. "You've said all there is to it, Lane."

"Of course, there's a way . . . another way," said Lane.

"Yes, there's another way," said Campbell softly. "A sure way."

Lane took out his handkerchief and wiped his brow. He resumed his pacing, thinking harder, perhaps, than he ever had thought in his life. After all, he was the sheriff of the county. It was his duty to enforce the law. But did the present problem come under the head of any duty he was pledged to perform?

Campbell had taken out a cigar. Lane almost jumped as the match was struck sharply on the sole of Campbell's boot. "I suppose you would know how to . . . to do it that way . . .

27

without too much of a stir," he said pointedly.

"I wouldn't shoot a man in the back," said Campbell.

"I know that," Lane snapped out. "But you can outdraw him and outshoot him, and they say nobody ever had to coax him to go for his gun." The sheriff's tone was hard.

"So they say," said Campbell, looking Lane squarely in the eyes.

Lane pressed his lips tightly, and then he blurted suddenly: "Use your own judgment."

"You mean . . ."—Campbell rose, his right hand dropping gently to his gun, his fingers caressing its butt with the lightness of a feather—"the sure way?"

Lane was startled by the gesture and the deadly tone of voice. "As long as it is done right," he said with a significant nod.

"So long, Lane. It's a wonderful night outside. I reckon you'll be noticing it on your way home."

Campbell went out, leaving the sheriff gripping the edge of his desk, his face white.

The Board of Trade saloon was ablaze with carnival. The hanging lamps were yellow moons in drifting layers of smoke. The gaming tables were not as yet going full blast. But the bar was lined two deep with a jovial crowd. From somewhere in the rear a piano tinkled, and its sallow, pale-faced player looked over his shoulder at a familiar scene, a cigarette drooping from the corner of his mouth. In the corner of the room between door and window a man slept with his head pillowed on his arms on a table. It was the start of a typical Pondera night.

John Campbell took up his station at the end of the bar, around the crook, nearest the wall. He ordered a drink and permitted it to remain on the bar before him, a signal to the wise bartender that he wanted no more. He looked over the scene and almost immediately spied Pearlman with a small group, drinking and making merry in the center of the crowd.

From then on he watched him carefully, keeping back as much as possible to avoid being seen.

But Campbell's eyes were elsewhere, also. He was first to see the swinging doors burst open and two young men enter. The first of the pair to look over the room held Campbell's attention. His big hat was tipped back a bit, showing his dark red hair. His eyes were a blue that seemed shaded with green, and they sparkled magnificently as he took in the scene about him. He was tall, with wide shoulders, and the tapered waist of the born rider. Splendidly built, with an air of the adventurer—a swashbuckler—about him. He would be noticed twice in any company. His companion was a tall, slim youth—a blond—who gave one the impression of laziness and indifference. His gaze appeared languid. There was humor in his blue eyes, an almost effeminate turn to his lips. Yet something told Campbell that here was no fool, no hammock lounger.

The first youth, unmistakably Irish, breezed up to the bar and made a place for himself and his companion. "All right, barkeep, we're here," he sang. "I'm Ricky Odell, Irish like yourself, and that ought to give me a break. This is my pal, Slim Olsen. A good, honest, common name, better than Smith, Brown, and Jones all put together, and not excepting present company. Give us a drink, Mike."

The barkeeper grinned and others smiled. Here were two live ones from somewhere out for a time. Their hats and clothes and boots shrieked quality and taste in Western wear. They must have shaved after they got in. And they looked like ready money.

The drinks were served, downed, and paid for with astonishing alacrity. "Not so bad," said Ricky Odell, his white teeth flashing in a smile. "How'd you find it, Slim?"

"About the average," drawled the blond one, stamping himself as of Texas origin with the three words.

"That's the trouble with my partner, Mike," said Odell, addressing the bartender, whose name really was Mike, and who naturally delighted in a departure from the usual form of entertainment in the place. "That's the whole trouble," Odell went on. "He's a pessimist and misses the sunshine. He got that sunburn from trying to light cigarettes in a strong wind. Get out the little jiggers with the spots on 'em and I'll shake you for the house."

"Not me," said the bartender. "The house takes no chances and buys drinks three times a year, the Fourth of July, Christmas, and New Year's."

"Well, let's shake for the Christmas drink, and if I lose, I'll leave it as a present for the boys," said Odell cheerfully.

"And I'll buy the New Year's drink and you can give me credit for it," Slim Olsen put in.

Odell looked at him in admiration. "You see, Mike? You wouldn't think that boy had brains, would you? Well, that disposes of the Christmas and New Year's drinks, so let's get back to this drink. I hope you don't think I'm a gambler because I offered to shake for a little thing like a single guzzle around. So. . . ."

"Who wants to shake for the drinks?" came a high-pitched voice.

Odell and his companion looked down the bar from whence the voice had come. They saw a slender man, whose eyes seemed the biggest part of him at the moment. This was Pearlman. John Campbell had not taken his eyes from Odell from the time he had entered, save for a brief survey of his lanky companion. He knew Odell was not showing off, knew he was not brag and bluster; he saw something in this care-free, energetic youth that others missed. Now he edged around and joined the ring of spectators that gathered about Odell and Pearlman.

"I'm willing to do half the shaking," Odell announced, the tone of his voice changing somewhat.

"Get out the dice," Pearlman ordered the bartender. "Suppose you know how to throw 'em," he said to Odell with a trace of a sneer.

"The last time I shook dice," began Odell cheerfully, "I. . . ."

"Cut it," interrupted Pearlman. "We don't care about the last time you shot dice, nor about any time you shook dice. We want to see you shake 'em now."

"And you'll not be disappointed," answered Odell. "It was a trivial matter that I had to kill a man the last time I shook, and I hope it won't happen this time. Go ahead. Best two out of three." His voice had cooled.

Pearlman took the cup with the five dice in it that the bartender handed him. He rattled the dice absently as he stared at his youthful opponent. "If you think you're kidding me," he said slowly, "take the taffy out of your mouth and make it real."

"Put 'em out!" The words cracked on the air in a commanding tone. "I'm shaking with you and not trying to pick a quarrel. I don't aim to have my night spoiled."

Pearlman obeyed instinctively and not because he had been told to do so. Three aces showed when the dice stopped rolling. "I'll leave 'em," said Pearlman in a satisfied voice.

"Might be good," observed Odell, putting the dice in the box and rolling them out. "Three kings!" he exclaimed. "Close enough. That's one on me." He rattled the dice in the cup. "Obey Ricky Odell!" he cried to the dice as they rattled on the bar. "There's your three aces right back at you, mister. They must have got mixed up as to who was handling them."

Pearlman's face darkened. He threw a mixture. "One apiece now," he grunted. "Look these over now." He shook the dice out on the bar.

"I can see 'em," sang Odell. "Looks like two queens to me."

"I'll put two with 'em," said Pearlman, giving Odell a mean look. He swore as the three remaining dice showed with but one

31

queen in sight. He put the queen with the other two and shook the third time. The fourth queen came up a smiling heart.

"Four in three," said Odell, rattling the dice over his head. "Four in three and we will see." Two jacks came up on the throw. He scooped up the five dice. "Four in one, maybe two," he said lightly. "Mike, your dice don't like strangers. Here we go!"

Two tens were best. "That's enough!" cried Odell. "Pass 'em out, bartender!"

"You've got another throw," said Pearlman jeeringly. "Maybe you got four big ones in one the last time."

"And I've had such good luck since that I don't want to take any chances this time," Odell shot at him in reply.

Everyone laughed except Pearlman and John Campbell.

CHAPTER FOUR

John Campbell had moved closer during the play of words between Odell and Pearlman. He was in the front row of spectators when the youth gave the order to the bartender to serve all present. He noted that Pearlman didn't smile when the others laughed at Odell's sally. Pearlman wasn't done with his defeated opponent yet.

Odell turned, motioning and calling all to the bar. The crowd surged forward and Odell caught sight of the man sleeping in the corner with his head on his arms on the table.

"C'mon, old-timer, wake up and have a drink!" he called.

There was no response from the sleeping man. Odell's eyes flashed with gaiety as he turned quickly to the bar and picked up an empty glass. He stepped out and tossed the glass toward the corner. When it was over the sleeping man's head and about to hit the wall, a thundering report shook the room, the glass was shattered, and the pieces rained on the sleeper's head. He sat up, blinking as Ricky Odell sheathed his gun.

"Come along and have a drink," Odell invited. "The alarm just went off. You won't get another until Christmas."

The man, a derelict of the plains, brushed pieces of glass from the table, shook his hat, and walked uncertainly to the bar with a sheepish grin.

"Nice trick," Pearlman sneered as Odell turned to the bar.

"Waking him up?" said Odell pleasantly. "Oh, he can use a drink. He isn't turning it down, is he?"

"I mean the shooting part of it," Pearlman said angrily.

"Oh, that." Odell made a derogatory gesture. "As good a way to wake him up as any. Did you think it was an accident? How much for the glass, Mike?"

"More'n you can pay?" Pearlman put in.

Campbell knew something was coming. Pearlman had been drinking, and when he was doing that, he always became mean. And, drink or not, his steadiness with his gun never failed him; he was death with his six-shooter. Campbell considered quickly. There was a chance of gun play. There was a chance—a slight chance—that Odell might be able to beat Pearlman to it. If he did, Pearlman would cause no more trouble. If he didn't, Pearlman would have to get out of town, and he would be sure to tie strings to his going. No, if Pearlman were to be involved in a shooting, he must lose. Campbell kept in the second line just behind Slim Olsen, Odell's companion. But Odell was talking again. His voice was cold and clear; his expression had changed.

"I've never seen the glass yet that I couldn't pay for, mister. Maybe it's your private glass or something like that. Is that so, Mike?"

"Never mind the glass," said Mike, frowning at Pearlman. "You don't have to pay for that and it belongs to the house. We'll sweep up the pieces, too, without charge."

Pearlman's erstwhile companions had drawn away from him somewhat. They were chance acquaintances and had no intention of being embroiled in any trouble. Campbell's eyes were gleaming. When it came, he could step in to defend Odell, and if Pearlman went for his gun, it would be his last draw. Campbell would lose nothing by having taken the part of a young stranger who was already liked by the crowd.

"That's what you think," Pearlman shot at the bartender. "Any reason why you've got to butt in on this?"

"Yes, I don't want any trouble in this place," was the

34

bartender's quick retort.

"Don't be taking my part, Mike," said Odell. He turned to Pearlman. "You chose me out of the crowd to get sore at, now what's the big idea?"

"What was your idea in coming in here to put on a show?"

"If I'm putting on a show, that's my business so long as I'm able and willing to pay for it," was Odell's cool response. "I don't hear anybody else here kicking, and if any of your crowd has a kick to make, let him or all of 'em step out here and register."

Pearlman glanced over his shoulder, and when he saw that the men who had been with him had withdrawn, it infuriated him. "If they're here, they're too yellow to step out," he said in a loud voice, and waited for the space of several seconds. There was only the deep silence that reigned when he or Odell were not speaking.

"Seems like you haven't got any crowd," observed Odell. "I've got Slim here, but he never interferes with my private affairs. Are they all set, Mike?"

"All set," replied the bartender cheerfully.

"Here's to merry living, boys!" Odell cried, raising his glass. The next instant he had dashed it, contents and all, into Pearlman's face and his gun leaped into his hand. "Keep your hand where it is!" he commanded in a ringing voice.

Pearlman was momentarily blinded and those who could see saw his right hand on his gun.

"Going to shoot the glass out of my hand, eh?" accused Odell, as Pearlman wiped the liquor from his eyes.

At this vital moment, John Campbell leaped between the two. It had been inevitable that Pearlman would draw his gun. He might draw it now.

"What're you picking on this young stranger for?" Campbell demanded sternly, speaking to Pearlman and pushing Odell back with his left hand. "He didn't do anything to you. What do you want to make trouble for? You're a stranger yourself and none too pleasant at that."

Pearlman was looking at him through narrowed lids. Campbell, of all men, taking sides with a wild young brat. What was more, Campbell was fighting mad. He could see it in his eyes. He was daring him to draw. He wet his lips with his tongue. Campbell had made no move for his gun while Pearlman's hand already was on the butt of his six-shooter. He was sure he could beat Campbell to it, although he knew the larger and older man was fast as light. Then an enlightening thought came to him. Campbell did have a job up his sleeve and Odell was one of the men in on it. Probably his friend, Slim, was in on it, too. This was Campbell's way of telling him to lay off. He smiled a twisted smile. He would be as clever.

"All right, Sheriff," he said. "You win. But tell the guy to be careful with his rattle if he runs into me again."

Campbell was chagrined. He had given Pearlman the advantage and had taken a chance, perhaps, himself. But Pearlman refused to fight.

"Don't worry," he said harshly, "I'm not the sheriff. But I live around here and I aim to see fair play when I'm on the scene."

"Give me another glass, Mike, and we'll all take that little libation I gambled for," drawled Odell. "The tornado has blown itself out. Have a drink, pardner." He put a hand on Campbell's sleeve, and Campbell stood beside him without speaking until Pearlman had gone out. Shortly afterward, he went out himself.

"Who was that *hombre*?" Odell asked the bartender.

"Why that . . . he lives near here," the bartender evaded. "Name's Campbell. Mighty good sport and a good man not to meddle with."

"Seeing as how I caused all the racket around here," said Odell in his bantering voice, "I'll buy another round."

36

Campbell walked swiftly down the street. He believed Pearl-man would assume that he wanted to see him again after what had taken place and that he would go where he had talked with him some time before. Campbell was nettled, worried, uncertain. He could have goaded Pearlman into drawing, even if he had had to slap him in the face. And he could have got him for keeps, regardless of the fact that the man had had his hand on his gun. Furthermore, he could have gotten away with it clean. As a matter of fact he had the sheriff's permission to kill Pearl-man. And there was the rub. To force him deliberately into a draw and shoot him down would be plain murder. Campbell had had to use his gun on many occasions; he was privileged to cut notches in its butt, but he had never deliberately forced a gun play. And now he realized that it simply wasn't in him to force a gun play with Pearlman. But what was he to do? Pearl-man had gone off at the head this night; he was liable to do so again. He might even boast that he had backed down before Campbell because. . . .

Campbell swore outright and paused in front of the place where he had talked with Pearlman before. Above all things he wanted to go home, even if he could only stay a day. He wanted to see Hope, and John Campbell was a man who loved his wife who had stuck by him in the turbulent years. Matters were different now that Hope was home to stay. If he bought Pearlman off for a large sum, the man would go away. But he would know Campbell had good reason to give him the money, and when he ran short again, he would come back. Meanwhile, if Campbell went home for a day or so, Pearlman might go after Odell again and make it a showdown. Campbell swore again and went around to the rear door of the saloon.

He opened and closed the door silently and, giving way to a hunch, looked in the card room where he had met Pearlman early in the evening. He was startled to see his man sitting at the table alone, with a bottle and glasses in front of him. The sight angered Campbell. Pearlman was so sure of himself. He would drive Campbell to do it yet.

"Hello, pardner," leered Pearlman as Campbell entered, shut the door, and sat down at the table.

"Cut the pardner business," said Campbell shortly. "How'd you happen to come here?"

"I reckoned you'd want to see me after the play you pulled up at the Board of Trade," replied Pearlman, pouring himself a drink.

"You're hitting that stuff pretty heavy," Campbell commented. "You always get in bad when you go against it strong. I reckon the worst scrapes you've ever been in have come about through your drinking, isn't that so, Pearl?"

"I'm quitting with this one," said Pearlman. "I'd been running short for some time and stepped out for a few. I'm not drunk. I know you have got something up your sleeve and that that pair, Odell and the other, are in on it. You couldn't afford to see him shot up, which is not saying I'd have done it. You came into the play knowing I wouldn't draw down on you, and you gave the kid a signal with your left hand when you did it. I saw you touch him. If you had dared, you would have winked at me, but somebody might have seen it." Pearlman chuckled and winked himself.

Campbell smiled. He felt like winking, too. But his pleasure was not what Pearlman evidently supposed. He waited a few moments before speaking to get full attention from the man across the table.

"I've never thought you were dumb," he told Pearlman, leaning on his elbows on the table. "In this case you want to remember that I'd only seen you to speak to once after you got into town. I handed over five hundred, you remember? I wouldn't do that unless I had a reason. Suppose these two fellows, Odell and Slim, are in on a deal with me? Do you think I was going to give you an earful right off the bat?"

"You ought to have given me a hint," said Pearlman soberly. "That fellow was pretty fresh and there might have been some trouble."

"How could I give you a hint when he just blew into town?" Campbell asked softly. "Now do you begin to get it?"

"And he was supposed to blow in with a roar, eh?" Pearlman grinned. "Must be a deep one you've got coming up now, John."

Campbell winced. He didn't like to hear this man call him by his first name. It was almost an insult. But he must be careful; he must play safe.

"Suppose I say you're in on it," said Campbell softly. "Are you willing to begin taking orders and doing what I tell you to do?"

Pearlman was delighted. He clasped and unclasped his hands on the table and pushed the bottle and glass aside. "I know the first order," he said. "Quit that!" He jerked a thumb toward the bottle. "I've taken that one already, and I'm willing to start taking the others. You know me."

"All right," said Campbell grimly. "You are in on my play. The first thing I want you to do, and keep on doing, is to let this man Odell and his pal Slim alone. Ignore 'em completely. I don't want 'em to know who you are and you don't know who they are. See?"

"I get you," agreed Pearlman eagerly. "I'm listening."

"Don't pay any attention to this Odell, or the other, no matter what they do," said Campbell earnestly. "I want to keep you and them apart, understand?"

"I don't even know they're in town from this minute, boss," said Pearlman. "If they spit in my face, I'll apologize for being in the way. I'll lay off 'em as you say, but I'll watch 'em a little."

"All right," said Campbell, rising and leaning his hands on

the table. "The other orders are the same as always when you start on a job . . . quit the hard drinking, don't make a flash to call more attention to yourself, and keep your tongue where it belongs. Agreed?"

"You know me," Pearlman said a second time in satisfaction.

Campbell slipped out the rear door and hurried back up the street to the Board of Trade. He looked in, saw that Odell and his friend had settled quietly into a game, then went for his horse.

He was going home.

CHAPTER FIVE

About 1:00 in the morning Odell and Olsen went to the room they had engaged at the hotel when they had ridden in after sunset. They had won a moderate sum and were tired.

"Reckon we're going to have more trouble with that gun-fighter?" said Odell as they were undressing.

"Hope not," said Olsen laconically. "Don't want trouble so soon. If anybody should ask, I'm dead tired after the ride yesterday. If I get into trouble, it'll have to come marching right up under my nose."

"I feel the same way about it . . . now." Odell yawned as he blew out the light in the lamp.

They went to sleep without further conversation.

Pearlman played cards until dawn. When he went out to get his breakfast, he saw Odell and Olsen going to the livery. He stepped between two buildings and waited until the pair rode forth, mounted on horses that caused his eyes to glisten with envy. He saw them ride out of town toward the west. He wondered mightily where they were going. Instantly his suspicious mind was alert. Were they going to join Campbell somewhere? Had Campbell fed him a lot of syrup and made him promise to lay off them until they could get safely out of town? Pearlman, himself experienced in double-crossing others, was always suspicious that others were trying to double-cross him. He turned into a saloon for an eye-opener. He was tired.

Odell and Olsen rode out of town with the rising sun behind

them and the prairie a running sea of gold before them. Both were in high spirits. They galloped their horses for a spell and slowed to a swinging lope.

"Take a look at this land out here, Slim!" Ricky Odell called to his partner. "Flat as the top of a pool table. Look at the grass. And the cattle are in fine shape, too. Guess they haven't shipped yet. Look at those prime steers over there. Rich ranches in here, boy."

"And a good place not to be riding around loose," was Slim's reply. "I wouldn't try inspecting any herds, Rick."

Odell laughed. "We're on a trail, are we not? There must be a town up in the hills. It's well-worn. Look at the yellow grass and the color of the trail. Maybe it's a trail of gold, kid. Look at those mountains! You've never seen anything like 'em and neither have I . . . not so close, anyway. Boy, this looks like tough range to me. Maybe we'll run into some excitement, if we go up there."

"We don't have to go to no mountains to find excitement, Rick," said Slim, the practical one. "If you don't find it, you make it."

"Somebody's got to keep the wheels going around," Odell said. "I'll turn the wheels and you be the regulator. And just keep your eyes open around here."

At noon they halted by the stream that flowed down from the foothills and unsaddled their horses so they could graze and drink and rest in comfort. The pair sat in the shade and ate their lunch. They had a modest supply of provisions in the slicker packs on their saddles. Then they smoked and dozed, and it was midafternoon when they resumed the trail.

Cattle were to be seen on both sides of the trail and more than once they saw horsemen working the herds.

"Hello," called Odell as they neared the foothills, "here's

somebody coming to visit us! Let me answer any questions, Slim."

The rider proved to be young and good-looking, although there was a suggestion of temper in his eyes. He was better dressed than the average cowpuncher, possessed a more important air.

"You boys going up the trail?" he asked when he brought his horse up with them.

"We figured on it," said Odell cheerfully, reining in his mount as Slim did likewise. "No restrictions, are there?"

"Of course not," was the quick reply. The stranger was looking them over carefully. "You boys come from town?" was the next question. "I got a reason for asking. You look all right, though."

"You're talking a little ahead of where we're listening, aren't you?" asked Odell, his smile fading. "Why're you asking us all these questions in the first place, and what do you mean by saying we look all right? You looking for anybody in particular?"

The other frowned. "I'm Ira Crowell from Square H Ranch," he announced importantly. "Guess you've heard of the Square H."

"Nope. We haven't heard of the Square H. Cattle plant, I suppose," said Odell offhand. "What are you . . . a 'puncher?"

"My father owns the Square H," replied Ira with a trace of haughtiness. "I don't know whether I can trust you or not."

"Oh, so you're the heir," said Odell, lifting his brows. "A young big shot around here, I reckon. Well, you can trust us for one thing, Square H, Junior. We're not taking off our hats and bowing just because your pap owns a ranch."

"That's impertinent!" snapped Ira, but he looked up the trail with worry in his eyes. "I suppose you're going past the Campbell place?"

Odell pricked his ears. That was the name of the man who

had prevented a gun play in the Board of Trade, according to what the bartender had said. "If it isn't too far, we'll be passing it," he said. "We're going up in the hills a ways."

"It's right at the start of the foothills," said Ira. "You can't miss it. It's a big white house on the right side of the trail with a hitching rail in front of it. It's the only house you'll see up there."

"That being the case, I don't see how we can miss it," said Odell. "What about it?" He had overlooked Ira's remark about impertinence when he had heard him mention the name Campbell.

Ira looked around. "Well, I'm going to take a chance on you," he said finally. "I can't get away and I've got a letter I want left at the Campbells'. I'll pay you if you'll take it along and leave it there. There's bound to be somebody about."

"We don't need any money," said Odell, "and you've talked sort of rough to us, but I guess we can take your letter along. We won't have to lose much time delivering it, will we?"

"Not at all, not at all," said Ira eagerly. "They've got a hand who'll probably be around the yard. Just give it to him. I wish you'd take five dollars for your trouble, though, to make sure you won't forget it."

"We haven't got so much on our minds that we'll forget it." Odell frowned. "Where's this letter?"

Ira Crowell leaned from his saddle and handed over a white envelope. "We do these favors for each other, riding back and forth up here," he said with a thin smile. "Maybe I'll have a chance to do you a favor someday."

"Can't tell," said Odell, putting the letter in his shirt pocket without looking at it. "We'll pause up there long enough to deliver it. How's the old Square H doing these days?" He shook out his reins.

"I'm much obliged!" called Ira Crowell as they rode away.

They watched him ride southward out of sight as they proceeded on the trail. "He's the old man's son," said Odell with a laugh. "He knows it and wants everybody else to know it. Trying to give us the high brow. Let's see who the letter's for." He looked at the envelope, and then winked at Slim. "It's for a girl, the young sneak!" he called. "Her name's Hope Campbell. Remember that old duck who stepped in last night? His name was Campbell, so Mike said. Maybe this is the same Campbell, and maybe this is his daughter. If she is and she's pretty, she's got no business messing around with that guy, Crowell. He's a prig and maybe worse."

"We shouldn't have taken it," said Slim. "Maybe we won't see the place, after all. Don't forget we're strangers around here."

"I suppose us being strangers will affect our eyesight," Odell shot back. "Delivering letters to unknown people from unknown people is liable to result in 'most anything. For two cents I'd read it."

Hope Campbell was standing at the hitching rail as the sunset spread its magic over the land. Again she was dreaming, waiting for the purple mists and the knights who would ride noiselessly past, saluting her with silent kisses from their fingertips. Two horses came around the lower turn in the road. Hope drew back a step but stood there as she saw the laughing eyes and figure of Ricky Odell. He pulled up at the rail, with Slim behind him. He leaned on the horn of his saddle and looked at her as he swept his hat from his head, revealing his dark red hair that shone like clouded garnet.

"Are you Hope?" he asked in a soft, vibrant voice.

"Why . . . yes," answered the girl, a faint flush adding to her beauty.

"That's what your name should be," announced Ricky Odell.

"I know now why I rode so far into the hills. It was to see you. Now, I'd be willing to walk back."

Hope's lips tightened. "Did you wish to see me about something?" she asked in a precise manner. This young stranger was good-looking!

"Many things," Odell assured her. "I wanted to ask you if you saw any signs in the stars last night, if the wind whispered anything to you today, if a little bird didn't twitter in your ear the good news that I was coming."

It was impossible to keep back the smile that came to her lips. "You must be very important," she said in a laughing voice.

In a moment, Odell was off his horse, standing at the rail and looking across it at her. "I am very important." He nodded gravely. "I'm a messenger, for one thing . . . worse luck . . . and I make a business of being important when I meet a girl like you . . . which isn't often. In fact,"—he cocked his head on one side and observed her critically, "I don't believe I ever did meet a girl like you. You're like a little hummingbird with a rose in its bill."

Hope laughed outright. "Do you mean that to be poetical?" she asked, almost in a giggle.

Odell drew back. "What a thing to say," he said reprovingly. "Here I come riding, riding, riding through the dust and the heat and the rivers, streams, and gumbo flats, across the prairie and over the hills, to see you, and you . . . what do you do?"

"Why, I don't know," said the delighted girl. "What do I do?"

"You repulse my first timid advances," he accused, his blue-green eyes sparkling. "Do you think that's acting right?"

"You spoke about being a messenger," she reminded him quickly.

"Oh, yes. Merely by chance. I met a bedraggled creature down the trail a while back who evidently has the nerve to annoy you by writing you a note. He got off his horse and kneeled

46

down in the dust, and begged me with tears in his eyes to stop at your place and deliver this note." He drew the envelope from his pocket. "Do you want to read it, or will I just tear it up?" He made a move as if to tear the envelope in halves.

"Give it to me," the girl commanded. "So this is how you learned what my first name is. I'll read this later."

"Hello!" exclaimed Odell. "We're going to have company, and if I'm not mistaken, I've met your father before, Miss Hope."

John Campbell was striding toward them, frowning heavily.

CHAPTER SIX

When John Campbell reached the little group, he stood for some moments, looking from one to the other of them, his brow furrowed with perplexity. He recognized Ricky Odell and Slim Olsen at once as the two youths who had nearly had to shoot it out with Pearlman down in Pondera the night before. But why were they here? And talking to Hope?

He spoke first to his daughter. "Go into the house, Hope," he ordered. "I'll find out what these two want."

"This one brought me a note sent up by Ira," said the girl, indicating Odell, who immediately smiled at her. "I suppose they're. . . ."

"Will you please go in the house, Hope?" her father interrupted.

As she walked to the house, however, she sent a smiling look at Odell over her pretty shoulder. This left Odell in a very pleasant frame of mind. He put on his hat and looked at Campbell whimsically. "Small world around here," he observed. "I reckon I should thank you for breaking up that gun play in town last night. We couldn't find out anything about that mean-faced *hombre*. Could you tell us who he is?"

"He's a good man to stay away from, I'll tell you that," said Campbell. "Did you see him again afterward?"

"Sure. He came in that place and sat in a card game, meek as a lamb. You'd've thought he didn't know we were there. If he'd got fresh the second time, I might have had to bore him. He was still playing when we quit early this morning."

"Didn't do much drinking, either, did he?" asked Campbell.

"Took one drink while we were there, that's all I saw," replied Odell. "You act interested in him although you stopped him proper last night. Is he a friend of yours, if I might put the question?"

"He's a dangerous man," said Campbell, "and I didn't want to see you two run up against his gun. He's fast and sure."

"Of course," said Odell coolly. "That's the way I like 'em."

"You don't want to get any big ideas in your head around these parts, young fellow," growled Campbell. "You've got to grow all the way up to match the crowd that hangs out on this range."

"It seems like we're always running into tough ranges," Odell observed with a side glance at Olsen who still sat his saddle on his horse. "Isn't that so, Slim?"

"Getting so we don't expect anything else," drawled Slim.

"Where are you two from?" Campbell demanded.

Odell hesitated. He didn't want to anger Campbell—he told himself he wouldn't even think of angering the father of a girl like the one he had been talking to—but he resented Campbell's attitude just the same. "If it's all right with you, we won't say," he said slowly. "Of course, if you're a sheriff. . . ."

"I have nothing to do with the law," Campbell broke in. "You needn't be afraid to talk to me."

"Then it'll be all right if we don't say much," decided Odell.

"How'd you come to get up here?" asked Campbell curiously. "And how come you brought a note to my daughter from that young Crowell?" His distaste for Ira was reflected in his tone.

"He met us on the road and asked us to favor him by delivering the note. Told us where the place was and offered us five dollars, which we didn't take, since we're not broke, nor near it."

"Humph." Campbell clearly was puzzled and uncertain how to handle the pair. He hesitated over the next question. Then: "Did you start for here in the first place?"

"Nope. We'd never have known where your place was if that son of the Square H hadn't told us. When I heard the name Campbell, I wondered if it might be you and decided to find out. Mike told us your name after you left the Board of Trade down there last night."

"I see," said Campbell, scanning Odell's face keenly. "You started out early, I suppose."

"At sunrise," Odell affirmed.

"Yes, I see. Did this . . . that fellow you had trouble with last night see you go? Did he see what direction you took, do you know?"

"We didn't see anything of him this morning," Odell answered. It was his turn to be puzzled. "He might have seen us ride west out of town, for all we know. Do you think he would follow us?"

"Not exactly," said Campbell, although that was just what he suspected. Pearlman might follow the pair to attempt to spy on them, and himself for that matter. And it wouldn't be hard for Pearlman to learn where he lived. He shot a quick look down the trail.

"Look here," said Odell in a sharper tone, "I can see by the way you act that you're thinking he might have followed us. There's something between you and that gunman. We didn't want to make any trouble, and don't want to make any now, but if we can be of any use to you, say so and we'll be right and ready this minute."

"I don't want you to have anything to do with that fellow," said Campbell shortly, "and you can't be of any use to me.

Where are you going? You're not going over the mountains, I can see that."

"How can you make that out?" demanded Odell.

"Because you're carrying such slim packs," replied Campbell. "It's no jaunt over the Divide and there's nothing this side of it."

"No town up this way at all, eh?" said Odell, looking up at the climbing ridges, purple in the first flush of the twilight.

"That ain't half of it," said Campbell. "There's no town on this side and no town on the other side until you get out of the mountains. All you'll see going over this trail is a small mine, a few prospects that're being worked, and some cabins. You haven't got grub enough in the first place, and in the second place you'd find it mighty hard to get a fresh supply on the way. I'm telling you this for your own good."

"Thanks," said Odell. "As a matter of fact, we didn't intend to go over the mountains. We wanted to see what they looked like. We might not have gone this far if it hadn't been for that Crowell fellow giving us the message to deliver and us thinking that you might be the Campbell that Mike told us about." He turned and spoke to his companion. "Get off that horse and rest it a bit, Slim. Maybe this man can give us some information."

Campbell frowned and looked again down the trail. He didn't relish the presence of Odell and Olsen on his place. He knew Pearlman's suspicious nature and underhand methods. There was only one particular way in which the gunman could be of service, and Campbell was not interested in the peculiar services that the man could give at this time.

"What do you want to know?" he asked Odell, when Olsen had dismounted. "I haven't had supper yet, you know. I don't mean to cut you short. . . ."

"That's all right," Odell interrupted. "We can wait till you've had your supper. We're not in any great hurry."

"No, no," said Campbell hastily. "I've got time to hear what you have to say, only . . . make it brief."

"That's fair enough. You know this country pretty well in here, I take it," said Odell. "You've lived here quite a while?"

"Why, yes," confessed Campbell, growing suspicious instantly.

"Well, we heard there was some land up here open to entry," explained Odell, "and we came up to look the country over. It looks pretty good. The two of us expect to mark off a hundred and sixty acres apiece, two homesteads. We don't have to live on it for six months after we file and by then it would be about spring and a good time to start. Can you tell us about this land?"

Campbell was staring at the young speaker with his mouth open. Then he swore gently. He seemed about to make a hot retort, thought better of it, and, after looking from one to the other of his visitors, he spoke in a gentle voice. "Do you two come from cattle country?" he asked.

"Yes," Odell replied. "Does that make any difference?"

"You ought to know that it makes a difference . . . a big difference," said Campbell coldly. "Strangers don't come into a cattle range and file on homesteads. You've got the wrong idea. Anyway, this is cattle country and nothing else, and will be cattle country longer than you and your pardner will be anywhere."

"We're not saying that it won't," replied Odell calmly. "In fact we don't want it to be anything else. But we want a piece of land in here and we're entitled to it. What's more, we intend to get it. We're not trying to butt in on cattle range with any other kind of proposition, but we want the land while it's good and while we can get it."

This speech made Campbell angry. "Do you suppose the stockmen in here would be fools enough to let any land stay

open on their range?" he demanded harshly. "You couldn't file
on an acre for there isn't any open land left. It was all taken up
long ago by the men who work the range."

"On the contrary, the Land Office down in Great Falls
showed me where there was quite a bit of land left open, and
the government ought to know," said Odell confidently.

Campbell swore again, then his face grew stern. "Listen to
me," he said in a voice that compelled attention. "You two didn't
come up here to file on any land." He spoke slowly, holding
Odell's gaze locked with his own. "You know that as well as I
do and I'm sure of it. You know better than to try that. And that
shooting of yours last night, Odell, wasn't any accident. You're
gun wise and able, too able, maybe, for your own good. You
made an entrance down there that wasn't just haphazard. Maybe
I'm wrong, but that's the way I feel about that stunt. Now,
whatever you have in mind up here, you'd better forget it. I'm a
long way from being the law or having any connection with it,
and I'm probably the one man who can tell you straight that
you can't get away with anything around here."

"You're talking as if you didn't like our looks," said Odell
without hesitation. "Not only that, Campbell, but you're jump-
ing at conclusions. There are plenty of men who can handle a
gun and you're one of them yourself. Just for your own private
information, I'll tell you that I wasn't scared for a minute . . . a
split second! . . . to draw with that gunfighter last night and I
don't care who he is. What's more, if he meddles with me again,
I'm going to slap his mouth and let him go through with his
bluff or the real stuff, whichever it is. We're not up here to put
anything over, but if we want a couple of pieces of land, we're
going to get 'em. I've been around cattle most of my life, and so
has Slim. I know just how pig-headed stockmen can be. What
you just told us has made me decide to stick around here for a
while. I've never been chased out of any place yet, and I don't

53

propose to be chased out of here. I mind my own business, too."

"Well, you're not minding your own business very well in sneaking around up here," said John Campbell sternly. "What I said about your chances to file on homesteads goes. You're strangers, you won't tell where you came from or anything else about yourselves, and because of that you're open to suspicion. So far as I'm concerned, you can pick a fight with anybody you want, and go to. . . ." He paused suddenly and both youths looked in the direction of a small, crab-like man who was hurrying from the shadow of the trees near the downtrail.

"What is it, Vagle?" asked Campbell sharply.

The man pointed toward the dip in the trail and said something in a low, croaking voice. Campbell was instantly alert.

"Take these men's horses and get 'em out of sight out back," he ordered briskly. "Take the men with you and hide 'em, understand? Go along with him and keep out of sight," he told Odell and Olsen. "That'll be doing me a favor, if you don't mind." His eyes were snapping.

"Sure," said Odell readily. "We'll lead the horses. Tell your man to show us where to go."

As they were rounding a corner of the house, they heard the dull echoes of hoof beats on the trail from the lowlands. Campbell had taken his station at the hitching rail. It was almost dark.

CHAPTER SEVEN

Vagle led the two around the house and showed them where to tie their horses in the trees behind the barn. "Can't hear them in this place," he said, peering at Odell and Olsen in the semidarkness. "You friends of Mister Campbell?"

"Yes," said Odell readily. He was looking at Vagle queerly. Something about his manner and the look in his eyes did not appear just right.

"You come," said Vagle, and led them to a small shack-like building that proved to be a storehouse and blacksmith shop combined. "You stay here," he said. "Keep still and wait till I come for you." He nodded energetically and left them.

Odell peered out the door and saw the man creep through the trees on the left and disappear in the direction of the trail. "Two can play at that game, Slim," said Odell in an undertone. "There's something going on around here we ought to know about. Maybe we're mixed up in something bigger than we thought. You wait here and I'll slip through the trees out there and see what I can see . . . or hear."

He went around the side opposite from where Vagle had disappeared. Before he could see the trail, he could hear the voices of two men, one voice sounding more plainly than the other. Presently he could see the opening where the trail ran and soon he could hear what was being said.

"You've got no business to come up here, Pearlman, and you know it!" It was Campbell speaking and he was angry. "If I'd

55

wanted you up here, I'd have told you where I was going or I'd have sent for you. You're overstepping the line."

"Yeah? How about those two prairie rats coming up here? That's all right, eh? And how do I stand?"

Odell recognized the voice of the speaker, who Campbell had called Pearlman, as that of the gunman who had threatened him the night before. He pursed his lips. Pearlman, eh? He didn't know him and could not remember ever having heard the name before. But there was some connection between the two men. This was why Campbell had stepped into the play the night before. Had he been afraid that Pearlman would get the worst of it in the encounter?

"What do you mean by prairie rats?" Campbell snapped.

"Those two you said were in with you on this next deal," replied Pearlman. "I don't know 'em except by the fake names they gave last night. What're they doing here? Why should I work in the dark when I don't know what it's about?"

"What makes you think they're here?" asked Campbell mildly.

"I saw 'em ride out of town this morning, going west," was the surly answer. "I had a hunch, and later when I found out that you lived up here, I started out behind them on this trail. I followed their tracks on the trail to this spot. They were fresh tracks and there ain't no fresh tracks going on from here. I can see that by the stars. I've been a trailer all my life."

"You've never been on a more dangerous trail than this, Pearl," said Campbell in a voice that showed he was in dead earnest. "You said you'd obey orders and I gave 'em to you. I told you to stay in town and now you're here. How do you explain that?"

Although Pearlman did not know it, he was playing with death. Odell sensed this and listened breathlessly for Pearlman's reply.

"I'll tell you, Campbell, and you can't blame me," said Pearlman, lowering his voice. "You left town last night after you talked with me. But you went up to the Board of Trade before you left, and for all I know you gave a signal to those two. And bright and early this morning they lit out and they came up here. You tell me to stay away from 'em, and stay in town and all that, and how do I know but what you're planning to leave me holding the sack?"

"In your narrow mind you're suspicious of me giving you the double-cross, isn't that it, Pearl?" asked Campbell.

"Oh, I'm not saying that, but. . . ."

"But you're thinking that," Campbell interjected. "You've had so much experience in that sort of work that you think everybody else plays the game the same way. Now, suppose I tell you to kick in with what you've got left of that five hundred I gave you yesterday, and light out . . . slope for good? Ever think of that?"

There was a short silence. "Yes," said Pearlman easily, in a voice redolent with confidence, "I've thought of that, Campbell. But it might be a bad thing to do. I probably wouldn't go, and. . . ."

"And I'd have to kill you, is that what you're thinking?" suggested Campbell, his voice smooth to the danger point.

"Something like that, yes," Pearlman drawled. "But you wouldn't want to do that, would you? It would stir things up, and start the home guards to talking, and your daughter would be asking questions, and. . . ."

"Stop!" Campbell commanded hoarsely. "Stop, or I'm liable to let you have it right here, you rotter!"

Pearlman stopped, and Odell could hear him breathing hard. Pearlman was liable to get it any moment. Odell's own hand had dropped instinctively to his gun. So this gunman was using the presence of Hope to protect himself. Odell's lips curled in contempt. He almost felt that he had a personal grudge against

Pearlman for that very reason. If Campbell did shoot, he would leap out and take the blame. And there was that man called Vagle, also listening.

Campbell finally gained control of himself. "I've got your number, you rat," he said finally. "You've come up here to try and shake me down for a bunch of dough to shut your mouth. Why, you slimy snake. Because I took you in on one job and let you make more money than you ever made in your dirty life, you think you've got a life's income coming to you. You confounded ass. I stopped the sheriff from jailing you as suspicious. So far as you and me are concerned, we're through. There's just this much more, Pearlman"—his voice seemed to be hissing through his teeth—"you've bummed around with a lot of different people. This is the second time you've met me. Be careful of the third time, if there is a third time."

"I'm not the only one," Pearlman piped defiantly, but with less confidence.

"You're the only one so far as I'm concerned," said Campbell. "You're across the line now, Pearlman. Why I'm giving you a chance, I don't just know, unless it's because I've never yet forced a man to draw. You can't get your gun out of its holster before you'll be carrying my lead. That isn't a promise, Pearlman, that's a threat."

Odell saw the gunman turn to his horse. He half expected him to try a trick draw. But Pearlman evidently knew better. As he swung into the saddle, Campbell's gun seemed to pop automatically into his hand. Pearlman saw it and shook out his reins.

"If your sheriff wants to jail me, he'll have plenty of chance," he said with a faint suggestion of a sneer.

"He won't bother you," said Campbell. "When you start, which will be after I've said what little I have left to say, you won't try to sneak a shot over your shoulder, remember. A funny move and I'll drill you if I have to do it in the back. I'll give you till sundown tomorrow to get out of Pondera and off this range."

Odell waited no longer, and as he stole back through the trees as fast as possible, he heard the thunder of flying hoofs signaling Pearlman's speedy departure. He slipped into the blacksmith shop and closed the door quickly.

"Just as I thought," he told Slim Olsen in a cautious tone. "That gunman we ran up against in town last night followed us up here. His name is Pearlman. He thinks he's got something on Campbell and he wanted money to keep still. Tried using the girl to protect himself and shake down Campbell. I figured he'd threaten to tell her unless Campbell came across. But Campbell beat him to it. I looked for Campbell to shoot him, but he didn't. He gave him till sundown tomorrow to get out of town and off this range. Seems like he thought we were in with Campbell on some kind of a play . . . shady, I think. We got to be careful, Slim, because I'll tell you as a friend that I've got to see more of that girl."

"You have to see more of all of 'em," Slim remarked dryly.

"But this one's different," Odell protested. "Did you ever see one to beat her?"

"Not in looks, but you can't tell about 'em just by that," growled Slim.

"Slim, won't you ever get over that affair of yours down south?" said Odell, exasperated. "I wouldn't let one girl put me to the bad on a bet. The world's full of fresh ones. You're getting to be a woman hater, and it ain't natural . . . not for a fellow your age, anyway."

"We won't talk about my affair, as you call it," said Slim in a cool voice. "One of these days you'll get yours, and then it won't be all honey and roses. If it wasn't for my trouble down there, I wouldn't be with you up here, savvy?"

"Forget it, Slim, and . . . listen. There's somebody coming."

They stood in the darkness until the door was opened and they saw the tall figure of Campbell. "All right, boys," he said amiably, "come on out. Just like Vagle to put you in here. I didn't mean to be . . . er . . . inhospitable, but I didn't know who it might be coming up the trail and, as it turned out, it's just as well he didn't see you."

"Suppose we would be out of order to ask who it was," said Odell as they joined him in the space behind the house.

"No," said Campbell slowly. "No, I believe I'll tell you. It was the man you had the trouble with last night. His name is Pearlman. He followed you up here."

Odell was astounded at Campbell's frankness. He wondered how much he would tell them. "What did he follow us for?" he asked. "Thought he'd take a pot shot at us in the hills, maybe?"

"He could tell by your horses' tracks that you didn't go any farther than here. But he couldn't prove it unless he saw you, and I saw to it that there wasn't any chance for him to do that. But I can tell you that he's got it in for you, right and proper. He thinks you're connected with me in some way and that's why I butted in last night and stopped the gun play. He's pretty sore at me, too. I gave him until sundown tomorrow to get out of town and off the range."

Odell tingled with excitement. Campbell was telling them the truth. For a few moments Odell was on the point of confessing that he had overheard the talk. Still, that didn't seem necessary, and he didn't like the idea of explaining why he had eavesdropped. And—could he really explain it?

"Do you think he'll go?" asked Slim in his lazy drawl.

Campbell shrugged. "I hope he does," he replied grimly.

"Is there anything we can do to be of assistance?" asked Odell.

"Yes. Keep away from him. He'll pick a quarrel with either of you the minute he sees you. If you can stay away from town tomorrow, it would be a good thing. He may be waiting for you when you ride in tonight. I have a sort of a bunkhouse here and I can put you up if you want to stay."

"I believe we'd rather go back, eh, Slim?"

"That was what I was thinking." Olsen nodded. "I guess we can keep out of his way if you want us to do that, Mister Campbell."

At this moment there was a flutter of white at the rear door of the house. "Father, aren't you going to ask those men to have some coffee and a bite before they go on?" It was Hope's voice.

"I hadn't thought of that," said Campbell in a low voice. "Yes," he called to the girl, "we're coming in now!"

"We don't want to make any trouble, Mister Campbell," said Odell, squeezing Slim's arm. "We've got some lunch in our packs and we won't take so long riding back as we did coming up. We took it easy on the way up here."

"No, come on and eat," said Campbell. "Vagle!" he called. The man came shuffling from the barn. "Put these men's horses in the barn and feed 'em while we're eating supper," he ordered.

Then he led the way to the house. He left them on the small back porch while he went inside a few minutes. When he called them in, they found a small table set in the kitchen with cold meats, fried potatoes, biscuits, pie, and coffee. "Hope you boys won't mind eating here," he said. "It's on account of the womenfolks . . . you will understand."

"Mighty fine of you to give us supper." Odell smiled. He had a good smile, and Campbell smiled back as they seated themselves at the table, but both could see the change in the older man since his talk with Pearlman. He had a weight on his mind and appeared tired.

"He's taken on a job, if Pearlman doesn't leave town tomorrow," Odell told his companion across the table in an undertone.

"He'll have to ride down there and make good," Slim agreed.

"He doesn't want to do it," Odell whispered. "But it seems

like he's got to do it on account of the girl. It's hard luck, pal."

They began their meal with splendid appetites sharpened by the long ride and the crisp, cool air of the hills. They could hear Campbell and his family talking in low tones in the dining room off the kitchen. Now and then they caught a few words of the conversation, and thus learned that they were not talking about anything that had happened in town or at the house. There were two feminine voices and it was not difficult to distinguish the voice of Hope and the voice of an older woman who they heard addressed as mother.

"Nice folks," Odell said softly to Slim Olsen. Slim nodded.

Then they heard a chair pushed back, someone rose, and came into the kitchen. Ricky Odell's heart jumped as he saw the girl. She was beautiful in a low-cut dress and bits of sleeves that showed her arms. Her smile brought one from both youths.

"Want some more coffee?" she asked, taking the big pot from the top of the stove. "Of course you do. Your cups are empty."

"We can use it," said Slim in a droll voice.

"He means we would be pleased to have some more," said Odell, still smiling. "Slim doesn't know much about how to talk to ladies. I reckon this is only the second or third time he's eaten in a house."

Even Slim had to laugh at this. "You can tell her all about it," he said to Ricky. "You're the mouthpiece for the firm."

"And it's a good thing I am," Odell asserted. "Don't you notice how perfect my English is, Miss Hope. And I haven't been to college, either, although everybody thinks I have. Don't you think I look intellectual, Miss Hope?"

"You look much like an Irishman." Hope laughed.

He touched her arm and whispered to her as she filled his cup. "Honey doesn't mean anything to me any more, now that I've seen you."

"Sounds like the title of a song," she whispered back.

"You're a sweet little tulip and I'm going to see more of you," he said in her ear. And before she could raise her head, he kissed her behind that same ear. "Whoa!" he exclaimed loudly. "Cup's full!"

Her cheeks were glowing with a pink flush, and she was looking at him out of wide, staring eyes. He jerked a thumb toward the door into the dining room and put a finger to his lips. "Could I have a little more butter?" He grinned.

"There's plenty on the table," she said severely. "Look around and reach. If you want more coffee, call out."

His eyes held hers as she put the coffee pot back on the stove and went into the other room. Slim was eyeing him queerly with his brows arched. "You ain't been late anywhere yet, have you?" he said in a low voice.

"I've been ahead of time some places where I wasn't invited," replied Ricky with a pleasant smile.

They finished their supper without calling for more coffee, although Odell was sorely tempted to do so. He didn't care anything about the coffee, but he did want another look at Hope Campbell. But thought of making her father cross and possibly suspicious held him back. Slim watched the struggle with a grin. "Well, you finished," he said. "Don't you want some more coffee?"

Ricky shook his fist at him, and they pushed back their chairs.

John Campbell heard them and came out at once. "All set?" he said. "Have enough to eat, boys? It was kind of you to ride up with the message for Hope and go out of your way, and we're thanking you for it."

"Don't bother," said Odell as they rose and took up their hats. "And thank you for the supper. We didn't expect it, and that made it taste all the better. I guess we'll be going." Would Hope come out when she heard?

They went out before she could appear, if she felt so inclined.

Campbell led the way to the barn and soon they were mounted on their horses in the yard. "Keep your eyes out," said Campbell, "and try not to run into that Pearlman. I'll see you in town tomorrow. And don't say anything about locating on any land up here . . . not yet, anyway. So long."

"So long!" they called as they rode away.

There was a flutter of white on the front porch as they made the trail and turned back down the way they had come. Odell waved a hand.

CHAPTER EIGHT

John Campbell sat in the living room of his house after his visitors had left and his wife and Hope had done the supper dishes. It was a large, comfortable room, lighted by a big lamp on the table with its ornate shade. A small fire was burning in the fireplace, for there was a nip in the September air at night. There were easy chairs, a wide couch with its head smothered in cushions, a music box, a bookcase, and a stand upon which were two blue birds mounted in a glass case. A comfortable room, truly, with a deep, soft rug under foot, and reproductions of well-known paintings in neat frames on the wall, together with family pictures in oval, brown wood frames, and some Indian relics over the mantel.

John Campbell was cognizant of all this, and of his wife who was sewing beside him in front of the fireplace, and Hope who was reading a book nearby. Now that Hope was home to stay, he was home to stay, too. He felt a glow of satisfaction and instantly the look of worry was again in his eyes. For across the shadow of his threshold lay the dark possibility of Pearlman's presence on that range, and the chance that another might come.

Campbell could not wipe out his tempestuous past with a mere wave of the hand and a smile. He had made such amends as he could. Insofar as it was within his power, he was square with the world. He was not wanted anywhere and no arm of the law was trailing him. But there were former associates like Pearlman, and therein lay the danger. He was not satisfied with his treatment of Pearlman this night. Always he had been the cool and calculating leader, holding his anger in check. Had he lost his head entirely with Pearlman? He feared this was true. But why should he lie to the man, cater to him? It probably was a mistake to give Pearlman his notice. In any event, he would have to live up to his word. He could not deliberately shoot the man down. But surely Pearlman would have sense enough to go. And Campbell believed he could smooth over anything the man might say before he left. The whole town would know he had taken the part of the two young strangers to prevent a gun play. That was in his favor. The sheriff would help. He had no positive enemies he knew of on this range or in town. He could snap his fingers in the face of gossip.

These thoughts brought relief. He emptied the ashes in his pipe, filled it carefully with good tobacco, lit it, and puffed with more contentment and confidence in his heart. He looked at Hope, immersed in the book she was reading. He could hardly realize that this beautiful girl was his daughter. Men would be coming into her life, for she was one to attract men and to make them love her, even though it might be a caprice on her part. And it would be a lucky man who won her. At this thought Campbell stirred in his chair. He could not bear the thought of her going away. Then he and the wife he loved would be left alone, in the rambling house in the foothills, to live the rest of their lives. John Campbell, sturdy rock of the range, was far from young in years.

"What did Ira Crowell have to say in his note, Hope?" he asked.

Hope looked up from her book, but there was no smile in her eyes. "He's coming up tomorrow night or the next to visit us," she replied. "He wants me to go to a dance with him in Pondera."

"I see," acknowledged her father. "Did he say when?"

"No, he just said the next one, and I don't know when that will be. Maybe it won't be until the rodeo."

"That will be three weeks from now," said Campbell thoughtfully. "Do you think you will go?"

"I . . . don't know," replied Hope, wrinkling her pretty brow. "Of course we all will go down for the celebration then, won't we, Father?"

"Yes," said Campbell with a swift look at his wife, who nodded. "We will all go and you can dance with anybody you wish, and if you want Ira as an escort, it's all right with me. I want you to have as much pleasure as possible. Do you . . . like being home?"

"Of course I do, Daddy." The girl laughed and rose to give him a hug. "I love it. And Vagle says Bismarck will be ready to go tomorrow, but I have to be careful of him at first. It was so nice of you, Father, to get me such a fine horse."

"He's a thoroughbred," said Campbell with satisfaction, "and there ain't a mean streak in him. I reckon he's about as fast as anything on four legs on this range. Did you tell her what else was coming, Mother?"

"Yes," said Jane Campbell with a light smile. "How could I keep it a secret? And you said it was so big she'd guess what it was long before it got up here."

Campbell laughed in delight. "Sent clear to Minneapolis for that piano," he told Hope. "Since you've learned how to play one, I thought you might as well play a good one. Ma and me will be glad to hear the music. It's something we've missed. And I'll bet your mother still can sing, too. She used to sing better than any girl I ever knew. Real singing, I mean, not just humming around the house. You wait and you'll see." His voice was full of pride, and his wife flushed rosy red as she looked at the two of them.

"Then we'll have a great time, won't we, Mumsey?" said

Hope, kissing her mother.

John Campbell smiled contentedly—until he remembered again.

Later he went out and found Vagle in the little bunkhouse. The man was sitting by the table, playing solitaire with a pack of greasy cards. He threw the cards aside as Campbell entered and his eyes lit up.

Campbell stood by the table, looking down at him. "You saw who was here tonight?" he asked.

"You mean the one man . . . the one you talked with?" asked Vagle eagerly.

"The one who came after the young fellows you brought back here," said Campbell. "I guess you were listening in the trees, eh?"

"Yes. I heard." Vagle's eyes narrowed and he scowled. "He's no friend of yours. Are you going to kill him?"

"I hope not," said Campbell. "Now, Vagle, you mustn't say anything about it to my wife or Hope, understand? Not a word . . . not a single word. It's just you and me that know about him, see?"

"Yes, I see," said Vagle. "That man's no good. He came near getting a bullet from you, eh? I was ready, too, in case you needed me. I'm carrying my gun till he is gone for good."

"That's all right." Campbell nodded. "Now, listen, Vagle, and get every word I tell you. If that man should come here when I go to town tomorrow, shoot him before he can get to the house. Don't give him a chance, for he's quick, see?" Campbell made a motion at his hip. "I don't care where you shoot him, but don't let him get to the house at any time if he comes back. If you have to do it, don't tell anybody until I get back. I'll do the talking, Vagle, you understand? Don't let him get the drop on you and get to the house, if he comes."

Vagle's eyes gleamed. He nodded his head slowly. "I know,

boss. He won't get farther than the hitch rail. I'll tend to him."

"But be sure he's the man," Campbell cautioned. "You'll know him for sure if you see him? Good. You can talk to anybody else who might come along. But don't talk to him . . . just stop him."

"I know, I know," said Vagle with that wild, eager look. "And I keep watch tonight, just like I keep watch every night when you go away. Vagle guards this place and don't you forget it."

"Here's something else I brought you from town," said Campbell casually. "I forgot all about it till tonight." He drew a pipe from a pocket and handed it to the delighted cowhand. "That's a good one, so break it in right," he finished. He walked to the door. "Now, remember, say nothing to the womenfolks," he cautioned, opening the door.

"I'll remember," said Vagle impatiently. "I heard what you said."

When Campbell had gone, Vagle sat at the table examining the pipe with a pleased look in his eyes. Then he rose, strapped on his gun, donned a warm coat and his hat, and stole out into the night to take up his vigil.

Hope was first to go to bed upstairs, leaving her father and mother sitting in front of the coals in the fireplace. She knew they would want to talk, because her father had only come home early that morning and after a light sleep had been out looking over the place all day. It had thrilled her to have her father back at home, and it had caused a great feeling of joy in her heart to hear him say that he was going to stay at home. After all, Hope knew little of her father's comings and goings, except what her mother had seen fit to tell her. She had been away to school in Great Falls so much that he almost was a stranger to her. But now all would be different.

John Campbell smoked quietly before the fireplace, and his wife sewed silently. Campbell had something on his mind, something to say, and Jane Campbell knew it. She would wait until he was ready to talk.

"I did a pretty good business this late summer and so far this fall," he said presently. "I worked as far east as Culbertson and shipped some fine cattle. Was talking to Tom Lane in town, and I guess he kept track of me because he knew I'd been in Culbertson. He's acting more like a friend than a sheriff . . . not that he would have any law business with me. The folks in town all know that Hope is back to stay, and I told Tom a thing or two."

"You're not going out again this fall, are you, John?" asked his wife. "It's so good to have you home, so good to know. . . ." She ceased speaking with a sly look at him.

"I know, Jane. No, I won't be going away again that I know of. I think I'll run more cattle, if I can make a deal for more range. Crowell has more range than he needs and maybe I can arrange with him. Otherwise, I've put matters in pretty good shape. I may not have lived exactly right some of my life, but I'm good for a long time yet and I can finish right."

"I always knew it would come, John," said Jane, smiling at him. "You've been straight for three years now, and that's too good a start to fall down on. Besides, there's Hope."

"I know," agreed Campbell. "I understand. It's a wonder you've stuck by me the way you have, Jane. Maybe you've loved me better than I thought, and I've always loved you. That's the part of it I never could understand. Why should I have kept on after . . . ?"

"Don't talk about it, dear," his wife pleaded. "Let's close that part of the book and keep it closed."

"That's what I want to do," he said softly, "but . . . it was opened today, dear, or, rather, last night."

Jane Campbell put down her sewing. "I knew you had something on your mind, John," she said slowly. "Now tell me about it, for that's the only thing to do . . . the thing we've always done."

"I saw Pearlman in Pondera before I came home," said John slowly, picking his words carefully. "He was in with me on that Benton business that I fixed up later, you'll remember. He needed money, and I gave him five hundred dollars till I could figure out what to do. I told you about the two young fellows who were here tonight. Well, he was the man they had trouble with, and I stepped in ready to drop him if he went for his gun. He didn't, worse luck. He was up here today. He was the one I talked with out by the trail. He has a notion that I'm planning another job, the fool, and he wants in on it. He talked pretty strong and I gave him till sundown tomorrow to get out of Pondera and off the range."

"John, was . . . was that wise?"

"Maybe not. I'm wondering myself. But I can't keep passing money out to him to keep his mouth shut, and I somehow can't just pick a fight with him and force him into a gun play, although Lane is willing that I settle it that way. I'm figuring that he'll go . . . for he knows he'll have to face the music if he stays . . . and if he talks before he goes, I guess I can hush that up easily enough. If it wasn't for Hope . . . but there's no use talking about that."

"No," said Jane in a low voice. "You will . . . go down to town, then?" Her lips quivered as she spoke.

"I'll have to. But I'm pretty sure he'll be gone. Somehow I've got an idea that he's being crowded from some direction, but I don't know the direction. But he was about broke when he came here."

"You mean you think he's done something and fled up here to get away, or get you to help him?" asked Jane.

"Either that, or to try and take me for plenty of money. I won't stand for it. He's a rat and he's not going to make trouble

71

for us if I have to . . . I'll stop him right, Jane, if I have to, that's all there is to it."

"Yes, I suppose you would have to," said Jane, staring into the glowing coals. "Oh, I hope you won't have to, John. It just makes me wretched to think of it, and Hope . . . wouldn't she be sure to hear about it?"

John Campbell didn't answer. Instead he said: "With Pearlman out of the way, there's only one who might . . . who I wouldn't like to see show up. Outside of him, the whole world can come here."

His wife was looking at him with wide, frightened eyes. She wet her thin lips and a pallor came to her face. "John," she whispered, "do you mean Brackett?" She shuddered as she pronounced the name.

"Yes, Jane, I mean Brackett," he replied frankly. "If he knew . . . if he thought I had quit and was settled down and comfortable, he might be afraid I'd say something in time. He might be jealous. He would be more likely to be just plain mean and ornery and come out of curiosity. He would want more than this cheap Pearlman, more than I could give or agree to. I have to face that . . . if the time should come, Jane."

Suddenly his wife threw up her head. "Yes, John, you have to face Brackett, if he should come, and you have to deal with this Pearlman, who I think will run away by the way you speak of him, and there's only one way to do it. Bring matters to a head and shoot it out with them, wipe them off the face of the earth, just as they would try to do with you. You've got Hope to protect, and me and our home to protect, and you'd best do it in the way you know how. I would be willing to do it myself."

John Campbell took her in his arms and kissed her. "You're a brave little woman," he told her, "but maybe we're just borrowing trouble. I've got a hunch that everything is going to turn out all right and I'm going to work to that end. Now you cry a little, and we'll forget about it, and go to bed."

Vagle kept watch. His eyes were clear, his steps steady as he moved about the place, with the moon high in the night sky and the breeze chanting in the branches. An intruder would have found himself unfortunate.

CHAPTER NINE

When Ricky Odell and Slim Olsen rode away from the Campbell place, they kept a sharp look-out. There were trees on the left of the trail and Pearlman might have concealed himself and be waiting in ambush. After they had rounded the turn below the house, the right side of the trail was clear.

"Let's go!" called Odell. "He might try to pot-shoot us."

They sent their horses flying down the trail, which gradually wound around and over the easy ridges and down to the upper slope of the prairie where it was open and flat, with the plain offering no opportunity for concealment.

"I'll bet I know what Pearlman did," said Odell, his voice carrying to Olsen's ears clearly in the still, night air. "He rode away as fast as he could because he wants to get to town and guzzle a few drinks after Campbell gave him a good bye and his orders. He's the kind that would want a few under his belt, so he could think."

"That's the way I look at it," Slim replied. "He doesn't look like good medicine to me."

"I thought Campbell was going to plug him sure," said Odell. "I don't see whatever kept him from doing it except that his wife and the girl would hear the shot and would have to know what had happened. It's going to make it mighty tough on Campbell if he comes to town tomorrow and finds Pearlman still there."

"He won't be there, so don't worry," said Slim confidently.

"That's the way I've got it figured out," said Odell. But he was not thinking that Pearlman would not be on hand for the reason that was in Olsen's mind. He was sure of what he was saying for another reason entirely.

Their horses shook their heads and raced across the prairie, eager to run in the crisp night air, eager to get back to the warm barn. They had to be held in check. Both animals were thoroughbreds, sleek of body, strong of neck, with tapered legs built for speed. The youths rode with the ease of those born to the saddle.

As they sped on, Ricky Odell was thinking hard. He had made out from the talk between Campbell and Pearlman that the two men knew each other of old. It was all too evident that Pearlman thought he had, or really did have, something on Campbell. He had suggested that there were others. Campbell had accused him of coming into the country to shake him down for a lot of money. If Campbell didn't pay, Pearlman would tell what he knew to Hope, or would see that she got the information some way. It was the blackest form of blackmail. Odell's blood boiled as he thought of Hope being used as a foil. He liked Campbell, too. If Campbell had lied to Pearlman, he must have done so to stall him off. Yes, that was it. Campbell had wanted to stall him off until he could decide what to do about him. Odell sat up in his saddle with a start as he remembered the happenings of the night before. Wasn't it possible, probable, that Campbell had stepped into the brewing gun play in the hope that Pearlman would draw down on him? Wouldn't it have given Campbell an excellent chance to drop his enemy with the approbation of the big crowd present? Slowly, as he pieced his conjectures together, Odell wove a net of reasoning that gave him a better idea of Campbell's position. In time he came to believe he knew what the situation was and how to relieve it. Pearlman had to be gotten rid of for the protection of Hope.

He began to whistle and Slim Olsen looked at him quickly in the light of moon and stars. Odell seemed happy. He had been silent a long time. This sudden outburst was a danger signal.

They rode without talking, making twice as fast time as they had made on the way up, and, of course, not stopping as they had at noon during the day for lunch and a doze. It was shortly after midnight when they galloped into Pondera and put up their horses with strict orders as to their care. Then they went to an all-night café to eat.

"I reckon I could guess where Pearlman is this minute," said Odell, while they were waiting for sandwiches and coffee.

"I'd say the Board of Trade," drawled Slim. "His kind of place."

"Right," Odell agreed. "Probably got a good start at the bar by this time. If we went up there, we'd likely run into him."

"And he would more'n likely see us," ventured Slim.

"Sure, there's a good chance he would." Odell nodded.

"From what you've told me you heard him and Campbell talking about, he hasn't got any great love for us," said Slim. "You say he called us a couple of prairie rats. That ain't exactly friendly talk. If we was to go up there, Rick, we'd probably have trouble."

"He'd have to start it," Odell pointed out as the sandwiches came. "I wouldn't pick any fight with him any more'n Campbell would. And if he did start something. . . ." He left the sentence unfinished, and they ate their sandwiches and drank the coffee.

When they were rolling their cigarettes, Slim spoke. "Now, Rick, what's on your mind? You've got something on it, for I know you well enough to see the signs. And it's serious, too . . . mighty serious, I should say. I know you better than you think."

They were the only customers in the place, and the waiter was back in the kitchen. Nevertheless, Odell lowered his voice almost to a whisper when he answered his companion. "Slim, just how fast do you think this Pearlman is with his gun? You saw him ready to draw and shoot that glass out of my hand at the bar last night. You're a good judge of gun handling. How did he go for his gun?"

"Fast," Slim answered. "He went for it like he meant it and he sure would have cracked that glass. I was watching him like a hawk and had my hand on my own gun. If he had jerked his, I'd have jerked mine, just in case he tried to shoot you instead of aiming at the glass."

"Do you think I could beat him to it?" asked Odell thoughtfully.

"Now that's no kind of question to ask me, Rick. I don't know. How can I know when I haven't seen him in full action? If I told you I thought you could, and anything happened, how do you think I'd feel? I think I know what's in your head right now."

"Let's hear your guess," said Odell, frowning.

"You're figuring that Campbell's in a mess. That if he comes down here tomorrow and finds this Pearlman here, he's got to get busy and that'll be bad medicine. You're thinking of the girl, too. And the big thing you're thinking is that, if you were to get into trouble with this gunfighter and put him out of business, you'd be doing Campbell a good turn, taking a load off his mind, and helping the girl."

"Slim," said Odell with a glance of admiration at his friend, "you're a wonder. You're a natural-born mind-reader. From start to finish you just recited exactly what's in my mind in every last detail."

It was Slim's turn to frown. "You'd be playing the fool," he said in full voice, and then, lowering his tone again: "How do you know that Pearlman won't light out in the morning? Campbell's no slouch with his gun, you can see that. He's got all the manners and earmarks of a go-getter with a six-shooter.

When he stepped into the play last night, don't you suppose he was ready to draw and shoot it out? Maybe that's what he wanted. You didn't see Pearlman going for his gun, or trying to jerk it out. I believe his hand was on it. And he had good reason to draw down on Campbell today, if he had wanted to. He's afraid of him. All right, if he's afraid of him, he sure ain't going to lay around here and have to draw with him, for that's what it would amount to, and you know it."

"I know," said Odell, his brow wrinkling. "But in the meantime, even if he does intend to slope out of here, he's got time to get drunk and blurt out everything he knows. And he'd have plenty of listeners, too."

Slim was becoming exasperated. "You've always got an excuse," he growled. "Even if you did intend to mix with him, there'd be no sense in doing it till you see whether he's going to leave or going to talk. I don't like to see you step into a gun play with a man we haven't got a line on. You're fast . . . you're powerful fast . . . but this fellow may have a trick or two up his sleeve that Campbell knows about and you don't."

"That's true," Odell assented.

"Well, I'm just wasting time and breath talking here with you," said Slim in disgust. "What do you want to do?"

"I'm going to take a chance and visit the Board of Trade," Odell announced, his lips tightening. "I want to see what's going on, anyway. But that doesn't mean you've got to come along, Slim, you. . . ."

"Cut it," Slim broke in. "You know I've got to go along with you. If you've made up your mind, let's go." He slid off the stool at the counter, paid the score to the waiter, who came in at the opportune time, and Odell followed him out the door into the darkened street.

They had almost reached the Board of Trade when Sheriff Tom Lane came out the swinging doors and stopped abruptly before them. The youths could see his star of office gleaming on the left side of his soft shirt, under his coat lapel.

"I'd like to have a word with you two," said the official, studying them intently by means of the beam of yellow light that streamed from a window of the saloon. Mike had given him an exact description of the pair and he now recognized them at sight. "Aren't you the fellows who came near pulling a gun play in there last night?" he asked in a moderate tone.

"We're the two who were in there last night when some other guy tried to pull a gun play on us," Odell replied. "We were minding our own business, Sheriff, as you must have heard."

"Yeah? Well, maybe I have heard about it." He continued to study the men before him searchingly. "You're strangers around here, too, aren't you? I mean the same as that other fellow?"

"We don't know a thing about the other fellow," said Odell quickly. "Never saw him before and have no idea why he should pick on us. As for ourselves . . . we're strangers. But we're not looking for any trouble, and we're paying our way as we showed last night."

"Where have you been all day, sleeping?" asked the sheriff carelessly.

"Nope, we rode out west to see the country. We've never been this close to the mountains. We thought we'd ride up there and maybe there would be a town we could look over. We've heard that mining towns were hot stuff. We stopped at a place in the hills and found out we were wrong about the towns, and came back here." Odell was seeing to it that they were square with the sheriff. This would be an advantage if there should be trouble with Pearlman, which he anticipated. He was talking straight from the shoulder.

"Hum. That would he Campbell's place you stopped at, wouldn't it?" asked Lane. "Big white house on the right going up?"

"That's the right house and the right name." Odell nodded readily. "He gave us the lay of the land, told us we weren't packing enough grub to go into the mountains, invited us to supper, and we breezed back."

The sheriff had been listening alertly. "Campbell was the man who stopped the gun play last night, wasn't he?"

"The same man," replied Odell. "We had no idea of where he lived and he was the last man we expected to meet up there. It was pretty square of him to step in last night, too, because we've heard that *hombre* who got fresh is a gunman."

"And I hear you're not such a bad shot, yourself," remarked the sheriff dryly. "Did you know Campbell, by any chance, before you wandered into these parts, boys?"

"Look here, Sheriff," said Odell earnestly, "let's get this straight and have it over with. I don't blame you for asking questions of strangers and we're prepared to answer 'em. We're from southern range, came up here to look the country over, and we don't know a soul in town, except by chance, and never knew anybody here before we came. Is that plain?"

"Oh, all right," he said. "I have to ask questions. It's part of my job, you know. So long, and be careful."

He walked away, and the youths entered the Board of Trade.

The saloon was teeming just as it had been the night before, except that there were more at the card tables and fewer at the bar. They found a place at the upper end of the bar and Odell signaled to Mike. "We're drinking beer, for a change," he said to the bartender, "and not much of that."

While they were waiting to be served, they looked along the bar and saw Pearlman immediately. He was spending money, and therefore had a small group about him. They seemed to be listening hard to what Pearlman was saying.

"He's down there shooting off his mouth already," Odell told Slim Olsen. "But that bunch of barflies don't look as if they took much stock in what he's saying. Anyway, we squared ourselves with the sheriff, and, if anything starts, he won't be able to blame it on us. Get me, Slim?"

"He's seen you in the mirror behind the bar," said Slim.

"Just sneaking a look," said Odell. "I'll shoot one back if I can catch his eye."

Slim pursed his lips. Odell's tone, and what he said, convinced him that his companion was going through with what he had been considering at the first chance. Slim's own right hand caressed his gun. All because of a girl Odell had met but once, he told himself with a wry smile.

"Your friend is in a mean mood again tonight," said Mike in an undertone as he served the mild drinks. "Running off at the mouth mostly, though."

"What's he talking about?" asked Odell, dropping a coin on the bar.

"Oh, he's sore at Campbell, you know . . . that fellow who stepped in on the play last night," replied Mike. "He doesn't want to mix up with that old-timer, though, or he'll just naturally get his fool head shot off."

"Well, now, listen, Mike," said Odell earnestly. "We're visitors up here, you might say, and we're not looking for trouble. If we can't come into this place and take a drink and play a few cards as long as we mind our own business and pay our way, it'll be just too bad, that's all. I don't know why that fellow picked on me last night, but I want him to leave us alone. But I'm not going to take anything off him, either."

"Don't blame you," said the bartender, "and if he starts anything tonight, I'll stop him mighty quick."

"You stay out of it," said Odell. "I've been given the lowdown on that *hombre* and he's bad clear through. Don't take a chance."

"I'm here to stop trouble, if I can," said Mike as he moved away.

Odell had been watching Pearlman in the mirror and he saw the man's eyes blaze with angry fire as he noted the conversation being carried on. His face was dark, and he had ceased talking when Mike walked down the bar.

"How're the hot-shot twins, tonight?" he jeered at Mike.

"You mind your own business," returned the bartender. "If you start any trouble in here tonight, it won't be so good for you, get me?" Mike's tone was sharp.

"Who, me start trouble?" said Pearlman, simulating innocence.

"You heard me," Mike said sternly. "This is a first-class place and we don't stand for any rough stuff."

Pearlman's eyes had narrowed. He was all too evidently angry at the bartender for taking sides with Odell and Olsen, as he thought. "Friends of yours, I suppose?" he ventured. "They got away lucky with their rough stuff last night. Must be friends of Campbell's, too. Tell 'em to have a drink on me and I congratulate 'em."

"They're by themselves," said Mike, "and minding their own business. I don't reckon they want to be bothered drinking with you." Although he had not intended to do so, Mike had touched off the wrath that was slumbering in Pearlman's heart.

"Won't do no harm to ask 'em," he said, trying to speak in a cheerful voice. "Hey, you two down there! Take a snort on an old prairie wolf."

Odell touched Slim lightly on the arm and made no reply. He looked into the mirror and caught Pearlman's eye. His lips curled slightly. It was done deliberately and it was enough.

Pearlman swung away from the bar and strode up to the pair with his eyes blazing. "Willing to buy drinks last night and make a big show but lame when it comes to drinking without much of an audience, eh?" he said sharply.

Odell whirled on him. His eyes were cold, his voice like ice. "Listen, you, we're minding our own business and not looking for any trouble. You started the row last night and you seem to be figuring on starting one tonight. Now I'm telling you straight to lay off us."

All eyes in the room were directed at the trio as Odell's voice rang through the place.

"Oh, I see," sneered Pearlman. "Did Campbell tell you to say that?"

"You heard me, and I'm saying it," Odell shot at him. "If you've got any brains in that low-brow head of yours, you'll let us alone. We're strangers here and all that, but we're not taking anything from you just because you don't like us. All we want is for you to leave us alone."

Out of the corner of his eye, Odell saw men nodding to each other. He was in the right. What they didn't know was that Odell was insidiously leading Pearlman on. His face had gone a bit gray.

"Been up to Campbell's place today, eh?" leered Pearlman. "Think I don't know? Got some job on somewhere, eh? Think I'm so dumb? Going to help him pull a double-cross on me, his old partner, eh?"

"I don't know what you're talking about," said Odell sternly. "I don't know anything about your affairs or any double-crosses. But you watch out that you don't run into a triple-play."

"Oh . . . meaning you and your partner are together?" said Pearlman in a menacing tone. "A gun apiece, eh, and threatening me."

Odell turned to Olsen. "Go over on the other side of the room," he ordered. "This gent seems to want to confine himself to me." Slim went to the side of the room, his eyes never leaving those of Pearlman.

The crowd had moved back from the bar and the men were leaving tables that would be in the line of fire, if shooting should come. Mike stood helplessly behind the bar. The situation had got out of his hands.

"I'm telling you again to lay off me," Odell said loudly.

"And I'm telling you that you're trailing with Campbell because you're sweet on his girl!" snarled Pearlman in a rage. "You can't fool me, you prairie rat!"

"But I can teach you not to insult me or a girl," said Odell. The next instant the slap of his hand across Pearlman's mouth echoed sharply in the room.

There was a scramble to get out of range, and then the place shook with the roar of guns. Odell leaped to the left, his smoking gun at his right hip, as Pearlman leaned against the bar, firing aimlessly. Then the gunman slipped to the floor, sprawling on his face. A murmur came from the crowd and a long-drawn sigh of intaking breath.

"Come on," Odell said, white-faced and sheathing his gun. "Come on, Slim, he wished it on himself and everybody here knows it!"

They hurried out the door, leaving the place in an uproar.

CHAPTER TEN

As soon as the two were out of the place, Odell whisked his partner, Slim, into the shadows of a space between two buildings and spoke hurriedly and authoritatively. He took Olsen by his coat lapels to emphasize his words. "Listen, Slim, you're going through with me, aren't you?" he said in a voice deeply earnest. "You'll go through, won't you?"

"I don't see how I could get out of it," Slim replied in a cool drawl. "You know I'd go through with you, don't you?"

"Yes, Slim, I do. You're my friend, and maybe the only one I've got. Now, there's more to this maybe than we thought, and when Campbell finds out what has happened, he'll come across. You know exactly why I shot that tinhorn, but keep that to yourself under all circumstances. I nagged him on, but I guess I did it in a way that none of 'em could detect. I was in the right and every man in the joint knew it. And he egged me on with his foul talk and drew first. The draws were pretty fast, but I believe Mike, at least, saw him go for his gun a fraction of a second before I jerked at mine. Didn't you see it, Slim?"

"I was watching for it and naturally I saw it," said Slim in a gloomy voice. "You're getting too fast, Rick."

"I had to be in this case," said Odell sharply. "Now you go straight to the sheriff and explain to him just how this came about. Put in all the details, drag it out, stall him just as long as you can, but always tell the truth?"

"Then he'll throw me in jail and say if I've given it to him straight, I'll tell him where you are," remarked Slim with delicate sarcasm.

"Tell him you don't know," ordered Odell stoutly, "and you won't know for that matter, guess as much as you please."

"All right, Rick," said Slim. "I'll stall him to the last split second. But I reckon I know where you're going and I 'spect he'll get the same notion in his head. So long."

They parted with Slim Olsen hurrying to the sheriff's office and Ricky Odell disappearing in the shadows behind the building.

Slim lost no time in getting to the jail, and arrived just as Tom Lane was about to leave his office, two others, who evidently had sped to the official with news of the shooting, being present.

The sheriff looked surprised, and then pleased. "Why, come right in . . . er . . . come right in. I thought you fellows had bolted town right after the . . . accident."

"We didn't," said Olsen, giving the two other men a sharp glance. "These men have to be here?" he asked with a frown.

"Sure not," said Lane agreeably. "We were just talking over some business and. . . ."

"Well, I'm here to explain that business and maybe I can give you more information than they can," said Slim coldly.

The two men had started for the door. "So long, boys," said Lane. Then to Slim: "You always jump at conclusions?"

"Don't have to in this case," was Slim's calm retort. "What did you hear, Sheriff?"

"I heard your pal, Ricky Odell, put that man Pearlman he quarreled with the other night in a pretty bad way, in one of the fastest gun plays ever staged on the range," said the sheriff slowly.

"In a bad way!" exclaimed Slim. "Isn't the man dead?"

"He might be by now," Lane confessed. "You fellows wanted

him dead, didn't you?"

Slim stared for a few moments with his mouth open. "Why, when Rick is goaded into drawing down on a man, after that man has already made a healthy start for his cannon, Rick usually draws fast and accurate and shoots the same way," he explained.

"Oh, so he's a gunfighter, eh?" droned the sheriff. "Draws fast and shoots accurately. They've got to be that way if they're to make any progress at their trade."

Slim sat down with a look of exasperation on his tanned face. "Sheriff, let's be square, because we're going square with you. I'm in on this play as much as Rick, for I backed him up and was tickled all over to do it. I'm Rick's friend, and when I tell you that I've spoke a mouthful. Ricky is fast with his gun, but he's not a gunfighter and never picked a fight with a man in his life. I've known him since we were kids, and this is his first killing. He's all broken up over it. Trembling and sweating and swearing, and I had to get him out of the way. Was afraid there might be some of that Pearlman's gang around to take the thing up, and Rick couldn't hit the side of a barn in the shape he's in. He's shaking like a leaf and I doubt if he could pull a gun, let alone shoot it right now. I told him to get out of sight, go anywhere, and he told me to tell you he'd see you later. He dodged in the dark and I don't know where he went. I'm here to represent him."

Sheriff Lane had listened intently, and had repeatedly searched the speaker's face. It was his business to know considerable about men. Here was a young man he thoroughly believed to be telling the exact truth. But the connection with Campbell, which he suspected—that was quite a different matter. "They call you Slim, do they not?"

"Olsen is the last name," scowled Slim suspiciously.

"Very well, Olsen it is," said the sheriff genially. "I understand very well, from what I've heard from a reliable source, that Pearlman picked a quarrel with Rick as you call him, and Campbell stepped in to prevent a possible shooting affray. Isn't that so?"

"Yes," snapped Olsen, "and we were mighty glad of it. We came here minding our own business to see the country. We'd never been so close to any real mountains."

"That's all right." Lane nodded. "And you told me this night you'd gone up to the foothills and had happened on Campbell's place up there and had had dinner with him. Isn't that so?"

"That's the unvarnished truth, Sheriff."

"Now when you came back tonight, this Pearlman picked on you again and said some things that practically compelled Odell to match guns with him. So?"

"Every word of it, and there are plenty who will say that Pearlman actually went for his gun first," replied Slim stoutly.

"In the meanwhile," said the sheriff shrewdly, leaning on his desk and looking his visitor in the eyes, "didn't Pearlman go up there to see Campbell? I expect an answer straight from the shoulder, since you say you're being square."

Slim's gaze was steel-blue. "I cannot answer that question."

"Why not?" Lane shot crisply.

"Because Campbell stepped into that first fracas, because you found out from us tonight . . . we told you willingly enough . . . that we'd had supper with Campbell after stumbling upon his place up there, and because there seems to be something queer about the whole business, and you seem to be linking us with this Pearlman and Campbell in some way . . . and you're not going to do it."

"How do you know I'm not going to do it?" asked Lane angrily.

"Because we came here on our own, not knowing a soul in town," rang Slim's voice, "and all you've got to do to find it out

for yourself is ask a few questions around, because this Pearlman picked on us from the moment we breezed up to the bar
and Ricky started to have some fun at his own expense with
everybody but this tinhorn willing, because Campbell, who we
didn't know at all, butted in on the play, because we visited
Campbell by accident, and because this Pearlman tried to get
Rick tonight for no reason we know of. You can't link us up
with anybody or anything. I'm going to answer no tricky questions, Mister Sheriff. Ricky Odell and me are on our own."

The sheriff re-lit his cigar, puffed on it, turning his eyes from
the youth, and then spoke pleasantly: "I have to look at all
angles in a case like this. We don't have many shootings around
here, and we don't like 'em. I've got to ask certain questions,
and, you not living here, wouldn't know why. I'll have to repeat,
Olsen, that you said you both were going to play square."

"We will stand that way, Sheriff, but we're not going to
answer any questions about anything we don't know about. We
will answer questions that have to do with us directly."

"You mean, of course, that Pearlman didn't go to Campbell's."

"We were not in a position to see Pearlman if he did come."

"Why not?" queried Lane, with a look of sudden interest.

"It was nearly dark when we got there and we talked to the
girl out by the hitching rail." He paused, knitting his brows, for
he had to be careful, and knew he was on dangerous ground.

"Never mind the girl, for she'd keep any young fellow hanging around," said Lane amicably. "I think Pearlman said
something about a girl in the ruckus tonight. Leave her out and
go on."

Slim had had a needed respite for quick thinking while the
sheriff had been talking and now he went on confidently. "Her
father saw us out there and came stamping on the scene. He
recognized us, told us there were no towns in the hills, and that

we didn't have grub enough to go over the mountains, and invited us to have supper before we started. We agreed and went around back to put up our horses, and wash up for supper. We were hungry and there wasn't a bit of sense in turning down the invitation."

"Of course not," agreed Lane with a friendly smile. "Now tell the truth, Slim, for I know there was a rider followed you two up there. It may be I know more than you think, so don't get yourself and your friend in a tangle."

Slim nodded grimly. "There was a rider," he said slowly, "but it was about dark, and we were in back, and couldn't see him. We're not going to try and identify any rider we couldn't see. He stopped out front a short while, rode away, and Campbell came back and we went in to supper. That's our story and if you know any different, make the most of it. But you can't hang anything on us out of that business."

"Why, boy, I'm not trying to hang anything on you," said Lane impatiently. "I merely wanted to be sure if it was Pearlman that went up there, and thought maybe you could help me out."

"I'm afraid we can't do anything in that direction," was Slim's cool response.

Lane remained silent for some little time, which suited Slim. Slim realized that he wasn't exactly stalling the sheriff. He was battling his wits against those of the official, and he was taking care to protect Ricky Odell and himself, although he had Odell foremost in his mind.

On Lane's side there was more than a bit of shrewd admiration for his youthful adversary. He, too, knew they were engaged in a battle of wits. That Slim Olsen was clever—more than ordinarily clever—was evinced in the way he had handled the matter of Pearlman's ride to the Campbell Ranch. He had acknowledged in time—and at the time he thought was proper—

that there had been a rider at the Campbell place, but that in no way could he or Odell know that it was Pearlman. And he had effectively stopped Lane's advance in that direction. No dumb, wandering cowpuncher, this boy. He now advanced from another quarter.

"Slim, I've thought of something else," he said with a slight wrinkle of his brow, puffing thoughtfully at his cigar. "Maybe you boys don't know that Pearlman was up there, and maybe I don't. We'll let it go at that. But, if it was Pearlman who rode up there, and if he followed you there, or if he thought you had ridden up to see the man who had stopped that first gun play and were keeping out of sight, wouldn't he feel mighty sore at you boys?"

"He might . . . on general principles," Slim conceded.

"There you are," announced the sheriff in triumph. "He suspected you had been there, he had got no satisfaction out of Campbell concerning anything he had in mind, and when you two drifted back to town and into the Board of Trade, it just naturally made him so mad he picked a fight without thinking of anything except getting even with somebody?"

Slim scowled and looked steadily at Lane. This was no dumb sheriff. And the question he had just asked was a poser. It was a dead out for Ricky and himself. He decided to take advantage of this and find out what the joker in the question was. "That's probably the way of it," he said, nodding. "He let his imagination run away with him, or he found out we had gone up there. It made him sore to think we may have taken up with our protector the night before, and he picked a fight with us and forced Ricky into a gun play at sight." He was watching Lane closely.

"Of course," beamed Lane. "Then Pearlman must have known you went up there, see? And he had to ride up there to make sure. He just rode into town a bit before you fellows came in. Don't you suppose that he must have been the mysterious rider you spoke about?"

Slim smiled broadly. "Sheriff," he said quizzically, "you're good. There ain't no doubt about it . . . you're good. Now let's try another angle and maybe we can get somewhere. What connection is there, or was there, between Campbell and this Pearlman? Explain the whole tangle to me and maybe what Rick and me saw might shed some light on what you're trying to get at."

But Lane frowned. His fresh attack had proved to be a boomerang, and he had no intention of explaining Campbell's connection with Pearlman, because he was becoming more and more convinced that there was a more serious connection between the wise youths and Campbell. He was almost on the point of believing that Campbell had sent them to town to kill Pearlman. But why should he do this when he had the chance to do the job himself when he had stepped into the first play in the Board of Trade? His head felt as if it was tired of thinking. One thing was sure. He would get nothing out of Slim Olsen. At present the youth was a match for him. Later—it might be different.

"I can't tell you anything without telling you too much," he scowled. "If you don't know about anything, then it's for your own good. I guess we'll call it off, for the present."

"I suppose you'll want to hold me," said Slim.

"Hold you?" Sheriff Lane appeared surprised. "What do I want to hold you for? Everybody knows that Pearlman deliberately forced a gun play and got the worst of it. I'm not holding you. You're free to go as you please and do as you please. I think I'll take some air myself a little later. Go ahead." He waved a hand toward the door.

It was a masterstroke, and Slim Olsen went out with his brow furrowed in thought. What did Lane have up his sleeve? He walked through the cool, crisp air of early morning to the livery.

"My pardner's horse here?" he asked casually.

"Sure," answered the barman. Then, seeing the look of perplexity on Olsen's face, he said: "He hired a fresh horse and rode out of here 'bout an hour or so ago."

"Thanks," grunted Slim, and, tossing the man a dollar, he went out, proceeded to the hotel, and went to bed.

CHAPTER ELEVEN

It was glorious dawn when Ricky Odell drew rein near the Campbell place in the foothills. He paused to look back over the golden waves of plain, sweeping into the sunrise. The little creek, flowing down from the higher ranges, sparkled and the river laughed and the air was sweet with the morning songs of the birds. Ricky removed his hat and waved it across his horse's head, as if in salute to this radiant universe. He turned his horse and caught sight of a rider coming down the trail. Instinctively he struck for his gun butt. Then raised his hand in another salute, which ended in a bow and the sweep of his hat, as the rider drew up beside him.

"Are you a sun worshipper?" asked Hope Campbell, radiantly beautiful with her hair spinning gold in the sunlight, and her lips breaking into a saucy smile. "I saw you wave your hat at it."

"Miss Campbell, this is not the time for trivial nonsense," he said soberly. "I saluted the dawn, the sun, the beauty of the plain, the singing of the happy birds, and thanked God for another day." He bowed again.

There was a queer light in the girl's dancing eyes that faded gradually. "I almost believe you are in earnest, Ricky Odell," she said seriously.

"I am in earnest, dear girl," he said severely and with an air of injured dignity that, sincere or otherwise, was splendidly done. "I am a lover of beauty . . . beauty of Nature, beauty of horseflesh, beauty in a woman. I'm even appreciative of a beauti-

94

fully played hand at cards." He arched his brows in a simulation of superiority.

"In the face of all this"—Hope Campbell laughed delightedly—"Ricky Odell, you're a fraud." Her voice was good to hear.

"It's a good thing you're not a man," he said with a ferocious scowl. "Besides that, you should be a little more considerate and have more courtesy. I hadn't finished what I wanted to say, or had intended to say."

"Oh, I'm sorry," she said in a voice of repentance. "Please excuse my interruption, Mister Odell. Honestly I thought you were just joking, but now I see I took too much for granted. You are in earnest, and when an Irishman is in earnest, well . . . that means something."

"I wish you wouldn't keep on with that Irish stuff," he said irritably. "Don't you like Irishmen?"

"I have nothing against Irishmen," she answered flippantly.

"That isn't answering my question," he said, "but here's one you're going to like, so you better take a good look at him while the light's good."

"Oh, indeed. Now that's interesting. I've been looking at you, too, now that I think of it. I'll grant you this, Ricky, dear, you're a novelty because there's nothing dull about you."

"Very well, I accept your apology. Now, Hope, sweet, we'll get back to what I was saying about beauty. We'll take it by sections and pass over the beauties of Nature because we're both very familiar with them. We'll pass over the birds, too. My favorite is roast grouse, and I suspect you wouldn't turn up your nose at one, either. But take the beauties of horseflesh. That is a fine animal, which is honored by having you on its back." He looked appreciatively at the fine points of the black charger, Bismarck.

"You're well mounted yourself, Mister Odell," she commented.

"Any horse that carries me, Miss Hope, is proud to eat my oats," he said sternly.

"It's a very good horse," said Hope gravely, "but when Bismarck is in shape, I can outrun you. This is the first time I've ridden him since his sprain. Vagle says I must be easy with him for a week or more."

"Yeah? And who's Vagle? Never mind. I know. He's that old-timer you've got working for you up there. Looks queer to me. But that horse. . . ." Odell was looking the animal over critically. "Yes, Miss Hope, if that horse can live up to its points, it can beat mine . . . and I'll bet yours is the only horse hereabouts that can do it."

"Why, Ricky. . . ." She stopped short in confusion. The name had come out so naturally.

"That's all right, Hope," he announced cheerfully. "That's what it's going to be from now on. We're friends, are we not? And don't friends call each other by their first names?"

"I suppose so," said the girl doubtfully.

"Of course they do," agreed Ricky Odell. "And you know when they've been friends a while . . . a boy and a girl, I mean . . . bimeby they . . . well, no matter." He shrugged and smiled. The smile went with the sunrise and she returned it. "Now, you were about to thank me or something for saying that I believed your horse, Bismarck, could outrun mine, isn't that so?"

"I was going to say it was very kind of you to say that," she confessed. "But I'm not sure at all . . . Ricky."

"Listen, girl, I paid your horse a bigger compliment than you think." He gestured impressively. "This horse I'm on isn't my own horse a-tall. I rode my own horse pretty hard yesterday and last night, and I hired this horse to ride up here this morning." He threw a look over his shoulder down the back trail and she noted it and realized that it had seemed perfectly natural to meet him like this in the early morning, whereas he must have come on some mission. She wondered.

"Now my own horse, which is in the livery down in Pondera, is a mighty fine animal . . . fast and enduring . . . and when I say I think maybe Bismarck could beat him, I am saying something. So! You see?"

"Yes, that is a compliment, Ricky. And I'm beginning to wonder why you hired a horse and rode up here so early in the morning."

"Oh, that?" He waved the matter aside with a sweep of his hand. "I'll tell you later. I want to go through with this beauty business, now that we've settled the horseflesh matter. You will remember I said I was a lover of beauty in a woman?"

"You seem to find beauty in everything," she replied, her cheeks blooming with rose.

"Well, I don't," he said shortly. "I see no beauty in . . . in a lot of things. There's no sense mentioning them. But I do see beauty in a woman, and in a girl . . . and with the sun spinning gold in your hair, and your laughing, tantalizing eyes, and your saucy lips, and the grace of you in the saddle, Hope . . . you're the most beautiful creature I ever laid eyes on. And if you think I'm fooling, I'll drag you down off that horse and kiss you."

Hope listened, her eyes wide, her lips parted. She lowered her gaze, then raised it with her eyes flashing. "I don't think you should have said that, and spoiled it all," she said with genuine regret in her tone.

"Why not?" he asked in surprise. "It's true, every word of it, and it comes straight from my Irish heart. I've fussed around with girls, Hope, and flattered 'em to see 'em smile. Any fellow will do that, if he has red blood in his veins. But I am not flattering you, girl, and you didn't smile. It won't spoil anything because I came out frankly at the start. You have too much

97

sense for that."

She was looking into the distance, across the flowing gold of plain to the clear blue horizon in the south. She felt a desire to be alone, to whirl her horse and speed away. But she didn't. She looked at the frank, serious face of Ricky Odell, and believed him. It was not hard to look at Ricky. He had dropped his hat. She felt a sudden urge to swerve her horse and pick it up for him, but his next words stopped her.

"When do you get any sleep?" he was asking. "I find you in the evening and I find you in the first of the morning."

"Why, I sleep at night, silly!" She almost giggled.

"But you can't sleep at night," he protested.

Her brows went up. "No? And why not?"

"Because the stars would sing to you, and the moon would have no control over them and would shout to them to shut up, and that would wake you up. And then you would hear the mockingbirds and other little night birds about your window, and the stars would start singing twice as hard, and when they do that tonight, you'll think of me . . . and that'll make it worse than ever."

"Ricky Odell," she exclaimed, her eyes laughing, "I might have known it! All Irishmen are born poets."

"And born lovers, too," warned Ricky. "Can't you see a romance when it's budding right under your pretty nose?"

"Ricky, why did you come up here this morning?" she demanded, flustered but stern nevertheless.

"Well, tell the truth, I came up to see your father," he confessed a bit ruefully. "You see, I have to be truthful with you . . . I never could lie to you, Hope . . . but I wish I came up thinking I might by chance find you riding out like this. This has been the most enjoyable half hour of my life, honestly. Is anybody up but you . . . besides you, I mean? My grammar falls down terribly in these high altitudes."

"Never mind your grammar, Ricky. What do you wish to see Father about?" There was a worried look clouding her pretty eyes.

"I can't tell you that, girl. I'm merely a messenger."

"Is anything wrong?" she asked quickly.

"Not that I know of," he replied, shaking his head. He gripped the horn of his saddle quickly and dived down with his right, retrieving his hat. "I suppose he's up by now."

"Yes, I reckon so," said the girl slowly. She pressed her lips tightly, then: "Ricky, you said you would never tell me anything but the truth. Please tell me this. Is there any trouble or anything like that? There was a strange rider here last night and I could tell by Father's voice that he was angry. Mother asked me not to go out on the porch. And Mother and Father were still talking downstairs in low tones when I went to sleep."

"Your father has been away for some time, hasn't he?" said Ricky gently. "It's only natural they would have many things to talk about. Why, I'm surprised if you're worrying about anything. I met your father first down in Pondera. I met him accidentally up here the second time. We're somewhat like friends, already. Is it strange I should come up with a message for him? I can't tell you what it is about. It wouldn't be fair to my trust, would it?"

She looked into his clear eyes, and for the second time that morning she believed him fully. Her eyes roved happily over the vast panorama below them—the limitless plain, the blue rim of the horizon, the mounting sun, the silver ribbon of river trailing its robes of green. She looked back at Ricky Odell, strong, almost handsome, his hat set at a saucy angle on his head. Why, it seemed good to be there in the glory and freshness of the morning with him at her side.

"Come on," she said gaily, "we'll go home and I'll coax Dad to make you stay to breakfast."

And away they went—to find John Campbell waiting for them at the hitching rail in front of the house.

Chapter Twelve

As they rode up to the rail and reined in their mounts, Hope called cheerfully to her father. "Look what I found on the up-trail," she said. "Don't forget to make him stay for breakfast, Daddy. He's ridden clear from town."

"Hope, turn your horse over to Vagle and go into the house at once!" her father commanded.

There was a long silence during which father and daughter looked steadily at each other. The girl's cheeks had paled and Odell gritted his teeth.

"That isn't any way in which to speak to me, Father," said Hope in a low, steady voice.

"Are you going to do as I say?" roared Campbell in a rage.

In a trice, Hope was off her horse. She walked straight up to him, her face almost white. "I will obey you in anything that is reasonable, Father," she said in a strong voice, holding her head high, "but not when you address me in such a tone of voice. You seem to have forgotten, in the time I've been away, that I am your daughter."

"And in the time you've been away you've been taught to disobey your father . . . is that it?" demanded Campbell angrily.

"I have been taught to conduct myself in such a manner that I will be treated with respect," was the girl's spirited rejoinder. "I have never treated you as anything but my father. I expect as much respect from you as from any other man."

Campbell sputtered and calmed down. A glint of admiration

came into his eyes. This girl, holding her head high before him, was a Campbell, sure enough. "All right, Daughter, please go to the house," he said.

"Very well, Father. I'll send Vagle for Bismarck. I'll tell Mother you're staying to breakfast, Mister Odell." She smiled at him, nodded coolly to her father, and walked rapidly toward the house.

"Is this any of your work?" Campbell demanded of Ricky.

"You're doing your daughter an injustice when you ask that," said Ricky coldly. "Why, I've only met her two or three times, and each time by accident."

"Then take care that you don't meet her again, by accident or any other way, understand?" said Campbell harshly.

Odell slid from his saddle, threw the reins over his horse's head, and confronted the irate man at the rail. "It's funny," he drawled, "that a man can get up on such a morning as this feeling the way you do. I'm twenty-one, free, and white, and with nothing in my past I'm ashamed of. I'll meet your daughter every time I can, regardless of the circumstances."

Campbell's face darkened. It was some time before he could get words out of his mouth. "Why, you . . . you. . . ."

"Cut it!" Odell interrupted curtly. "I have that right!" He looked Campbell squarely in the eyes, and his own eyes were hard. "Don't try it, Campbell," he warned, "for I'll beat you to the draw. That's one reason why you should keep away from your gun, and there's another reason far more important."

Campbell never knew how close he had been to the point of drawing. Odell's worlds stopped him. "What other reason?" he shot through his teeth. The idea of this stripling opposing him!

"You don't think for a minute that I rode up here on a hired horse this morning for nothing, do you?" asked Odell calmly.

"I don't give a hang how you got here!" Campbell exploded. "What do you want?"

"I want to talk to you a minute or two, and then I expect to accept Miss Hope's kind invitation to stay to breakfast," said Odell. "Maybe I've got pleasant news, and maybe it isn't so good, but I thought it important enough to bring it to you and you'd better calm down and receive it coolly."

Despite his anger, Campbell was keenly interested. "What's the news?" he asked with more composure.

Odell's eyes narrowed a trifle. "Early this morning," he said slowly, "I shot and killed your man Pearlman in the Board of Trade in Pondera."

"You what . . . killed him?" Campbell managed to gasp out.

"Exactly," confirmed Odell. "He picked a quarrel with me the minute Slim and me went into the place. I was careful . . . very careful to let him put himself in the wrong. He bullied and insulted me, and mentioned your daughter. I slapped him in the face and let him start for his gun. Then I dropped him for keeps."

"But . . . but. . . ." Campbell seemingly could not believe his ears. "But Pearlman was one of the wickedest gunmen I ever knew," he blurted.

"He was wicked this morning," agreed Odell. "I believe he was shooting off his mouth about you when we came in . . . not that anybody would believe, of course. He was buying the drinks. You'll remember you'd given him till sundown tonight to leave town. I don't think he would have stayed. But he wanted revenge on somebody, and Slim and me figured he was taking it out on us. It wouldn't have made any difference, for he'd have got it anyway, after the cracks he made. I thought you'd want to know what happened . . . from me."

Campbell was visibly shaken, his eyes no longer glowed with anger, and his face had gone pale under his tan. He kept wetting his lips with his tongue.

"Tell me just what he said before the . . . what happened?" he asked in a dull voice.

"I don't know what he had been saying before we got in there, as I told you. When we came in, Mike came hurrying up and we bid for a couple of beers. Neither me nor Slim drink to any extent. I saw Pearlman at once, through the mirror, with a crowd, drinking a ways down the bar. Then he ordered a drink for the house and we ignored his invitation. He came up to us and made a crack that I had been ready to buy drinks the night before, but fell down when it came to showing off without an audience. I told him to lay off us, that we were not looking for any trouble but were minding our own business. I put this across hard, two or three times, so the crowd would be sure it was not me who was pushing the fight. Then he said we, Slim and me, had been up here and as much as declared we were helping you to double-cross him in some way, hinted we had a deal on."

Campbell swore and looked toward the house. No one was in sight except the crab-like man, Vagle, who was coming for Hope's horse. "Don't say anything while he's here," cautioned Campbell. "I'll talk stock talk till he's gone."

When the hand had taken away the horse, Odell resumed. "I told him we didn't know what he was talking about and to leave us alone. He as much as accused the two of us as being ready to take him on and I sent Slim across the room, making it a two-man play, for I was getting mad fast." Odell paused and nodded slowly to the older man to warn him of what was coming. "The next crack he made was that I was trailing with you because I was sweet on your girl and he called me a prairie rat. I thought I'd taken enough and slapped his face. I let him make a move for his gun, and plugged him in the heart."

Campbell's lips were pressed into a thin, white line. "You had to do it," he breathed, looking down the trail. "There wasn't any way out of it. Especially after . . . after. . . ." He shot a quick look at Odell.

"Exactly," Odell said grimly. "I couldn't let him go on and

bring Hope's name into it. He was the kind to do it."

"I won't have to go down to town today after all," Campbell muttered vacantly. Then his eyes lighted up and he stared at Odell. "Listen, young fellow, you must be a wonder with your gun. I reckon you knew pretty well that you could beat Pearlman to it. You just said a while back that you could beat me to it. And you knew I had to go down today and settle with Pearlman if he didn't leave town. Isn't that so?"

"Yes, that's so," Odell acknowledged promptly.

"Well, are you sure you didn't pick the fight with Pearlman so that I wouldn't have to go down there today?" asked Campbell pointedly.

Odell's brows lifted. "I have told you the circumstances just as they happened," Odell again grew cold.

"But you won't deny that if you did do this thing to take the trouble off my hands, even though I didn't ask you to do it, you would, in a way, have a club over my head. Isn't that so?"

Odell's lips curled. "It's a mighty cheap way of looking at it," he said. "Perhaps I've got you wrong, Mister Campbell."

This had its effect. "No, no, I guess I didn't realize what I was saying," he put in hastily. "You had to do what you did. Still . . . you could have stayed out of there."

"I'll stay out of no place for any man," was Odell's hot retort. "There's no reason for anyone to pick on me or on Slim, unless it's because of the fact that you butted in on our side that first night. Everything seems to have happened the wrong way after you made that move. What was your idea?"

Odell's words crackled on the air and John Campbell stared at him with a startled light in his eyes. The youth spoke the truth. Why had he stepped in? Because at the time he thought he would make Pearlman draw and end it himself. He didn't dare to answer Ricky Odell's question and tell the truth.

"It seems to me," Ricky drawled, "that the best way out of it would be to tell me what's behind all this and then Slim and me will know how to protect ourselves. It's no more'n fair. I never killed a man in my life till now."

Campbell fell back. He felt guilty, and he knew his face was red and that his eyes must be giving away his thoughts. "Where's your pardner, Slim," he asked in confusion.

"I sent him to the sheriff to tell him exactly what took place," replied Odell. "I told him to tell nothing but the truth and to leave you and the rest of it out of it, and to stall the sheriff off until I could get word to you. I don't know what kind of a mess I'm mixed up in. What's more, if you don't tell me, I'll go to the sheriff himself and demand a showdown."

"That won't be necessary," said Campbell quickly. "And I guess you've cleaned up what mess there was. Yes," he concluded grimly, "that's about what you've done." He turned. "Vagle!" he called. Then to Odell: "Come on and Vagle will take care of your horse. You better stay to breakfast until I have had time to think."

When Vagle had taken the horse, Odell went up the steps to the porch, sat down, and proceeded to roll a cigarette. He had just lit it when Hope Campbell came out. He threw it away and took off his hat immediately, rising.

"You needn't have done that," said the girl. "I don't mind a man smoking in my presence, for I'm used to it."

"I don't think I better take so much liberty at first," he said gallantly, with a bow and a twinkle in his eyes. They had stepped to the porch railing.

"I don't feel I should be afraid of any liberties from you, Ricky," said Hope with a smile. "You're a gentlemanly sort."

"In my rough way, Miss Hope," he corrected. "I reckon I've got plenty of competition among the blue bloods hereabouts."

"You mean Ira Crowell," she accused. "Why didn't you tear up that note you brought from him?" she taunted.

106

"You're forgetting I hadn't met you yet." He smiled. "And after I had met you, it was a good excuse for meeting you, an alibi. But I wouldn't swear I'd be a messenger from him again."

Hope laughed. "I get plenty of notes and know lots of boys, but I hope you won't think I'm a flirt," she chided.

"Not so far as I'm concerned, you're not a flirt, Hope."

She looked away quickly. "Don't you think this is a pretty place?" she asked, changing the subject with a feeling she was on dangerous ground. This Ricky Odell was not to be trifled with and she was not accustomed to men like that. As for Ira Crowell—he was silly. The others. . . .

"This is a beautiful place," he told her with an honest ring to his voice. "Look at the sun filtering through the trees and dropping golden spangles on the grass. And those high mountains wearing purple shawls. It's my first time in the hills."

"I have a name for it," she said, somewhat dreamily. "I call it Prairie's End. It is that . . . in more ways than one."

"It's a pretty name," said Ricky. "But if it's that, it must be the beginning of something else."

"Come to breakfast!"

They turned and saw Mrs. Campbell in the doorway.

CHAPTER THIRTEEN

It was a sprightly breakfast, with John Campbell at the head of the table, his wife Jane at the foot, and Hope Campbell and Ricky Odell on either side. Hope and Ricky kept up a running fire of banter into which Jane frequently interjected a sprightly remark. John Campbell was quiet, mostly, and moody. Time after time, Odell caught the older man regarding him curiously. Jane served the breakfast of baked apples, sausages and eggs and griddlecakes, biscuits with wild honey, and fragrant hot coffee.

"This is the liveliest breakfast we've had in this house since we lost our boy," said Jane thoughtfully in an interval of silence.

John Campbell dropped his knife and fork and looked at her, almost crestfallen. Then he quickly resumed eating. There was an awkward pause and Odell thus learned for the first time that there had been a boy in the family. He looked at Hope, who smiled faintly.

"Bismarck is almost himself again," she told her father. "Mister Odell paid me a compliment today by saying he believed Bismarck could beat his own horse."

Campbell looked suspiciously at the youth.

"I was riding a hired horse at the time," Odell explained lightly. "But I wouldn't be surprised if Bismarck could give my own a run for the money."

"Hope's horse is a thoroughbred," Campbell muttered.

"Someday when Bismarck is himself and you have your own

horse, we'll have a race," said Hope merrily.

"That wouldn't be fair . . . with you riding him," said Odell.

"Why not? I ride well, don't I, Daddy?"

"I mean, I would have to let you win," laughed Odell.

"Which shows he's a chivalrous young man, Hope," said her mother, while Campbell scowled sullenly.

"If that's the case, I'll get Vagle to ride him," returned the girl. "Vagle can probably ride as well as you, Mister Odell." There was a mischievous look in her eyes when she glanced up at him.

"I lay no claim to being a marvel in anything," Odell said.

Thus it went, back and forth, with Jane frequently joining in, and John Campbell remaining taciturn and thoughtful as if he were hardly conscious of the food he was eating. All had noticed that Ricky Odell's table manners were not those of the average cowhand. Jane and Hope appreciated this, while it increased Campbell's suspicions. He could not get away from the fact that the youth who sat at his table had just killed one of the fastest gunmen he had ever known. He couldn't be expected to overlook that fact, either. And here he was, eating in a most mannerly way, carrying on a conversation that he made little short of brilliant with his witty sallies and clever repartee. Campbell always had been suspicious of men who could talk lightly and entertainingly. Yet Odell had faced him in an entirely different manner out by the hitching rail. He had talked straight from the shoulder, without mincing words. He had given Campbell such a vivid description of what had taken place in town that Campbell could easily form a mental picture of the scene in the Board of Trade when Odell's gun had blazed death into Pearlman's heart. And it was the indirect reference to Hope that had precipitated the shooting. That fact made him squirm, but he was not satisfied that Odell had not brought on the clash, insidiously and subtly led Pearlman to his doom. Of course, later, the sheriff would be sure to be involved. Campbell decided to go to town with Odell, and the decision cheered him somewhat.

Campbell and Odell left the house together and sat on a rustic bench in the yard where the trees drew back from the trail. Campbell filled his pipe and Odell rolled and lighted the usual brown-paper cigarette.

"What do you suppose has happened to your friend Slim?" Campbell asked casually.

"I suppose the sheriff held him and is waiting for me to come in," was the answer. "I sent word by him to the sheriff that I would report, which I intend to do this morning."

"Humph," grunted Campbell. "I'll have to go in with you."

"I don't see any necessity for it," said Odell earnestly.

"Well, you don't know Tom Lane, that's all. He's the sheriff. He'll want to see me. He probably knows you fellows were up here yesterday and he more'n likely knows that Pearlman followed you up. He'll want to know why the crowd was here. I'll tell you this much, Odell, and be careful not to talk to anybody about it. I'd known this Pearlman before and he thought he had something on me. He was trying to take me for a bunch of money to keep his foul mouth shut, but he went too far when he came up here. That's why I gave him his notice. You did the job I'd have had to do if he failed to leave. Now you know all I'm going to tell you. Pearlman is gone and you haven't anything to worry about." He was thinking of Brackett, the only man he really feared, but he had no intention of mentioning the name.

"I'm glad I was of some help," murmured Odell.

"Hello! There's another visitor coming," said Campbell. "I can hear him on the trail. Hustle out of sight behind the house till I find out who this rider is. Hurry!"

Odell sped away, but he walked slowly back when he saw the newcomer was Slim Olsen, who dismounted near Campbell.

"Let me do the questioning," he suggested to Campbell as he joined them. "I reckon Slim can talk easier to me. What happened, Slim?"

"Nothing," drawled Olsen. "He told me he had nothing against me and I was free to go and do as I please. I found out you'd hired a horse at the livery and suspected you'd come up here. I came along to pass you the news that he expects to see you, but says we were in the right."

"*Pshaw,*" growled Campbell. "I'm the man he wants to see."

"He didn't say any such thing to me," Slim announced.

"Didn't he ask you if you had been up to my place?" asked Campbell. "Didn't he mention me in any way a-tall?"

"Well, yes," Slim confessed, "but he didn't say he wanted to see you. He asked if we hadn't been up this way yesterday, and I told him we had stumbled on your place. Didn't see any use in concealing it. The thing he tried to get me to confess was that Pearlman had been up here. He tried every way he could to trip me into admitting it. Seemed to be more interested in that than anything else. I steered a roundabout course and didn't tell him anything he seemed to want to know."

"Well, I'll have to tell him," said Campbell wryly. "And that will finish this business. Odell can tell you what I told him a minute or two ago, so you'll understand why Pearlman was here and why you boys haven't got anything to worry about. But you better get some breakfast, Slim, and when you're through, we'll hit for town." He rose to his feet, looking suddenly old to both youths.

Vagle came running from the trees on the opposite side and whispered excitedly to his master. Campbell waved him away.

"Guess I won't have to go, after all," he said, his face growing stern. "You boys hide out back there. The sheriff's coming up the trail. That's why he let you loose, Slim . . . to see which way you would go. But he can't touch you boys, at that. Slope, and

I'll have it out with him here and now."

Odell and Olsen hurried to the rear of the house where Ricky told his friend what Campbell had told him. "And now," he said, "I've got to see Hope and tell her." His lips tightened.

"Tell her what?" Slim demanded in a puzzled voice.

"Tell her that I killed a man," replied Odell tartly. "Do you think I'm going to let somebody else tell her first?"

Slim shrugged his shoulders. He looked around the corner of the house. Then he nodded soberly to Odell. "It's him . . . the sheriff," he announced. "Campbell stopped him at the rail."

At this moment Odell caught sight of Hope near the rear porch of the house. He called to her softly, and when she turned, he held up a warning finger and hurried toward her.

"I've got to see you alone," he said breathlessly when he came up to her. "Isn't there some place . . . where I can talk to you a minute or two?"

She led the way to an arbor at the side of the house where they couldn't be seen. When she saw his eyes, a swift look of concern came into her own.

"What is it, Ricky?" she asked anxiously. "You're excited."

"And I have good reason to be," he said soberly. He put his hands on her shoulders and looked down at her. "You remember what I told you, Hope . . . that I would never tell you anything but the truth?"

"Why, yes," said the girl. "And I've believed you, Ricky. Oh, something is the matter just as I suspected." A mist came into her eyes as she spoke, but it didn't develop into tears.

"Yes, something is the matter. Now you mustn't interrupt me, Hope, you must listen to everything I have to say, at least I ask you to. I have to hurry, for the sheriff is here." He paused to make sure they were alone, and in that pause she threw an arm about his shoulders. He could feel her breast swell, feel the tension in her soft, warm body so close to him, and for a moment his perspective was blurred and he was overwhelmed with a burning desire to possess her, to love her and protect her and have her for his very own.

"Last night . . . or early in the morning . . . I killed a man," he confessed unsteadily, holding her tightly to him as if he were afraid she would slip away. Her eyes were closed and he kissed them. "I had never killed a man before," he went on in a stronger voice. "It shook me up a bit and it was your appearance, like an angel out of a dark sky, this morning, that drew me out of it. A man cannot think dark thoughts or remember unpleasant things and look at you, girl. I wanted to be the first to tell you."

She opened her eyes. "I understand," she said clearly.

"There was no other way, Hope . . . I swear it," he said fervently. "The man was a gambler and I think some kind of an outlaw, but I'm not at all sure. I'm not trying to hide behind anything. I had to do it. He forced the fight but I let him do it because I believe he was a scoundrel. When it came to the draw, it was to be one of us. I saw to it that it was him. They can't do a thing to me, Hope, but that isn't the point. It's a fact we can't get around . . . that I've killed a man. Maybe your father will tell you about it, but I won't. That's what I wanted to tell you, that . . . and one other thing."

As he ceased speaking, she looked up at him. "It seems as though I'd known you for years, Ricky Odell," she said softly. "You come out of nowhere, without notice, and bring something . . . something exciting, almost boisterous, sometimes sad, into my life. But I can tell by your eyes that you are being truthful with me. I'm so sorry, so awfully sorry, to hear this, Ricky. It gives me a chill all over. It makes me feel . . . oh, I don't know how it makes me feel. What . . . was the other thing you wished to tell me?"

There was a long pause before Ricky spoke. "Hope, I'm as

good as most of 'em . . . and that's all I've got to say in my favor. I swept out of the clouds and met an angel. That was you. I knew it the moment I saw you. Something queer happened inside of me. I've no right to tell you what I'm going to tell you. I'm going to tell it to you even if I never see you again. You won't understand it, perhaps, and maybe you won't believe it. It's something I've never told a girl before. Oh, if you'll only believe me. Hope . . . I love you."

"I know it, Ricky. Maybe it's just a fancy at this time, but you honestly believe it. No man has ever told me such a thing before. Not that they haven't tried, but they've always stopped short and bungled, and I've never urged them on. I don't know how I feel, but I'm a different girl when I'm with you. You're not just a cowpuncher, Ricky Odell, and I don't believe you're just a gambler. Tell me, Ricky, are you a gunfighter?"

It seemed as though the sun shone in her face at his smile.

"I'm not that, Hope, in any sense of the word," he declared. "I had to work fast last night and folks may put me down as one. But they're wrong. I had to learn to handle a gun, Hope. There was no way getting out of it. I had to learn even while I was a kid with 'em lifting me into a saddle on a real horse." There was a note of humor in his voice, but his eyes were not smiling. "But I'm not a gunman, as they take the word on the range."

"Then I guess that's all that matters," she said in a low voice. "Yes, I . . . guess that's all I care about."

Then his eyes lit with the brilliancy of a sparkling star. He drew her to him, her head a flood of gold upon his shoulder. He bent over her and kissed her lips, and felt her thrill. Then he drew away as suddenly. He had looked out and saw Slim walking toward the front of the house. The sheriff knew they were there, then.

"I've got to go out and take part in the conversation,

sweetheart," he told her lightly, setting his hat at its usual angle.

"Ricky!" She threw her arms about him and kissed him impetuously. "Don't let 'em put anything over on you."

Her eyes were shining and he laughed in utter abandon. "Why, Hope, sweet, I've been looking for your sort all these twenty-four years that're hanging from my shoulders. I'll get you yet. So long."

When Ricky walked jauntily out of the arbor to the front of the house, he saw Sheriff Lane, Campbell, and Slim Olsen standing near the bench where he and Campbell had talked earlier in the morning. He strode toward them. Ricky felt different this morning, more confident, more aggressive, with a feeling of jubilation behind it all. Hope must love him and that was all in the world that mattered; for the rest of it, he didn't care a snap of his fingers. As he drew up to the little group, he looked squarely at the sheriff.

"I'm reckoning I'm the man you want to see," he said in a crisp voice. "If you had waited around a bit, I'd have been back to town and in your office by noon."

"No doubt," remarked Lane dryly. "Why did you hot-hoof it up here so fast after the killing?"

"To tell Campbell, here," replied Ricky shortly. "He's the only person hereabouts that has shown any friendliness toward Slim and me, and I thought he ought to know what had happened. He gave Pearlman his notice last night and I wanted him to know that it wouldn't be necessary for him to go to town today."

"So Pearlman was up here," said the sheriff sternly. He turned to Slim. "And you lied to me."

"He didn't do any such a thing," protested Ricky. "Slim didn't see Pearlman. I saw him because I sneaked out here through the trees and watched and listened. Don't think I'm not telling the truth." He looked at Campbell. "Didn't you tell him?" he asked.

"Sure I told him," said Campbell promptly.

"There you are, Sheriff," said Ricky impudently.

"You see Pearlman and you heard what was said up here, and you went back to town for the very purpose of dragging Pearlman into a gun play and shooting him down," Lane accused sternly.

"I have plenty of witnesses that Pearlman picked the fight almost the instant Slim and me entered the Board of Trade," said Ricky in a ringing voice. "He forced the business from the start, with me telling him time and time again to lay off us and leave us alone. Would he do it? Fat chance. He was out to get me from the beginning. He carried it to a point where I slapped him in the face. He could have chosen a fistfight if he had wanted. But he went for his gun. Then I gave it to him for keeps."

"I don't suppose Campbell, here, sent you to do that very thing," suggested Lane.

"Confine your conversation to intelligent remarks and questions," shot Ricky. "You know better than that."

"We'll assume he didn't," snapped Lane. "But you could have pulled Pearlman along in that business. You could have urged him on to a showdown for the purpose of killing him."

"We'll assume I did," Ricky retorted swiftly, "but just how and by what means could you prove it? I'm telling you straight that Slim and me are visiting up here, not at this place, but in this country. We're minding our own business. Do you think I'm going to let anybody like that Pearlman run me out or take his insults? Not on your life. It was the first time I ever killed a man. Do you think I thank him for it? Here we are. You know the facts. Now, Mister Sheriff, what're you going to do about it?"

"Me? I'm going to ask Campbell for a glass of his home-made blueberry wine," replied Lane blandly. "Come on, John."

Ricky and Slim watched them walk away and then stared at each other blankly.

CHAPTER FOURTEEN

Ricky and Slim were about to sit down on the rustic bench when a voice called to them from the front porch. It was Hope, standing at the top of the steps beckoning to them.

"C'mon, Slim," ordered Ricky, taking his friend by an arm. "No more kitchen for us. We're in right this time."

"Leave it to you," grunted Slim. "And by the way, Rick, that sheriff's no fool. I had one of the hardest two-fisted word battles with him I ever had in my life. I thought maybe he would follow me up here, but I couldn't see that it would make much difference."

"It hasn't." Ricky grinned. "You handled your end perfect."

By this time they had reached the bottom of the steps and Hope was a vision of loveliness above them. Her eyes sought Ricky's, asking a question.

"All clear sky," he told her. "And this wretched prairie tramp has something on his mind about . . . er . . . breakfast."

"Why, I didn't say any such thing!" blurted Slim, his face growing red to the roots of his hair.

Ricky stepped back, apparently aghast, while Hope's laugh rippled on the breeze. "Look at him, Hope!" exclaimed Ricky. "He's blushing! I've known that lad since the time when they used to set us down on the prairie to play with a prickly pear and this is the first time I ever saw him blush . . . except when cashing in a satchel full of poker chips!"

"Come up on the porch," the girl invited. "I knew you'd

want some breakfast, Slim, and you're going to have it in a minute."

"You're not going to take him into the dining room, are you, Hope?" said Ricky anxiously. "I don't believe Slim has been inside a private house in. . . ."

"That'll do!" Olsen interrupted. "Miss . . . er . . . Hope, you needn't be afraid of my table manners, nor of my appetite, for that matter. And if you wish to offer me some breakfast, I shall be most pleased to accept, since I suspect this roughneck already has had his." He concluded with a slight bow.

Hope looked at him and at Odell with a puzzled smile.

"That's all right, Hope," said Ricky cheerfully. "Nothing wrong with him. He talks like that."

So Hope laughed again and went inside, promising to call Slim in a minute and leaving them to their cigarettes on the porch.

Slim looked at Ricky appraisingly. "So you've put her on the list, too, eh?" he said. "Didn't take long, either."

"Now lay off that stuff," Ricky warned. "I've told you already where I stand in this business. I'm not fooling, Slim."

"That's all right with me," responded Slim. "But don't try to make me the butt of any of your jokes. I can sling a little language myself, and mix some sarcasm and irony where they'll bite harder than humor, boy, and I'm telling you."

Ricky looked at him in surprise. "I didn't intend to make you the butt of any jokes, Slim," he said slowly. "I wouldn't hurt your feelings on a bet, if I could hurt 'em as a friend. But I'm happy this bright, sunny morning and I'm not telling you why."

"You should be," Slim decided aloud on general principles. He threw his cigarette away as the girl came again to the door.

"Come on, Slim," she said pleasantly. "And I'm going to wait on you myself."

"Then maybe I won't be able to eat," grumbled Slim as he

followed her inside.

Hope had put his breakfast on the table, and now, as he sat down, she brought in the coffee. Slim began to eat without hesitation and she watched him, feeling a bit awkward. There were several questions she would have liked to ask him, but she couldn't bring herself to put the queries.

He looked up at her suddenly. "What time did Rick get up here?" he asked.

"At sunrise," she answered with a smile. "I was out for a morning ride on Bismarck and met him on the trail."

"Huh. The sunrise trail, eh? Do you like Ricky very much?"

The girl flushed and then cooled at the direct question and his straightforward gaze. "Why, yes," she replied. "It isn't hard to like Ricky, is it? Don't you like him?"

"Yes," answered Slim shortly. "He's my pal, so why wouldn't I? Just want to tip you off that he's a pretty good sort. Heard about his trouble? He said he was going to tell you."

"Yes, he told me," said the girl eagerly. Perhaps this queer youth was going to tell her something more.

Slim Olsen waited until he had finished his meal. Then, over a last cup of coffee, he looked at her steadily and spoke again. "You don't want to hold that business against him," he said slowly, earnestly. "Rick couldn't get out of it. The man he had to shoot . . . to protect his own life . . . picked the quarrel and forced it to a gun play. Rick was lucky enough to beat him to it, that's all. He's square both ways from the jack. I wouldn't like it much if he really liked any girl and she gave him the run-around."

As he drank his coffee, Hope flushed again—this time with annoyance. "If you've finished," she said coldly, "we'll go out on the porch."

"Don't get mad at me, Miss Hope," he said as he rose from the table. She learned to her surprise that he had a good smile.

"The boys call me a woman-hater, but I'm not. I'm just . . . I don't understand 'em and I don't believe any other man does, Ricky the least of all. And just because I'm sticking up for him in my queer way, don't think that that boy's any angel. Come on."

Hope laughed, and was happy again, and they went out on the porch.

"Did he leave anything?" Ricky Odell inquired mildly.

"He left me with a good impression," laughed Hope.

Ricky looked quickly at his friend in genuine surprise. Slim favored him with a supercilious glance and a faint smile.

"I learn more about the fellow every day," Ricky sighed.

At this juncture, John Campbell appeared around the corner of the house. "You two go out in the bunkhouse and catch some sleep," he commanded. "Vagle's waiting to show you a couple of nice, clean bunks. You didn't have any sleep last night and none too much the night before. You're going to need a clear head because we're all going to town as a sort of formality, so the sheriff says. Now do as I say. Look at that fellow!" He pointed to Slim, who was caught yawning.

"It was the breakfast," Slim explained lamely. "I always yawn after meals."

This brought a laugh from Ricky. "Let's go," he told Slim. "We can stand some sleep and we'll ride down in the late afternoon."

"That's right," said Campbell. "Come ahead. Here's Vagle now. Hope, I'll tell you and your mother what this is all about later. Boys will be boys, and I'm an old man and a foolish one, at that. Nothing even to think about. All right, you fellows, come along."

Ricky sat on the edge of his bunk after he had drawn off his boots and stared through the window at the sun-flecked green of the trees. Slim was undressing, and he looked sharply at his friend from time to time, frowning slightly. By the time Slim was snug in his bunk, Ricky had gone so far as to pull off his shirt. His finely muscled arms and shoulders gleamed brown against the white undershirt. It was a tan that came from swimming in the rivers to southward during the long, hot summer.

"What's eating you, Rick?" demanded Slim.

"I'm . . . I'm just thinking," said Ricky in reply.

"Thinking about that girl, I suppose," Slim conjectured.

"You guessed it the first time out," replied Ricky.

Slim sat up in the bunk. He couldn't remember that he had ever seen his partner in just this mood before—not over a girl, at least. Well, this Hope was about everything a man could want.

"You in earnest about that girl, Rick?" he asked sharply. "I mean, are you actually hit?"

"I'm hit harder than you think, boy," was Ricky's quick retort. "A whole lot harder than you think, take it straight from me."

"*Humph*," grunted Slim. But there was a slight film of worry in his eyes. "You might as well tell me about it, Rick. I'm not fooling, you know."

"I told her about the shooting this morning, Slim. Oh, I didn't put in any plug for myself and didn't give her any details. I just said I had to do it. In a way I lied, just as I've lied to all of 'em in a way. To get right down to cases, I did lure that Pearlman on. I did it to . . . well, you know why I did it. She asked me just one thing. She wanted to know if I was a gunfighter, and I told her no. That was true enough. And I told her I had to learn to be lightning with my gun, and you know that's true, Slim, don't you?"

"How well I know it," admitted Slim.

"And you just about had to learn, too," said Ricky vehemently, "living there on the ranch with us. You know how Dad was. After they put his gun arm out of commission, he swore he'd make me the fastest man with a gun that country had ever seen. Why, Slim, we were both lugging guns around almost as soon as we could walk. They gave us empty guns to play with. Dad used to keep me at it three or four hours at a crack, and you with me lots of times. You're mighty fast yourself, Slim, but it's as natural for me to pull a six-shooter in a wink as it is to rub my eye if I get something in it!"

"Sure." Slim nodded. "I know it, Rick. But you never shot anybody before. Did you tell her that?"

"I think I did. Yes, I'm pretty sure I did. But I told her something else, Slim, that was more important than this shooting or anything else . . . the most important thing I ever told anybody in my life, so help me."

Slim Olsen was watching him closely. He was listening intently and he was thinking hard, thinking ahead of Odell's story. "What did you tell her, Rick?" he asked quietly.

"I told her that I loved her," Ricky confessed slowly. "And I meant it more than anything I ever said. I told her so that she believed me. And I held her in my arms and kissed her. She's the sweetest girl I ever met, Slim, and I want her and I'm going to have her. I'm declaring myself."

For some time Slim was silent, looking out the window. He was silent so long that Ricky looked at him curiously.

"Do you believe me, Slim?" he asked in a low voice.

"Dog-gone it, yes," blurted Slim. "And there's the rub. Play square with the girl and I'm at your back every second in any kind of a play. She's the real goods and a lady if I ever saw one. But let's get some sleep, Ricky. We can't tell what'll come up next, and we've got to be wide-awake and careful."

John Campbell had a large root cellar built into the side of a slope behind the barn. The stream flowed just beneath it. It served as a refrigerator in the summer and it was warm in the winter. He kept his vegetables and other provisions such as meat, ham, and bacon there, and in addition a stock of several jugs of the home-made blueberry and elderberry wine that Sheriff Tom Lane had mentioned when he and John took leave of Ricky and Slim.

Campbell and the sheriff sat just outside the root cellar in the shade, for the September sun was hot. In a month they could expect the first blizzard, harbinger of the Indian summer and the winter to come. It was about this that they talked as they sipped the sweet wine, each waiting for the other to lead the conference into the channel that it was bound to enter.

"I guess it's up to you, Tom, to say what's on your mind," said John Campbell finally, with a steady look at the sheriff.

"I've got two or three things on my mind, naturally," was Lane's answer to the challenge. "And I suppose I might as well get 'em off. There's no use in you and me stalling each other, John. And first of all, I'll confess I'm suspicious about your connection with these young bucks. You protected them that first night, although we both know now that there wasn't any need of it, for this Odell is sure-fire fast with his gun."

"You'll remember what I told you in your office that night," said Campbell. "I told you about Pearlman being in town and I told you what he wanted. We had a little talk about it and, if you'll remember it just this once and then forget it, you just the same as agreed with me that the only way out was for me to get Pearlman into a gun play and do for him. That's the night these young fellows got into a mix-up with him and I butted in expecting to have to draw with Pearlman. He fooled me and I didn't have the chance. That's the way that was, and that's the way I met this Odell and Slim."

"I know you said you wouldn't match guns with Pearlman any way except fairly," said the sheriff. "Then they came up here and stumbled on your place and found you?"

"Exactly. They've told you about it, eh? They were going over the Divide without enough grub and thought they would come to a town. Ira Crowell gave 'em a note to deliver to Hope and told 'em where the house was. That's how they came to know this place." Campbell didn't see fit to tell Lane anything about the youths' talk of taking up homesteads.

"That tallies with their stories," the sheriff said, frowning. "And Pearlman came up that night."

"That's right," Campbell conceded. "I sent 'em to the back of the house to keep out of sight, but Odell, as he says, stole through the trees and heard every word that passed between Pearlman and me . . . which was pretty hot. I gave him till sunset today to get out of town and off the range."

Sheriff Lane whistled softly. "I see . . . I see," he said. "Now I begin to understand. Odell knew what you were up against."

"I suppose so, but. . . ."

"Let me go on with this," Lane interrupted. "Odell likes your daughter. Oh, don't blow up, don't you think I've got eyes? He didn't want you to get into a gun play with Pearlman, partly or wholly on her account. Can't you see that? I thought maybe you deliberately sent the two of 'em to town to get Pearlman. I even thought you might have some kind of a deal on with them. That was what Pearlman hinted when he accosted Odell. They went down there and Odell egged Pearlman on in a slick way, protecting himself all the time, until he actually forced Pearlman into the finish where he didn't have a chance. As a matter of fact, it was the mention of the girl that caused Odell to slap Pearlman and bring on the shooting."

Campbell looked at him as though stunned.

"Now, listen, John," said Lane confidentially, "no one is going to know about this except you and me. Those fellows won't tell. Didn't I try for an hour to get something out of that Slim, and wasn't he too slick for me? There's a boy that's as bright as a dollar, before it leaves the mint. And Odell is one gunman out of a thousand. They're still standing around down in town talking about his draw against Pearlman. It was like blinking your eye quick. As I've said, we've got to see the county attorney as a sort of formality, but I'm going to let this thing go as it is . . . on the face of it. There'll be no charge against Odell."

"A gunman is right," observed Campbell. "but so danged young. And the other . . . smart you say? And looks like a dummy."

"Exactly." Lane smiled. "I'd like to know more about that pair and I'm going to let 'em run free, wide, and handsome. If anybody's on their trail, I'll soon find out. I can't say that I blame Odell much, under the circumstances. He's young and able . . . and maybe he did us a favor, after all. Anyway, Pearlman is out of the way. Are . . . are there any others, John?" He eyed the other carefully and saw Campbell's jaw clamp shut.

"No," shot Campbell through his teeth.

But Tom Lane read another answer in the cool, gray eyes. He frowned. "John," he said, lowering his voice a bit, "I know you didn't turn a trick all summer. I know about every move you made. You turned back from Culbertson after shipping some cattle from there. I've told you before that I'm willing to help and I'm telling you so again." He paused to light a cigar and finish his glass of wine. "I know now for a certainty that the cattlemen are going to make you a proposition, and, if you take it, it will mean that I'll have to make you a deputy. Sometimes it's nice and handy to be a deputy, John."

Campbell looked him straight in the eyes but could read nothing there. He was thinking of a man named Brackett. He wondered if the sheriff knew. But he wouldn't have asked him for the world. He put the empty glasses in the root cellar, swung the heavy door shut, and they walked down toward the house.

CHAPTER FIFTEEN

Slim was first to wake in the bunkhouse. He blinked one look at the window, the slant of the sunlight, and hopped out of his bunk with unusual alacrity. He shook Ricky Odell out of a deep sleep, sweetened with amorous dreams, perhaps, and brought him up into the full light of day, grunting in protest.

"Know what time it is?" asked Slim, looking at his watch that he had hung at the head of his bed. "We're not rooming here, you know, and it's half past four. Get busy!"

Ricky was out of his bunk in a twinkling and they dressed speedily. "Reckon his nibs, the law, has gone by now," yawned Ricky. "Wonder what this meeting with the county attorney is going to be."

"Oh, they'll ask you a lot of questions," replied Slim, "and me a lot of questions . . . which we probably won't answer . . . and the upshot of it'll be that they'll lock us up on general suspicion of being bad men to have around and end up by running us off the range in disgrace."

"Yeah?" Ricky grinned, making his way to the wash bench. "Then I'll just let you do the talking, Slim. You can sling words without making 'em mad, and twist their questions into answering themselves, while all I know is 'yes' and 'no' and 'go to blazes,' which aren't so good. You're the lawyer of this firm, Slim, old horse thief, so start thinking up the answers right now. Me . . . I've got to look at the beautiful scenery, and think fine thoughts, and keep our . . . what you call it? . . . morale up.

127

That's it. I've got to keep our general morale up and. . . ."

"Oh, shut up," Slim broke in. "And give me a chance at that water and soap. I've got my own comb. You'll have to coo-coo your sweet farewell to the damsel who's probably waiting with a basket of apples and a bag of doughnuts for you to wake up."

"Thanks," said Ricky, stepping aside with the towel. "An excellent idea, Slim. Nobody can say I picked a dummy for a pardner. But you mean temporary farewell, Slim. Don't get mad, for even the *hombre* who adds up words in the dictionary is liable to miss one once in a while. Now, if the old gentleman isn't around, I ought to be through with my temporary farewells by seven-thirty at the latest. And you don't mind looking after the horses, do you, Slim?"

His friend glared and snatched away the towel. "If you're not on your way by five o'clock, I'll miss my guess," he retorted.

Shortly afterward they issued forth from the bunkhouse and found the man, Vagle, near the barn. Vagle interested both of them. There was a furtive, cunning light in his eyes; he had a habit of snapping his fingers softly as his hands hung at his sides. His arms were abnormally long, while his legs were short and bowed. His face was tanned a leathery hue and was a map of intricate wrinkles.

He saw them and grinned, showing his yellow teeth. It was not pleasant to see, this grin, but it was evidently well meaning. He pointed a long forefinger at the house and said: "They want to see you? I'll tend to the horses."

"Gives me the creeps," said Ricky as they turned toward the house. "Wouldn't want him trailing me on a dark night."

"Cracked," was Slim's observation, "but a he-wolf guarding Campbell's door, I expect."

Hope Campbell came out before they reached the house. "I've got some lunch for you," she said, smiling. "You'll have to call it that, because it's cold. But there'll be hot coffee."

"Where's . . . ?" Ricky left the question incomplete, and looked about with a puzzled air.

"Father went to town with Sheriff Lane," Hope explained. "He said you two should have some sleep and ride in later. They went this morning."

"Now isn't that nice for the old gentleman to look after us this way," said Ricky with a sly glance at Slim. "That means. . . ."

"That we'll have to be moving along as soon as possible, Miss Hope," Slim supplied. "We'll grab this lunch and slope. Where is it?"

"Please excuse him, Hope," Ricky said in a pleading voice. "I sent to Kansas City for a book on ettyquit for him and it hasn't got here yet."

"Meanwhile, give me credit for having my hat off, Miss Hope," said Slim pleasantly.

The girl laughed as Ricky flushed and removed his Stetson.

"That was under the belt, you devil," Ricky told Slim in an aside.

"Go around to the front porch and see what you can find," Hope advised them as she turned into the house.

The lunch was quickly consumed, with the talk restricted and most of it coming from Slim. He kept them laughing with a series of utterly irrelevant remarks and episodes, mainly concerning himself, with a few humorous references to Ricky, and all the while he knew Ricky and Hope were waiting for a few words with each other before he and his friend left for town.

Lunch finished, Slim rose from the table abruptly and took up his hat. "I'm going for the horses," he told Ricky. Then: "Miss Hope, I want to thank you in the proper way for both of us for your kind entertainment. And I hope to meet you again."

He bowed slightly, ran down the steps, and disappeared around the house.

"Why, Slim's clever!" Hope exclaimed when he had gone.

"He's wiser than a lot of 'em might think." Ricky nodded. "We've been pals since we were kids, so I ought to know him pretty well."

She stepped closer to him. "Father told me about your . . . your trouble," she said softly, "and I know you were not to blame. Father knew that man somewhere and said he was a bad one. He even came up here trying to meet father again."

"Yes?" So that was the way Campbell had explained it. Good! "I'm going to have to ride down to town with Slim now," he said, "but I'm not going to leave town. I may have some sort of business up here, and, anyway, we'd stay for the rodeo."

"Well, that's good," said the girl with a hint of hesitation that he didn't miss. "I'll see you again, then." She had something else to say and he knew it.

"Where's your mother?" he asked.

"She always takes a rest in the afternoon and I let her sleep," the girl answered. She didn't see fit to say that she had let her mother sleep later than usual.

"Hope, you've got something on your mind," he told her soberly. "I expect it's something you want to ask me. What is it, dear?"

"Why . . . well, Ricky, when are you going to tell me more about yourself?" she asked, looking at him earnestly.

"I expected it," he said, smiling. "I haven't much bad to tell. But just now Slim and I are having a lot of fun by letting them take us as they find us. But I'll tell you what I'll do, Hope. I'll tell you all about myself on the night of the big dance at the rodeo, providing you dance with me. Is it a go?"

"That's a bribe, Ricky Odell," she laughed with sparkling eyes, "but I'll take a chance and promise."

He caught her in his arms and kissed her. Then he was down the steps, just as Slim showed, leading the horses. They waved back to her and caught the flutter of her handkerchief in the wind as they broke down the trail.

Behind them the sun was poised, as though hung from an invisible celestial string, for its drop behind the purple peaks. The prairie ran before them, and with them, in billowing waves capped with gold—driven by a restless wind. The river was languid in turquoise, as though waiting for the sunset to touch it with silver, when it would sparkle along hurriedly to meet the horizon moving in with the twilight.

"There comes a rider!" Ricky called to Slim, pointing off to the right where a horseman was approaching the trail from the south.

"I see him," Slim returned. "And I believe I know who it is."

"I was thinking," said Ricky. "I was wondering if it could be . . . it looks. . . ."

"That's just who it is!" Slim broke in. "It's our friend, Ira Crowell, heir to the H Square. I'd bet my saddle on it."

"You're right," Ricky conceded with a slow frown. "Wants a report on his message, maybe. Well, I'll give it to him. He must be hanging around that big herd down there where he can see the trail."

Slim smiled to himself. He knew by his partner's tone that Ricky suspected a rival in Ira Crowell, and he knew Ricky resented the fact that Ira was the son of one of the richest and most powerful stockmen in that range. This fact, ordinarily, would give him an advantage. Just how Ricky would discount that advantage was to be seen, and Slim looked forward to considerable entertainment.

"That's just who it is, all right," said Ricky. "Look at him slow down so's to be sure to meet us. Let's pull our horses to a walk, Slim, and make him wait."

"Sure." Slim grinned, checking his mount. "There . . . see? He's going to wait all right."

And wait Ira did, waving to them to stop as they approached. "Hello!" he called out brightly as the pair came up. "Back again, I see." He smiled patronizingly. Not a bad-looking fellow, the two friends decided, paying him more attention than on their previous meeting.

"Yes, back again," sang Ricky cheerfully. "Want to see some of the gold samples we got from our claim up in the big mountains? I don't see, I don't honestly, how you fellows down here can afford to monkey around with cows."

"Yeah?" said Ira derisively. "There isn't enough gold up there to fill a tooth. Any prospector will tell you that. That's galena country, silver and lead."

"Oh, well, we ain't got any teeth to fill . . . except with raw meat," said Ricky easily, with a wave of his hand. "What's on your mind, Ira?"

Ira scowled. He didn't relish such easy use of his first name by a pair of roving cowpunchers, but he felt he had to overlook it under present circumstances.

"Did you . . . ah . . . deliver my note to Miss Campbell?" he asked.

"Note? You mean that letter. Yes, I gave it to Hope, but I don't know what she did with it," said Ricky amiably. "I suppose she read it. Were you expecting an answer?"

Ira Crowell's eyes bulged and his jaw dropped. Then he found his voice. "Why, you . . . ," he sputtered. "Are you sure you delivered that note? How did you find out Miss Campbell's first name?"

"It was on the letter, don't you remember?" said Ricky, raising his brows while Slim chuckled. "Yes, it was on the letter, and I want to say, although maybe it's none of my business, that you've got good taste in picking 'em, Ira." He nodded gravely at the inarticulate youth who was listening with his eyes narrowing more and more with each word uttered. "And, listen, bozo," he continued, "I usually remember what I do, and any more questions like whether I delivered the letter or not will put you out of order."

"Why, you . . . you probably went up there and represented yourself as coming from me and met her," said Ira harshly. "I wouldn't put it past you to have opened the note!"

"I thought of that," said Ricky, squinting, "and if I'd known then what I know now, I'd probably have torn it up. Hope didn't seem to think, that is, she didn't give the impression of thinking that it amounted to much, Ira."

"Stop calling me by that name!" roared Ira. "My name is Crowell, and you'll please refer to Miss Campbell by that name. You've no right to call her by her first name. Who do you think you are, anyway?"

"I don't have to think who I am," retorted Ricky suavely. "I know who I am. I'm Ricky Odell, and pleased to meetcha. And this is my friend, Slim Olsen. . . ."

"Who doesn't give a whoop whether he ever met you or not," Slim put in energetically.

Ira's face darkened with anger, but he strove to control his voice. "Now let's get this straight," he said. "I'm Ira Crowell of the H Square, and my father is one of the biggest stockmen hereabouts, and you two seem to come from no place and have no place to go. Line riders, maybe. Is that plain?"

"That's what you think," said Slim, taking charge of the conversation. "We're ready at all times to hear the defendant."

Ira glared. "Very well," he capitulated. "I gave you a note to deliver in good faith and offered to pay you for the service. Now I ask you if you did deliver the note and you start to pull a lot of smart stuff on me. What's the big idea, you . . . ?"

"Let's talk on the ground," Slim interrupted sharply.

Ira jerked out his gun. "Don't move from that saddle!" he commanded, covering Slim with his weapon, which was a brand new .45. Both Slim and Ricky noted this.

"This is my saddle and my horse," said Slim coldly. "When I want to get out of the saddle on my own horse, I do it, like this!" In a moment he was on the ground with his horse between himself and Ira.

"Drop it!" The sharp command came from Ricky.

Ira looked at him in genuine astonishment. He hadn't even glimpsed the draw. Instinctively he let the gun fall from his hand. "Oh," he sneered, "a couple of road agents, eh?"

"Never mind," said Ricky in a hard voice. "Don't forget you pulled a gun on us. I guess you haven't learned that when a man pulls his gun in tough country, he's supposed to use it. Get off that horse! Pick up his gun, Slim."

In two seconds all three were standing on the ground.

"Listen, you," said Ricky to Ira, "we're not all born with silver spurs in our mouths, but we can be good people just the same. Now you're a nice kid, Ira, and all that, but it doesn't count with us whether you're the son of a big rancher or not. Get that into your head for keeps, because we're liable to run across you again, and we don't want you shooting off any funny talk. You drew down on us, or on Slim here, which is the same thing, and that's dangerous business. On top of that, you called us a couple of road agents. Suppose you had to prove it. Ever think of that?"

Ira's face was white with outraged dignity and anger. "I notice you're careful not to say much about yourselves," he blurted.

"Why should we?" asked Ricky calmly. "We don't have to tell you who we are. I told you our names, the only names we've ever used. I didn't have to tell you that. I did it out of the goodness of my heart. But I don't have to tell you anything further. You're a stranger to us, just as we're strangers to you. You came out here of your own accord and asked us to do you a favor by delivering a letter at the Campbell place. We did that little thing for you. It happened that we'd met Campbell before. You'll learn about it later when you can spare somebody from your ranch long enough to go into town and bring back the news. We're not coming back from our first trip, when we took your letter up. We're on our way to town from our second trip. Do you think you're the only guy around here that's entitled to go up there?"

"Sure he does," Slim put in with a nod. "He's the H Square heir, that boy. I'll bet if he takes his hat off, his hair is parted in the middle. Who were you going to shoot, anyway?"

"I'll defend a girl's name anytime," declared Ira in a heat.

"But you'll wait until you're sure it's got to be defended," Ricky put in. "At least with us you will. You're taking a lot for granted up Campbell way, I'm thinking."

"What do you mean?" cried Ira hotly.

"He means that maybe you've got competition," said Slim mildly. "He's playing square with you and telling you in his own sweet way that maybe you're not the only tea leaf in the cup. You should go out and have a heart-to-heart talk with yourself."

Ira's rage got the better of his judgment and he swung a wicked right for Slim's face. Slim hardly moved his head to avoid the blow. He feinted with his right, and Ira ducked into a left uppercut that sat him in the grass. The scion of the H Square looked about in a daze. Then his burning eyes met Slim's and he got to his feet, his face nearly black with anger.

"The fight stops right here," warned Slim in a dangerous voice. "We didn't want a fight with you, Crowell. We've had trouble enough without flirting with more. We did you a favor and when we started to kid with you a bit you repaid us by calling us names and pulling your gun. Now I personally am getting sore. If you make another pass at me, I'll knock you colder than a January blizzard, and that's a promise!"

Ricky saw that Slim meant what he said. "Lay off, Crowell," he advised. "Slim's mad, and when he's that way, he's a bad man to fool with. He's right. We don't want any fight with you. I had to flash my gun on you to stop you from maybe doing something you'd be mighty sorry for afterward. Suppose you'd shot Slim . . . then what?"

"Give me my gun?" Ira demanded of Slim.

"Sure." Slim broke it and spilled the cartridges on the ground. Then he handed the weapon over to its owner. "Take it home and leave it there," he said earnestly.

"I'm the judge of what to do on my own range," Ira gritted through his teeth. "And I've got you fellows' number. It won't be so soft for you the next time we meet, and that's my promise!" He swung into the saddle and galloped up the trail toward the foothills.

"Nice friendly sort," said Slim in a tone of contempt.

"And he's going up to the Campbell place to plug my stock up higher than those mountains without knowing it," Ricky observed.

"Looks like we've made a high-toned enemy," said Slim as they took to their saddles. "There goes the first wrench into the machinery of your romance, Rick. Let's beat it for town before somebody throws another one."

CHAPTER SIXTEEN

Hope Campbell ran lightly to the hitching rail when Ricky and Slim had left. Her thoughts were in a turmoil; her heart was racing. Ricky Odell had brought something new into her life—a thrilling, throbbing sensation that was almost an ecstasy, came and went, hot and cold, joyously and fearfully within her. In Ricky's arms she had been blissfully content, given him her lips, but, now that he was gone, a tremor of doubt, almost of fear, assailed her. She had known him, it seemed, for ages, yet it was still only a matter of hours. Was he an adventurer, after all? She knew nothing about him. But he had promised to tell her on the night of the rodeo ball. And she believed him.

When she turned back to the house, she found her mother on the porch. "Sit down, dear," Jane Campbell invited. "I slept longer than usual. Have they gone?"

"Yes, Mother. I prepared some lunch for them and they left right afterward. They will see Father in town."

Jane Campbell looked closely at the flushed face of her daughter. She knew the story of Pearlman and she had wondered if her husband had sent Odell to town to kill the man. Now she knew better, and she knew, too, that Hope's name had been indirectly involved. She had missed nothing during the visit of the two youths. Could Hope have fallen in love with Ricky Odell practically at first sight? If so, she could say nothing. For Jane had married John Campbell one month from the day she first had met him. And she fostered no regrets.

"Did you enjoy having visitors, Hope?" she asked kindly.

"Why . . . why, yes, Mother," replied the girl in surprise. "We don't have many visitors, you know, and. . . ."

"I know," said her mother, "especially young men. Do you like Ricky Odell, dear?" The question came with such frankness and suddenness that the girl was momentarily confused.

"Yes, I do. Don't you like him, Mother?"

"Very much," was the reassuring reply. "But we haven't known him long and we don't know anything about him."

"That's true," said Hope. "But you'll keep a secret, won't you, Mother? I know you will. Ricky has promised to tell me all about himself at the big dance at the rodeo. He asked me to promise to save him a dance in return."

"And . . . you promised?" asked Jane softly.

The pink was in Hope's cheeks again. "Yes," she murmured.

"Ira Crowell will be at that dance," the older woman said.

"I know it, and he can have a dance, too," said the girl with a slight frown. "But we're all going together, Father said . . . the family, I mean."

"Ira likes you very much," her mother reminded her. "You've known each other since you were children. You've been together in the Falls when you both were in school. Ira isn't such a bad boy, Hope."

"Oh, I know it," said Hope, tapping a foot impatiently. "He'll never let me forget we've known each other so long. He's always reminding me that he's 'cattle people' as he calls it, and says he belongs. I don't care if his father does own the H Square. Money and cows. Is that everything, Mother?"

"No," replied Jane gently. "But you have to be very careful of . . . of the other, dear."

Hope knew what she meant and looked at her mother quickly. "I like Ira, Mother, and I wouldn't say a word against him, but. . . ." She paused, looking straight ahead.

"You mean that you don't love him, Hope?" Jane suggested.

"I don't believe I know what this love is," said the girl wistfully. "How can a girl tell when she loves a man?"

"By her heart," replied Jane faintly. "It's a wonderful and treacherous thing, Hope. You can't play with it safely. Do you think you love this Ricky?"

"Mother!" Hope's cheeks flamed. "How could I? Why, I've only known him a few hours. I . . . I like him because he's different than . . . the others. You shouldn't ask me such a question. How can I answer it when I couldn't possibly know?"

Jane Campbell was silent. Her thoughts trailed back along the long, hard years. John, too, had been a gunman. She had known it when she married him. But Hope—it was different with Hope. But she was too wise to express a direct opinion. "After all," she said cheerfully, "it's silly to talk about such a thing. But you are all we have, Hope, dear, and you must know that."

The girl rose and put her arms about her mother's neck and kissed her. There were tears in her eyes. "You mustn't talk this way," she said in a trembling voice. "You'll always have me, Mumsey, sweet . . . always."

But Jane Campbell knew better and a chill came to her heart. "Yes, I know, dear," she faltered, "only, when you ever do feel you love a man, you must tell me. It's just your mother's whim, but will you promise, Hope?"

Without an instant's hesitation, Hope gave her promise.

"And now let's clear away this table," said Jane practically. "Your father will be late and he may stay in town all night. But we must have our supper."

They had not started supper, however, when Hope's alert ears caught the sound of hoof beats on the uptrail. She hurried to the porch as Ira Crowell came into view, riding at a canter.

He didn't stop at the hitching rail but rode on in as Vagle appeared.

He waved a hand to Hope and dismounted. "Take my horse, Vagle," he ordered crisply. "Water him, but don't feed him."

But Vagle turned away with a grunt and started for the barn. Crowell called to him in vain and slapped his riding boots angrily with the quirt he carried. Then Hope intervened by going down the steps.

"Vagle!" she called. The crab-like man halted and blinked at her with disapproving eyes. "Take care of Mister Crowell's horse," she commanded. "He's a guest. Are you forgetting that?"

Vagle came slowly back. "I do it for *you*," he said, flashing a dark look at Crowell.

"He's as crazy as ever," said Crowell, meeting the girl with a smile and taking her hands. "I'd have been up before, Hope, but you know how it is on the range now. We're shipping in a week or so."

"Come up on the porch, Ira," she invited, and as they went up the steps her mother came out.

"Why, hello, Ira," said Jane Campbell, giving him her hand. "You're such a stranger. But now that you're through school, I suppose you have half the ranch on your hands. Your father always said as soon as you started running the H Square, he would retire and smoke cigars instead of a pipe."

"I haven't got that far yet." Ira laughed. "But I'm learning. I'm not just punching cows and running errands, anyway. You are looking wonderful, Missus Campbell." He smiled.

"You'll stay to supper, won't you, Ira," Mrs. Campbell asked. "John has gone to town on business and may not be back until late. There'll be just you and Hope and me."

"Nope." Ira laughed again. "I'm stealing time off as it is, honest. Anyway, I wouldn't stay in these togs. I'm working cattle, Missus Campbell. I just ran up in a spare moment to see you and Hope. Did you get my note, Hope? I sent it up by a couple of questionable-looking strangers, but I took a chance on it being delivered."

"Yes, I received it," Hope replied. "Of course, I haven't had a chance to reply, and there was no hurry, Ira." She looked at him frankly.

Her mother had discreetly retired, murmuring something about supper. Hope wished she had stayed. There was something formidable about Ira this day. It thrilled her and frightened her.

"Let's take a walk under the trees," Ira suggested. "I haven't seen you in such a long time, it seems, Hope. I want to talk with you a little and then I must go back to the ranch. I've quit the schooling, as you know, same as yourself, and now I've taken hold and I'm . . . well, I've got a job on my hands. The H Square is a big ranch, and someday I'll have to take charge of it."

As they went down the steps into the yard, Hope could not but feel impressed by Ira's words. "I know you'll make good," she said in a tone that showed she meant it. "And you have the ability, Ira, no one has ever questioned that."

"All right, that ends the ranch talk. Are you going to the rodeo with me, Hope?"

"Why, Ira, we're all going. Father and Mother and me. We are going to stay the whole three days." She was thinking, however, of the third day, for it was to be that night when the annual rodeo ball would be held, with a big orchestra from Great Falls. "Of course, I couldn't go with you for the three days." She smiled up at him. "And you wouldn't want me to come back purposely to go down with you for one day, would you?"

"No. But I would like to be your escort at the big dance," he said. "We could go together for the whole three days if you . . . if we . . . but we haven't time for that."

"For what, Ira?" she heard herself saying in a faint voice.

"For something I want to ask you about later," he said softly. "This isn't the time, for we must be wholly alone, with the rest of the world shut out . . . just you and me with the stars breaking through the twilight. Maybe you can guess, Hope."

For a moment he had talked something like Ricky Odell and Hope caught her breath. She knew that Ira wanted to marry her, though he never had told her so. "Yes, we'll wait till then," she hastened to say.

"But you haven't answered me as to whether I can be your escort at the big dance the third night," he reminded her.

"Oh, Ira, we're all going together. You'll be there, and I'll be there, and Mother will be with me, of course."

"Naturally," he said. "But the other girls, at least the girls of your standing, Hope, will have, you might say official escorts, although that sounds like nonsense. Anyway, you will have to . . . or should dance the first and last dances with someone and don't you think it might as well be me, Hope?"

"Oh, very well, Ira, but listen. You may be my escort, but I will dance with whom I please, and I won't promise dances in advance, and, above all things, I will not be dictated to under any circumstances."

"That's all right, Hope," he said wryly, although he thought very differently. "There's something else I wanted to talk to you about. It may seem silly, but I . . . I'm always thinking of you, Hope, and always anxious about you. I believe I have that right."

Hope looked at the ground and made no comment.

"You remember I sent that note to you by two strange young fellows I didn't know, and didn't like particularly," he went on. "I offered them five dollars to deliver it because I couldn't get away at the time, honestly. I even told them where you lived so there could be no mistake. I didn't expect an answer right off. Did you meet those two fellows?"

Inwardly Hope bristled. Ira was using his old authoritative tone that came near to being proprietary. She resented it. "Of course I met them," she replied sweetly. "Father knew them and it was but natural. They stayed to supper the first time . . . when they brought your note . . . and were here again today. Didn't they tell you their names?"

The dark look again was in his eyes, but he didn't let her see it. "Why, yes. One said he was Odell, and the other was Slim something. I met them coming back today . . . this afternoon . . . and Odell insulted you, or nearly did so. I suppose it was his crude idea of a joke."

"Ricky . . . Mister Odell insulted me?" exclaimed the girl in an incredulous voice. "In what way, Ira?"

"I stopped 'em and asked if they had delivered the note and they got fresh," said Ira hurriedly. "This Odell . . . and I don't see why you call him Ricky . . . said they had delivered the note and he called you by your first name, as if he were an old friend or something."

"Oh, is that all," said Hope with a toss of her head. "Well, Ira, how do you know that he isn't an old friend, or at least a friend?"

"That's it, I don't know," sputtered Ira. "And I think I should know," he added firmly.

"Very well, he is a friend of mine," said Hope with spirit. "And the other is Slim Olsen, who is his best friend. Now, have you got it straight, Ira?"

"Well, I object to it," said Ira arrogantly. "No, I don't mean that," he added quickly, noting the look in Hope's eyes. "It's just that . . . well, I can't explain myself exactly."

"So it seems, Ira," said Hope. "There's Mother calling us to supper. Don't you think you can stay, Ira? It would be nice to have you."

"No, I can't," he answered shortly. "I'd have too many

explanations to make, for one thing, and I'm stealing time as it is. But I'll be up to see you again soon." He squeezed her hand and went for his horse.

Hope went for a ride after sunset, but no company of charging knights broke through the purple mist of the twilight. Instead, there were only two, and the leader laughed and threw a kiss to her, while the other rode stern, almost commanding.

She saw them again in her dreams that night and awoke to the sound of a voice. It was a mockingbird outside her window.

CHAPTER SEVENTEEN

When Ricky Odell and Slim Olsen rode into town in the early twilight, John Campbell met them at the livery while they were putting up their horses. He suggested that they have supper at the hotel right away, to which they readily consented, and he sent word to Sheriff Lane.

During the meal Ricky told Campbell of the meeting with Ira Crowell on the upper trail. "I'll admit I was kidding him along a bit, but it was because of the way he treated us. You'd have thought we were the dust under his horse's hoofs. Then he made Slim mad with one of his mean cracks, and when Slim started to get off his horse, Ira drew down on him. Slim dismounted just the same and I covered Crowell and made him drop his gun and get off his horse. I was pretty sore after he'd called us a couple of road agents in the bargain. We thought you ought to know about it."

Campbell was shaking his head. "Not so good," he said. "Crowell is one of the biggest stockmen on the range. But Ira must have run off at the mouth and the head, too. He doesn't intend to be mean, but he's got a queer streak just the same. What was the upshot of the business?"

"Slim told him where he was wrong and so did I," Ricky replied. "Then he made a fierce pass at Slim and dodged into an uppercut that put him on the grass. We finally persuaded him that we didn't want any fight with him and he told us he had our number and got on his horse and streaked for your place."

Campbell raised his brows and put his tongue in his cheek. "And it all came about because he wanted to know if you'd delivered that note to Hope, eh?"

"That started it," agreed Ricky, "and I happened to call Miss Hope by her first name, besides calling him by his. It seems I made a social error, and he wasn't slow in telling me."

"He told us just how important he was and what scum he thought we were," Slim put in, "and we just didn't feel like taking it, that's all. If it wasn't because he lit out for your place to tell goodness knows what, we wouldn't say a word about it. We're not looking for trouble, and the sooner folks around here find that out the better."

"I see," said Campbell as they got up from the table, with a worried look in his eyes. "Well, you forget him around town anyway."

They met Sheriff Lane in the little lobby of the hotel. He greeted them, and then spoke to Campbell. "Suppose we go up to Berry's office," he suggested. "He's expecting us and we might as well have it over this evening."

Campbell looked questioningly at his youthful companions.

"Who's this Berry you mentioned?" asked Slim.

"He's the county attorney," replied Lane. "It's a sort of formality, but it's necessary."

"All right," said Slim cheerfully, "let's go."

They found Berry waiting for them in his office at the courthouse. He was a thin, wiry man with a shock of dark hair that stood almost straight up and a pair of keen, dark eyes that seemed to be continuously darting glances in all directions. He greeted Lane and Campbell cordially and bestowed a frowning, appraising look upon Odell and Olsen. Ricky deliberately nudged Slim with his elbow, and Berry saw it. His eyes flashed and he moved some papers on his desk.

"Sit down," he told Campbell and the sheriff. Then to Slim and Ricky he said, sharply: "Take these two chairs in front of my desk." When they were seated, he sat down himself behind the flat-topped desk and, looking at Odell and Olsen, said: "I'm the county attorney, as you possibly know. Now, Odell, tell me just what happened in the Board of Trade when you killed Pearlman."

"I reckon the sheriff has told you all about that," Slim put in. "We've both explained to him and he has questioned the witnesses."

Berry looked at him, his eyes snapping, while Lane smiled behind his hand and winked at John Campbell.

"You speak when I address you," Berry snapped at Slim. He turned again to Ricky but was once more interrupted.

"Has any particular charge been filed against us?" Slim demanded. "You talk as if you were a court. We've explained, and explained, and. . . ."

"That'll do!" thundered Berry, half rising in his chair. "I'm the county attorney and this is a regular procedure to ascertain if there is sufficient evidence to ask an indictment. I'm not here to play around with you two, but to determine certain facts as near as possible."

"Very well, Mister County Attorney," said Slim, bristling, "but this is the last time we'll do any explaining except before a jury."

Berry's face was flushed with anger, but he managed to control himself. He again turned to Ricky. "Please explain exactly what took place in your altercation with Pearlman," he said crisply.

"Slim, here, does the talking in cases like this. He knows how to sling language better'n I do. This is my first experience of the sort, and his, too, for that matter. But I'm willing to let him look after the business." Ricky spoke in a light drawl.

"You mean to tell me you won't talk?" demanded Berry.

"Exactly." The word from Ricky cut through the room like a knife.

Berry leaned back, pressing his teeth against his upper lip.

"It's better that I should tell you, anyway," crooned Slim. "I was the closest and most expert witness."

Berry looked sharply at Sheriff Lane, who nodded. "All right," he said, "go ahead and don't wander from the subject."

In less than three minutes time, Slim told in short, concise sentences and terse phrases all that had taken place on the two occasions when they had met Pearlman in the Board of Trade and ended with the shooting, showing indubitably that Ricky was in the right.

"I'm going to accept your story at its face value," said Berry, "because it has been corroborated. But when strangers come into this county and become involved in a shooting scrape that results in a fatality we want to know something about them. I can, of course, hold you as suspicious characters."

"As long as you like," said Slim with a wave of his hand.

"Oh, I'm not going to do that," said Berry in a tone that was close to patronizing. He fussed with some papers on his desk. "Where are you boys from?" he asked amiably.

"We came here from Fort Benton," Slim replied readily.

"How long were you there?" asked Berry.

"Oh, a week or two," drawled Slim. "We've been traveling up this way for some time, looking at the country, enjoying ourselves, and this is the first trouble we've had."

"Well, it came from outside of this town, same as you two did," Berry snapped. "Where'd you come from originally, that's what I want to know."

"And that's what we're not saying," Slim shot back. "Now, it would be easy for us to name any number of towns from here to the Mexican border, and you'd have to accept the answer. But we don't propose to name any town or place except the right one, for we haven't anything to hide as to our past. But we have our reasons for keeping our whereabouts and our business unknown. We have that right, too, haven't we?"

Berry ignored the question. "What is your business?" he demanded sharply.

"Cut it," Ricky told Slim impatiently. "We're not telling our business, nor answering any more questions," he said to Berry. "All we want is to be left alone. We're going to wait and see your rodeo and we'll probably enter some of the contests and take down some of your prizes. And that isn't so long off."

Berry leaned back in his chair as though relieved. "Why didn't you say so in the first place?" He glared. "If you're here for the rodeo, there's no need to be so secret about it. Our rodeo is famous all over this north range country. And you needn't be so sure of copping any prizes. You may find the competition keener than you think."

Ricky smiled. Unwittingly he had given a perfectly good reason for their presence in Pondera, and he had given the county attorney a perfectly good reason to end the interview.

"Your friend, here," Berry continued, "will talk himself into a tight fix one of these days if he isn't more careful with his tongue. You can go, both of you, so far as I'm concerned."

"That's what I've always told him," assured Ricky. Slim had enough sense to keep still. "C'mon, Slim, let's beat it."

They went out, leaving Campbell and the sheriff with Berry.

CHAPTER EIGHTEEN

John Campbell left County Attorney Berry's office half an hour after the departure of Ricky Odell and Slim Olsen. He looked into the Board of Trade and several other gambling and refreshment places without seeing them. It was dark, with the night sky alive with brilliant stars, and yellow beams of lamplight slanting across the street. Since the youths had slept from morning until late afternoon, Campbell could hardly believe they had gone to the hotel and to bed, although he directed his steps toward it. There, to his surprise, he found Odell at the one small writing desk in the lobby apparently writing a letter. Ricky turned the sheet over with its inked face down as he approached.

"This is about the first time I've seen you quiet and in a thoughtful mood," said Campbell, as he drew up a chair and sat down. "Letter home?" he asked, filling his pipe.

"Yes," answered Ricky. There were several reasons why he should show proper respect for this man, and he did so now.

"Well, if you mail it here the address is liable to get to the sheriff or that other fellow, Berry," Campbell volunteered.

Ricky smiled in genuine admiration. "I'd thought of that," he said pleasantly, "so I'm not going to mail it here. We're going to take a run down south of here for a few days, and I'll mail it out of town. Do you want to know why we're keeping ourselves more or less of a mystery, Mister Campbell?"

"Well . . . I don't see yet why it's any of my business,"

Campbell evaded, betraying his curiosity by his speech and manner.

"It may be . . . later on," Ricky told him. "I made a promise to your daughter. In fact, we came to an agreement. I told her I would tell her all about myself on the night of the big rodeo ball if she would save a dance for me."

"She told you she would, I suppose," growled Campbell.

"She did." Ricky smiled. "So after the big dance, maybe she'll tell you. There's only one thing I'm afraid of, Mister Campbell."

"I can't imagine you being afraid of anything," was Campbell's sarcastic comment. He had noted Odell's respectful attitude.

"That's natural," said Ricky, "so long as I can see the danger. But this is in the dark. I'm afraid that Ira Crowell might make some kind of a fool move. He's going to take her to the dance, isn't he?"

"How do I know?" asked Campbell crossly. "That's Hope's affair and I don't just see where it's any of your danged business, to tell the truth. You think you can ride into strange range, take a fancy to a girl, and, bingo, she's going to fall for you hard at first sight? You have the wrong idea about Hope. I'm taking Ira's view of the matter and telling you hereafter to call my daughter Miss Campbell. She's just that to you."

Ricky bit his lip to keep back a sharp retort. "I've never had occasion to mention her name except to Crowell," he said instead, "and I used her first name on that occasion purposely because he was overbearing and fresh."

"You mean you did that little thing to try and show him that he had competition," Campbell corrected him. "I'll approve of any competition from any eligible young men on this range . . . who live here . . . in winning my daughter's good graces. That's a point you've overlooked, Odell. You've got to prove yourself something besides a would-be homesteader and a gun expert before you're straight with me, regardless of what you've done that you might look on as a favor."

Ricky's face was white. "I'll take that as agreed," he said, "with the understanding that I get fair play from you. As for the competitors you speak of, they're on the same footing as I am, so far as I'm concerned. If they're not able to look out for themselves, then they're not entitled to any good graces from anybody. I told you straight that I wouldn't stop seeing your daughter whenever I can, and I'm not taking it back."

"But you can make it some place besides the house," drawled Campbell, lighting his pipe.

"So that's it." Ricky managed to get it out calmly, although he was burning with fury inside. "And are you going to tell Miss Campbell that I'm no longer welcome up there, and why?"

It was John Campbell's turn to become angry. "It isn't necessary to tell her anything," he said sternly. "We'll leave her out of it for the present."

"Don't say we, because that's not understood," said Ricky crisply. "I'm not leaving her out of it for a minute. If you don't tell her that you've barred me from coming up there, and your reason, I'll tell her."

Campbell knocked the ashes out of his pipe upon the floor with an oath. Then he surveyed Ricky calmly through narrowed lids. "The only way," he said finally, "that I can put this matter on a . . . a neutral basis, would you say? . . . is to pay you off. You're a stranger to me, and I don't and won't feel under any obligations to a stranger. I've got a feeling that you've sort of taken advantage of me, but maybe it isn't fair to say that."

"You know it isn't," snapped Ricky. "You're trying to make me out as a paid gunman. I had you pegged just the other way around. Pearlman is the only man I ever shot, and I have blamed good and sufficient reason for killing another man on sight, and had that reason before I ever saw a blade of grass on your range."

"That settles it," said Campbell, a bit pale himself. "What's your price to forget this rough business?"

"My price is your daughter," replied Ricky softly, "and I'm calling her Hope to your face, because her name means just that to me."

With a move incredibly swift, he sent his gun spinning across the floor to the opposite side of the lobby. The clerk and two others in the room looked at them, startled.

Campbell's jaw clamped shut and his strong face darkened.

"Very well, I'll tell her," he said grimly, got up, and walked out of the place.

Ricky Odell crossed the room and picked up his gun. He had made it impossible for Campbell, angry as he was, to attempt a draw. He tore the letter he had been writing into fine pieces, reached out the partly opened window, and gave them to the wind. Then he went upstairs to the room where Slim already had gone to bed.

In accordance with an appointment made the night before, Campbell met with Sheriff Lane, County Attorney Berry, Adam Crowell, owner of the H Square, Alex Johnson, and Pete Lamont in the office of the latter at noon the next day. He had seen neither Odell nor Olsen during the morning and secretly hoped they had left town, but that they had not gone in the direction of his place in the foothills. Crowell, Johnson, and Lamont were the three leading stockmen of the district, and Lamont was president of the Chouteau Cattlemen's Association. Campbell was most interested in Crowell. He had known him for years, always liked him, and had helped on one or two occasions when the rancher had had trouble on his range. Just now, Campbell was wondering how much Crowell knew or suspected, and what his son Ira had told him. Campbell was pretty sure that Ira was in love, or thought he was in love, with Hope. But he knew the girl was not to be won by any show of wealth or family prestige. He was of the opinion that she liked Ira well enough, at least as well as she liked any of the other youths on that range, but this Ricky Odell had something that the others lacked. Secretly John Campbell saw something of his old adventurous spirit running rampant in the Irish youth. Jane had taken a chance and had married him in those days. She had stayed with him through the turbulent, trying years. Hope must not have such an experience. And Jane was entitled to peace and comfort, and everything his love could bring into her life to brighten it, in the years to come. With all this in mind, John did not frown upon Ira's suit. His meeting with Adam Crowell was cordial and their handclasp was warm and firm.

"Tom tells me you're going to stick around here where you belong, now that Hope's home to stay," boomed Crowell with a twinkle in his eye.

Campbell glanced at the sheriff, who was talking with Lamont. "You know, Adam, that confounded Tom seems to know more about everybody else's business than his own," he complained. "I'd naturally have to be home in the winter, for I haven't got any other place to go, and wouldn't want to go, if I did. But I suspect I'll have to go out again in the spring, though."

"There's plenty for you to do around here," said Crowell with a convincing nod. He was shorter than Campbell, but a big man, just the same. A typical stockman, with his shirt open a bit at the throat, a huge, gold watch chain across his wide expanse of vest, a round, tanned face with a medium mustache, and wide, blue eyes. "The Association's got a little proposition for you today, but later on you and me will have to get together and have a little talk. You might as well be raising more of your own stock as to be buying and selling somebody else's cattle. But don't mention it, for it's an idea of my own."

They were joined by others, and the conversation was general.

But Campbell could not forget the hint that Crowell had thrown out. The big stockman knew that Campbell's stock-raising activities were limited by lack of proper range. Crowell had range and range rights to spare. His idea might prove to be the most important thing in Campbell's life as he now intended to live it. It kept running in his mind as he listened to the others.

Lamont went and stood by Berry's desk. "We'll call this meeting formal without any ceremonies," he said pleasantly. "Campbell, our Association voted at its last meeting that we should have a man to keep an eye on our combined range. He will be invested with the proper authority by law and by the Association. He will be made a deputy sheriff, so he can exercise the authority of the sheriff's office if it should at any time be necessary. He will, in reality, be a supervisor of the range, protecting stockmen from encroachments upon their territory, aiding where such limits or boundaries of territory are undecided, assuming charge in case of cattle thefts or other disorder within the Association's domain. He will be known as the Association's general agent. We have considered the appointment of such an office for some considerable time, but the material for the job hasn't been at hand, and we do not wish to import any talent in such an important place. We are convinced that the best time to start protecting a range is when it is peaceful, and there are no end of duties that can fall under the jurisdiction of a general representative." He paused, and the others nodded eagerly as though to compliment him on a job well done. He had, in a few words, done away with preliminaries and needless explanations and details that could easily be taken up later. "You know our range like a book, Campbell," he continued, "and you know the men on it, particularly the ranch owners. We have decided unanimously that you are the man we want for this job. What do you think about it and what is your answer?"

John Campbell smiled broadly. "What with the sheriff, and the county attorney, and old Adam Crowell, here, and the rest of you fixing this soft spot for the last six months, and then gently but firmly shoving me into it before anything is said officially, I'd feel I was being pretty snooty if I didn't accept," he drawled.

"That," said Lamont, turning to Berry, who was smiling, "is what we can take as an official acceptance." He scowled at Campbell. "Berry is our attorney, even if he has a county job," he said. "He has a paper or two for you to sign, and the sheriff will have to make you a member of his outfit, and then you and me will have a conference the first day of the rodeo. Meanwhile, if anything comes up, you are to use your own judgment."

"That's fair enough," said John Campbell. "My first official act will be to drag this outfit over to the Board of Trade and buy it a drink."

As they walked out of the office, Campbell's throat tightened. Once more, in the parley of the range, he belonged. Whether this place had been made to order for him or not, he could not mistake the goodwill behind the source from which it had come. And Adam Crowell's hint of an idea was still in his mind.

CHAPTER NINETEEN

Ricky Odell and Slim Olsen had risen early, in the dark hour before dawn, and had gone to the only all-night café in Pondera for breakfast. A pale light showed in the east when they got their horses at the livery and rode forth. Ricky was again astride his own horse. Leaning to caution, they started east, circled the town to southward, and cut southwest to the river. Then, with the rising sun at their backs, they swung westward, far enough away from the main trail to be out of sight of any chance rider.

"I expect we'll have to cut straight through H Square range when we leave the river," Ricky told Slim, "and we don't want to be seen, that's a cinch."

"You've planned this expedition," Slim reminded him, "and it's up to you to take the lead. But Crowell must have a bunch of cattle scattered over his range, and where there's cattle, there's likely to be men, and where there're men. . . ."

"I know the rest of it," Ricky said sharply. "The first thing is to sight the cattle and stop then and there, and weave around out of sight. Savvy?"

"Sounds mysterious," was Slim's comment. "I think half the people up here think we're cardsharps, or cattle rustlers, or some such critters, to say nothing of being branded as gunmen. Even that leather-necked Campbell acts like he's got something behind his ear."

"That's me," Ricky said as they loped over the soft grass. "He doesn't like me butting in where Ira Crowell thinks he has a toehold."

"Yeah? And you figure to put a plug in with the girl before he has a chance to lay down the rules and bylaws. Is that it?"

"I'm not going to leave her for any length of time with what our friend Ira has to say to her," Ricky replied sharply. "I've got my end to hold up, and I propose to hoist it whenever I have a chance."

"Oh, I'm not blaming you," said Slim. "We going up to her place first?"

"No." Ricky scowled. "We're going out here and make this map I've got fit a couple of quarter-sections. We can read a cornerstone, if we can find one. Then, maybe. . . ." He stopped talking as he remembered Campbell's warning of the night before.

The sun hardly had climbed above the golden banners athwart the horizon when they spotted the first grazing herd. They came to a stop, and Ricky wrinkled his brows. "The place we want to hit is where the prairie joins the foothills, up west of the Crowell place," he announced. "There are two ways to get there. We can dodge through the H Square range, or we can turn north and hit the main trail. If anybody did see us leave town, they couldn't know where we were going."

"And if we go through Crowell's range, he has a reason to ask what we were doing there," Slim put in wisely.

"Then we'll go north," decided Ricky instantly. "If we run into Campbell, it's just none of his business, that's all."

"And if we run into Ira, he'll make it his business, that's what," said Slim dryly.

Ricky reined in his horse and looked at his companion with a frown. "What's the matter, Slim? You got any doubts about this business? I thought we'd gone all over it before."

"Oh, I'll stand by what we decided, Rick," answered Slim.

"The one thing about the business I don't like is that it may get us mixed up with the Crowell crowd. But if you're sincere in this affair with the girl, I'm right at your back, as I told you before."

Ricky thought a minute. "We'll play safe and keep clear of the Crowell angle," he said. "But we need more than the rodeo idea for being around here, for we'll be here after the celebration."

"Go ahead," Slim urged. "I'm with you."

But Slim could not rid himself of the persisting premonition of trouble in the move they were making.

The trail was clear when they reached it with no one in sight, east or west. They galloped for a time and slowed to a swinging lope. "We'll take it easy," Ricky called, "and then shoot past the spot where Ira hangs out!"

This they did, and as a consequence avoided meeting Ira, and also passed early enough in the morning to miss Adam Crowell on his way to town to keep his appointment with the others and hear the cattlemen's offer made to Campbell.

Ricky had his map out, and almost at the prairie's end, where it rolled upward into the slopes of the foothills, he swerved south. Soon, as near as he could make out, they were due west of Crowell's range, slightly above it where the creek that flowed down through the Campbell place ambled off into the southeast to join the river. Several squares denoting quarter-sections were marked as open to entry on the map.

"Now, we've got to find a cornerstone," Ricky said with a note of excitement in his voice. "We'll just have to keep apart and trail back and forth and around here till we find it. We're in the northwest section, I'm sure, but we've got to make certain."

They searched for nearly an hour. The stone would be buried in the grass and hard to find, as they knew. This country had been surveyed "on horseback", to use the term most frequently applied to the district.

Finally Slim cried out. "I guess we've hit it!" he shouted.

At this instant Ricky caught sight of a big black horse on the trail to the right and above them—the trail leading to and past the Campbell place. A second look confirmed his first thrill of expectation. It was Hope out for her morning ride on Bismarck.

He wheeled his horse and closed in on Slim, handing him the folded map. "Make sure of it!" he cried. "There are two quarters here together, northwest and southwest of the top corner section. You know as much about it as I do. And you've lost your watch, Slim." He whirled his horse. "Don't forget, Slim, we're looking for your watch!" he called over his shoulder.

Then he was off at a gallop to join the girl on the black horse.

Slim looked after him. "I've lost more'n that," he muttered. "And if he keeps on, I'll lose my mind." He dismounted to examine the stone.

In the search and subsequent excitement neither of them had caught sight of a number of riders below them who now disappeared in the timber and brush screen along the creek to southward.

"This is luck!" Ricky called out as he rode up to Hope and came to a rearing halt with his hat sweeping low. "I wanted to see you this morning and I was afraid I'd have to come to the house."

"Well, why not?" asked Hope, her eyes sparkling at the sight of him. "You know you're welcome."

"Did your father come home last night?" he asked quickly.

"Why, no," replied the girl with a look of surprise. "He said he might have to stay in town, so we didn't expect him. I thought you were to . . . to have a meeting today."

Ricky breathed deeply with relief and shot a glance back along the trail. No telltale curl of dust was visible. "We met last night," he explained. "The . . . that business is all settled. I saw your father before I went to bed and . . . well, I guess he'll have something to say to you when he comes back. No, don't ask me, for I cannot tell you."

Hope had flushed as she had been about to ask him a question and he saw that she had formed a wrong impression of what he and her father had been talking about and what the older man would have to say to her. "Is . . . is it about me?" she found herself asking.

"Yes, girl, it's about you . . . partly. But I don't want to talk about it. It's your father's business. I saw Ira beating it up to your place late yesterday after we went down."

"He came for a short visit," said the girl, her eyes clouding for a moment. She had forgotten Ira in the glowing, stimulating presence of Ricky. Then something dawned upon her. She looked at Ricky, startled. Had her father interfered? Ricky had spoken about not wanting to come to the house. Had her father forbidden him to come there? Hope's spirits surged in rebellion.

"I don't want to hear anything about it," said Ricky, "about Ira's visit, I mean. But I did want to see you this morning because I . . . I. . . ." He ceased speaking, with a light flush in his cheeks.

"Yes, Ricky, go on," she encouraged him. "Because . . . ?"

"I'm going away for a few days," Ricky got out, "and I don't want you to forget me. I'll be back soon. I wanted just a word with you to tell you again that I meant what I said in the arbor yesterday morning. You remember? I told you I love you. You can't forget that, Hope, for I won't let you."

"How do you know I'd want to forget it?" she asked shyly.

"For that, dear Hope, you must move your horse over closer." His eyes were brimming with a soft, glowing light and the world was forgotten.

"He isn't used to such a performance," said Hope dreamily.

In another few moments Ricky had his horse alongside. He leaned from the saddle and brought her lips to his. Her horse started, and she looked at him with sunlight in her eyes. "We're not in an arbor now, Ricky, and . . . oh, look!"

Ricky glanced around and stiffened in his saddle. Slim was sitting his horse where Ricky had left him, but down the creek a bunch of riders had burst from cover and were racing toward him. He was looking in the direction of Ricky and the girl.

Ricky shouted and pointed. Slim looked around, then back at them. Ricky beckoned, but Slim stood his ground.

"You must go back . . . quick!" Ricky told the girl. "Those are probably H Square 'punchers, and I have reason to think they maybe don't think much of Slim and me. Remember what I told you, sweetheart, and I'll see you soon."

He let his horse out in the direction of Slim and sped like the wind across the intervening distance. Just as he reached Slim, the nose of the black charger ridden by the girl showed at his side. He called to her, but she paid no heed. He saw her eyes flashing, and she was looking at the oncoming riders, who were almost there. Slim was afoot, his horse standing with reins dangling some few feet away. Just as the riders, led by Ira himself, came up to them, Slim raised his hand and shouted, waving them back.

"Don't let your horses step on it!" he cried, pointing to the ground. When they looked, they saw a splash of gold in the grass where the brilliant sunlight was reflected from the crystal of a watch.

Ricky grinned, but quickly suppressed it as Slim took a few steps and picked up his watch. He attached it carefully to a buckskin thong fastened to a buttonhole of his shirt. He looked at it carefully, held it to his ear, and dropped it into his shirt pocket, stuffing his sack of tobacco and cigarette papers in with it.

"I told you I'd stay here till I found it," he said to Ricky. "If it hadn't been for these gents attracting my attention in their direction, giving me a chance to see the glare of the crystal, I might have been here a week." He had stuffed the map into a pocket where it couldn't be seen. He nodded to the angry-faced Ira. "Much obliged," he said with a nod, turning toward his horse.

"What were you doing on our range?" Ira demanded harshly.

"You saw what I was doing here," Slim shot back as he gathered up his reins. "What were you doing? Going . . . or coming to help me find it?" He swung into his saddle.

Meanwhile, Ricky had looked carefully at each of the five men with Ira. They were experienced cowpunchers, regular hands, as he saw at once. There was no menace in the cold, searching look they returned him; no personal antagonism was in their eyes. But they made it plain that he and Slim were strangers, and that they were acting under Ira's orders. Indeed, they looked questioningly at Ira from time to time and listened keenly to what he had to say. But the young scion of the H Square seemed, for the time being, to have forgotten their presence. He now was looking at Hope.

"You had better go back to the ranch, Hope. . . ."

"I've already told her that," Ricky interrupted suavely.

"You shut up!" cried Ira, and immediately bit his lip as he realized he had made a mistake in the girl's presence.

"You see?" Ricky said to Hope with a dazzle in his eyes. "Isn't he pleasant? And this is only the third time we've met."

"I don't see any necessity for me to leave," said the girl in a pleasant voice, with a smile to the men behind Ira, who touched their hats. "I was out riding and met Mister Odell, Ira, and we rode over here to help Mister Olsen find his watch."

One of the cowpunchers chuckled, and Ira turned in his saddle and gave his companions a black look. But their faces were all sober.

"It just happens, Hope, that this Slim hadn't lost any watch," he said politely. "He and the other have been on our range this morning and I want to find out why. When strangers start moving around on our range, we are naturally curious about it. I wish you would go, so we can talk to them and not bother you."

"Oh, it isn't bothering me a bit, Ira," the girl returned sweetly. "You know how it gets rather dull up at our place at times, and I enjoy a little excitement, especially in the morning when I'm out for a ride. And, really, I was talking with Mister Odell on the trail when you appeared." Hope felt the undercurrent flow of feeling in the words that had been spoken by the three men, and she sensed that she was indirectly responsible for the situation. She had not forgotten Ira's disparaging remarks of the day before when he had spoken of Ricky and Slim, nor Ricky's fair statement that morning that he didn't want to hear anything about the meeting, but she glanced at him furtively, then she spoke to Slim. "Did you really lose your watch?" she asked.

"You saw me pick it up, Miss Campbell," returned Slim readily. "I'm not in the habit of throwing my watch around on purpose for some strange cowhand's horse to step on it." He looked squarely at Ira. "Why don't you tell her the whole business?" he demanded sharply. "Go ahead and tell her why you don't like us. Just because you were foolish enough to pull a gun on me and get planted in the grass for it is no reason you've got to go prowling around with a bunch of 'punchers at your heels whenever you see us."

"That's enough!" said Ricky in a commanding voice. "Look here, Ira! We were going up that trail. Maybe we took a short cut, maybe we were riding around to see the scenery, but we haven't been roaming around your range, and don't know if we're on it this minute. I've told you three times that we're not looking for any trouble with you."

"You're a liar!" flashed Ira in the heat of his rage.

Ricky's face went white as he turned to the girl. "I guess you'd better go, Hope," he said in a quiet but stern voice. "I've stood just about as much as I feel I should take. Please go."

Ira's eyes had narrowed to slits as he heard Odell call the girl by her first name. One of his men, close to him, was saying something in an undertone, possibly cautioning him.

"Please don't let my being here have any bearing on the situation," said Hope casually, tucking a stray wisp of hair under her cap. "This is really exciting, Ira. I suppose now there will be a fight." She looked at him with a question in her eyes.

"Not in your presence, there won't," Ricky assured her. "But Ira can choose his time and place, as long as it isn't in his front yard."

"If you go for that tin gun of yours, I'll shoot it into the next county!" cried Slim in a ringing tone of warning.

But the cowpuncher at Ira's side pushed ahead of him. "There's no use in this argument," he said, looking straight at Ricky, who met his gaze coolly. He turned to Slim. "The guns'll stay where they belong."

"That's sensible," said Ricky, holding the other's gaze. "Are you assuming the responsibility now?"

Ira made as if to speak hotly but the men with him murmured in protest.

"I'm working for the H Square and taking orders from Mister Crowell," said the new spokesman. "You're on our range. We'll take your explanation that you didn't know it. But you know it now, and the best thing you two can do is get off it."

Ricky's retort was swift and to the point. "If you've ever played cards, you'll know that some decks have a joker in 'em. We're playing with one of those decks right now and Slim and me hold the joker. We'll play it all ways, if necessary. We'll go back over to the trail now to avoid any further scene . . . which would be unpleasant . . . before the young lady. But I'm telling you straight that we haven't been, and are not looking for trouble with Crowell, there. And it's the first time I ever told a man that for the fourth time in my life."

"I'm not hearing it the fourth time!" Ira ejaculated. "And if I ever meet you in town, I'll show you that you won't want any trouble with me again!"

"And don't forget me, Ira," drawled Slim. "You didn't like me from the start."

"We'll let it stand as it is, then," said the H Square cowpuncher impatiently.

"Sure," said Ricky. "I'm agreeable."

Even Hope could see that these two men understood each other, that they were really trying to avoid trouble, while Ira was at a loss to decide what to do. In a moment she solved the predicament. "I'm going home," she said with a toss of her head. "If you'll ride to the trail with me, Mister Odell, I'll tell you the answer to give to the message you brought me. So long, Ira." Her smile was warm, and Ira thawed perceptibly.

"I'll see you tonight, Hope!" he called after her as she rode away with Ricky and Slim following.

"And the rest of us will get back to work," growled the cowpuncher who had acted as spokesman. "This looks like a personal affair, Ira, and you'll have to look after such things yourself."

"Go ahead," Ira snapped out insolently. "I'm going to the ranch."

CHAPTER TWENTY

When they came to the trail, and Hope reined in her horse, Ricky moved to her side while Slim held back, ostensibly rolling and lighting a cigarette. There was a slumbering light of worry in the girl's eyes. She looked back once to see Ira riding swiftly away in the direction of the ranch while the others were cutting back to the big herd of cattle in the distance.

"I'm sorry this had to happen," Ricky told her soberly. "I was afraid it might turn out as it did, and that's why I wanted you to go back. You can see there is no love lost between Ira and me, but I didn't want a ruckus with you present. This is the third time we've met, but don't take in any stock in what he threatened about the fourth time . . . if there is a fourth time."

Hope looked at him, her eyes serious. She knew there was tense rivalry between him and Ira. It had developed naturally and she couldn't have expected anything else. But Ira's attitude had indicated serious consequences, and she didn't want any trouble that she could rightfully blame upon herself. "What did Slim mean when he told Ira to tell me all of it?" she asked in a low voice. "About the gun and . . . the rest of it?"

"Slim is sensitive and Ira rubbed him the wrong way of the grain," Ricky replied. "It was nothing. It happened yesterday. Ira went to see you afterward. No, Hope, I don't want you to hear a word. I'm standing on my own. I love you, and I want you, and I'm willing to fight for you in the open and on the square and take my chances. Won't you please try and forget what you saw and heard today?"

"But Ira said next time he met you. . . ."

"Ira was excited," Ricky interrupted soothingly. "I'll see to it that he doesn't clash with me, and I'll hold Slim in check if I have to put a halter on him. You know, Hope, so far as I can make out, Ira doesn't know about my trouble in town."

"And when he finds out," she said anxiously, "it will be just terrible. The things he'll tell me. . . ."

"Are the things I'll make him tell me to my face," Ricky broke in sternly. "I won't fight for a girl behind anybody's back, and I won't let the other fellow do it, if I can help it. I won't back down on that proposition, girl. I mean it."

Hope's eyes sparkled momentarily, but again clouded. "You say Father has something to tell me, and I believe I can guess what it is."

"I have nothing to say, Hope . . . nothing except what I say for myself. It is for you to determine. I'll tell you much, as I promised on the night of the rodeo ball. At present some think we're here to take part in the rodeo contests. We'll let them think so, and we'll enter the contests, so far as that goes, for the sport of the thing. But what is holding me here, dear, is you. All I ask is to be allowed to answer any man who has anything to say behind my back."

"You can answer to me, Ricky Odell," she said lightly. "And I'll be ready to . . . listen," she added in a whisper which just reached his ears. She looked him straight in the eyes and smiled. It was like a dazzling ray of sunlight breaking through the dark, rolling clouds of a storm.

He reached and touched her hand for a moment. "I couldn't ask anything more than the chance to talk for myself, sweetheart. And now we've got to be on our way. I won't come up for a while, but I'll get word to you some way. Slim, c'mon and say so long to the lady."

"I reckon I'm to blame for this fracas, Miss Hope," said Slim, riding up to them. "And I'm to say something that Ricky's too soft-hearted or something like that to say. I'm. . . ."

"Just don't say it," interrupted Ricky with a frown. "I've told Hope all she needs to know. She doesn't want to hear about unpleasant happenings, and I've promised her that you and me won't have any trouble in town with Ira. Does that go with you?"

Slim lifted his brows. "Well, if the boy doesn't go clear off his head, and. . . ."

"That's enough," said Ricky sternly. "He's promised, Hope. C'mon, Slim, it's getting along toward noon and we've got quite a ride back. So long, Hope."

"So long!" the girl called cheerily, and waved to them as they rode down the trail into the prairie.

"Are the locations all right, Slim?" asked Ricky.

"Seem to be," was the answer. "But I'll tell you one thing, my buckaroo, you promised something when you said you'd keep out of trouble with Crowell. He aims to make trouble any way he can first time he gets to town and finds us there."

"All right, we'll wait till that happens," said Ricky, a bit grimly. "I told Hope I wouldn't fight no battle to win her behind her back, and I mean it."

"Well, don't forget he was up there today with a gang behind him," was Slim's dry retort. "That boy ain't taking no chances."

They rode back slowly, both seeming busy with their thoughts. Ricky could not keep his mind off Hope—the beauty of her, her sensible attitude, her apparent fairness, and, as he now believed, her regard for him. But he couldn't deny the fact that Ira Crowell had a certain advantage—an advantage that Campbell recognized. And any clash that Ricky might have with Ira would be detrimental to Ricky's cause. For Ira had standing in the community and his father was possessed of wealth and power. These things counted on the range just as they figured elsewhere.

Slim's thoughts were racing further ahead to the time when the elder Crowell would take a hand. For he felt sure this would come.

They rode slower than they thought, walking their horses much of the time, allowing the animals to choose their own pace. It was early afternoon when they finally came in view of Pondera. Almost at the moment they sighted the town they descried two horsemen on the road ahead. Both recognized John Campbell's form in the saddle.

"Well, here's the big bugaboo," sang Ricky, suddenly cheerful. "He'll probably want to know where we've been, and if . . . he's liable to have a lot of ifs on his mind, Slim, so let me do the talking if there is any."

"Don't worry, I'm through," Slim assured him. "I'm just wondering who's with him."

As they neared the pair they failed to recognize Adam Crowell, for neither of them had ever seen the H Square owner. But Slim was suspicious. He could tell a stockman at sight, and here was one, and an important one, if ever he had seen one. He finally decided the chances were about even that it was Crowell.

Campbell checked his horse as they met. "Been up to my place?" he asked Ricky in a pleasant voice.

"Not quite that far," replied Ricky in a reserved tone.

"Then maybe you've been to mine," Campbell's companion said pompously with a frown. "Is that so?"

"Where is your place?" asked Ricky coldly, resenting the big man's tone instantly.

"Oh, you don't know, eh? My place is the H Square."

"Then you must be Crowell," drawled Ricky. "No, we were not up to your place exactly, either, although we ran into your son and some of your men along the trail."

"It looks to me as if you're hanging around here to make trouble," said Crowell, easing his bulk in the saddle. "Now, I want to tell you something here and now, young fellow. . . ."

"Suppose you write it and mail it to us," snapped Ricky curtly, his eyes flashing. "There's been too many people telling us this and that, and we're in a hurry."

He touched his horse lightly with his spurs and he and Slim were off for town at a racing pace, leaving Campbell and Crowell to stare after them and then ride on, talking and gesticulating.

"You're the boy that can do it!" called Slim. "We can put Crowell on our list in red right now."

"Which is the color I'm seeing this minute!" Ricky retorted hotly.

Slim remained silent as they went on into town.

John Campbell took more than usual notice of his daughter at supper that evening. He had arrived but an hour before, giving as the reason for his slow return business in town.

"I rode back with Adam Crowell," he told Hope and her mother casually, "and stopped at his ranch for a short time. He's getting ready to ship."

He didn't look at Hope, who betrayed her interest in her alert gaze. The girl was wondering if he had talked with Ira and just how much Ira had told him if he had. Or perhaps Ira had talked with his father. In her heart she resented the very advantages Ira possessed. And now her father was already getting close to Adam Crowell again.

"Adam says I should go in for more cattle, Jane," Campbell told his wife. "I took a job today as general agent to oversee the Association range, and Crowell doesn't see why that should interfere with my going in deeper in the stock-raising business."

"You, why you should have done that long ago," his wife

reminded him.

"Yes, I know," said John slowly. "It has been mostly, well, all a matter of range. But Crowell says he has more range than he needs, and Johnson to the north seems to have plenty to spare, and according to Adam we can make an agreement that would give me all the range I need. Then there's range here in the foothills to which I'm actually entitled even if I've never used it."

"That sounds like a good proposition," said Jane, smiling.

Campbell glanced at Hope, but the girl failed to smile or make any comment. The significance of what her father had said came to her in a flash. Crowell, the greatest power on the range, was behind it all. He had used his influence to get her father the job of which he had spoken. He had arranged with Johnson to provide him with the range he needed. But Crowell would expect something in return and Hope believed she knew what that something would be. Ira's father had set the wheels of his wealth and influence spinning behind his son's suit for her hand. And immediately all thought of romance was blurred.

"It will make me," John Campbell was saying with conviction. "I can't overlook such an opportunity, Jane. I can't keep up buying and selling cattle and being away from home all the time. This is my place and I'm going to make something out of it. Especially now that Hope is home with us."

There it was. The sinister shadow of the club over her head. Her father and mother talked on, happy with the new prospect, and Hope excused herself early from supper.

She went out to the hitching rail in the purple mist of the twilight. No charging knights were abroad this evening in her imagination. But she saw the specter of a powerful face, keen-eyed and stern, and almost caught the sharp crack of a whiplash in the still, scented air. She was pale when she went to the porch, and there found her father.

"Sit down, Daughter, and let's talk a minute," said Campbell, puffing quietly on his pipe.

"I only went out for a minute," said Hope. "I should be helping Mother with the dishes."

"Bless you, child, she isn't near ready yet, or else she has finished. Sit down. I want to ask you something."

Hope saw that her father was experiencing difficulty in getting out what he wanted to say and she surmised that her mother was missing purposely so that her father could talk with her alone. She sat down.

John Campbell cleared his throat. "Was that fellow, Odell, and his partner up here today?" he asked finally, striving to make his tone sound casual.

"Not at the house," Hope replied. "I was out riding and I met Mister Odell down the trail and later met his friend, who had dropped his watch on the prairie and was looking for it."

"Then they were on the way here," said Campbell in a harder voice.

"I'm not sure of that," said Hope. "I suppose you heard down at the Crowell Ranch about Ira and a bunch of 'punchers riding up and asking Ricky . . . Mister Odell . . . and Slim what they were doing on H Square range?"

"I heard something about it," Campbell confessed, "and I can't say as I blame 'em. That pair has no business sneaking around up here. Did they say what they were doing on H Square range?"

"I don't believe they knew they were on it," said Hope with spirit. "As if it made any difference. No doubt you know there is a . . . a personal matter between Ira and Mister Odell. At least Ira has made it so, and incidentally he has made a fool of himself."

"I wouldn't say that," her father cautioned. "You must remember that Ira belongs here . . . was born here . . . and that

173

he comes of a pioneer family. He's entitled to more consideration than . . . than. . . ."

"Than who, Father?" the girl prompted. When he didn't answer, Hope resumed. "I understand the whole situation," she said firmly. "Ricky Odell said he had talked with you in town but he wouldn't tell me what it was about. And he wouldn't talk about Ira behind his back. But I saw and heard enough today to know that Ira hasn't been using his brains lately. He made a show of himself today, and when Slim urged him to tell me everything, he quit cold, as they say. But I caught enough to learn that Ira pulled a gun play on Slim and didn't get away with it."

"Are you taking sides with this Slim and Odell?" her father demanded sternly.

"I like to see fair play," the girl replied defiantly.

Campbell strove to hold his anger in check. "This Odell, with his devil-may-care air, his gun ability, and his laugh seems to have turned your head, I'm thinking," he said with a touch of sarcasm.

"Is that what you wished to tell me?" asked Hope, rising from her chair with flashing eyes.

"Just think it over and see if you don't think you'd better sit down and talk everything over with me," said her father. "Maybe you'll realize that I have a right to be concerned about this business."

"I'm willing to talk to you, Father, but I will not talk to you when you say such things to me," said the girl stoutly. "Ricky hasn't turned my head, as you say, with his personality, and Ira isn't going to turn it with his boast of belonging and being the son of a big rancher and all that. And I see quite clearly why his father is suddenly so anxious to help you."

Campbell gripped the arms of his chair. "You . . . don't want to see me succeed here?" he thundered.

"You know I do, Daddy," said the girl, patting him on the head and sitting down beside him. "But your business affairs shouldn't affect me personally, and I'm afraid it looks as though . . . well, I won't say anything more."

"And see that you don't," said John Campbell gruffly. "Crowell can't dictate to me, and he knows it." He scowled in the fading light. He wasn't altogether sure of what he said. But of one thing he was absolutely certain. If his daughter should fall in love, it would be far better that a substantial youth such as Ira should be the man.

"You've got to look at my side of it, Hope," he said slowly. "You're the only child I have. You're attractive . . . the prettiest girl on the range. Men will want you and in time you'll have to take one of them. You can't decide during any snap-shot love affair. The man who gets you must be a man in every sense of the word, and he must have something behind him. I don't want to interfere, and I know it's dangerous. But my thoughts are for you, and I can see what's going on right under my very eyes. That's why I had to tell Odell something last night and that's why I've got to stick to it. It's my duty."

"What did you tell him, Father?" Hope asked softly.

"I told him I had reason to believe that he liked you, or thought he did. I'd cautioned him before and he said he'd see you every time he could manage it. But I told him last night that we didn't know anything about him, and that until he had proved himself and had shown me that he was fair and square and above board, he would have to stay away from the house, and I meant it."

"Oh," breathed Hope slowly. "You told him he couldn't come here?"

"I did . . . until he shows that he has a right to come here."

"You know he promised to tell me all about himself the night of the rodeo ball. They're staying for the rodeo and are going to be in the contests. It isn't as if he intended to remain a mystery."

"No? Well, why is he waiting till then?" demanded her father. "Doesn't that look tricky? If he has an honest excuse for romping into this country like he has, why doesn't he tell you straight off . . . 'specially if he likes you?"

"He undoubtedly has his reason," said the girl with just a tinge of doubt in her heart. "If he can't come here, I'll see him at the ball and listen to him. I'm fair enough with him to believe him. But, until then, Ira cannot come here to see me, either. I told him he could be my escort at the dance, and I told Ricky I would dance with him. I'll keep both my promises. And that's all I have to say, Daddy."

Her father sensed that she was on the verge of tears. "That's all you need to say, Hope," he told her quickly. "Run in and help your mother, like a good girl, and don't think too hard of your dad."

That night John and Jane again sat until midnight before the coals in the fireplace, talking in subdued tones.

CHAPTER TWENTY-ONE

Hope Campbell slept fretfully. Once she awoke, looking out the window where the dark branches of the trees were interlaced against the cold, white light of the moon. She heard a soft sound that was not like that of any night bird. It was a weird crooning, rising and falling gently on the night air. At once it soothed, interested, and puzzled her. At times it resembled the cry of a loon and dwindled to the wail of a violin.

She rose noiselessly and looked out the window into the yard. As she did so, a shadow flitted near the trees from which came the sounds to excite her ear. She recognized the scuttling form of Vagle, like a huge bat, and it was he who was crooning in the wind. Hope would have called to him but it might have meant awakening the others in the house. She crept back into bed.

Vagle, the restless, standing his vigil during the dark hours. Why was this man always on the watch, she wondered? Surely there was none to come to harm them. But suppose someone should come in the night? Suppose Ricky Odell were to send a message, or come himself in some emergency? What would Vagle do? The girl tossed restlessly in her warm, white bed. She would speak to the man in the morning.

Hope was awake again with the first flush of the dawn. She performed her ablutions and dressed in her riding habit. An early ride on Bismarck would erase the signs of an almost sleepless night. The wind in her face and the red and gold of the sunrise would revive her spirits. She was nervous, tired, worried. She stole down the stairs and found Vagle in the barn. He already had her horse out.

"Vagle," she said irritably, "you've been up all night."

"Yes, I'm up all night," he said with his mirthless grin.

"Listen," said Hope, stamping a foot with impatience, "you were trying to sing last night. I heard you. You woke me up with the noises you were making. You must not do that again, do you hear?"

"You don't like that?" he said, as if asking the question of himself. "Too loud, maybe?"

"I don't like it loud or soft, or any way," said Hope, frowning. "Why do you stay up nights, prowling around as you do? Do you expect somebody to come here in the night?"

The man's eyes flashed with a startled look. "I keep watch every night," he said crossly. "I am supposed to do that. If you don't like it, I can't help it. Maybe somebody will come, maybe not, but I will be ready. If you don't like it, you talk to your father."

"But if someone did come," the girl persisted, "what would you do?"

Vagle bared his yellow teeth in another grin. "I stop him," was the answer, and his hand dropped lightly to the gun he wore.

"You mean you would shoot?" demanded Hope in an awed voice.

"If it was the right one, I would shoot if he didn't go away," replied Vagle with a series of comical nods.

But Hope saw nothing humorous in his speech or manner. "Would you shoot my friends who were here yesterday?" she asked breathlessly.

Vagle shrugged. "I dunno," he said in a noncommittal tone.

"You don't know!" the girl cried. "Well, I'll tell you so you will know, and I'll have Father tell you the same thing. You're not to shoot anybody I know, nor anybody at all. If someone comes, you call Father. You act like a child. Saddle my horse, Vagle!"

In another few minutes she was on the trail, riding east.

Hope came into the full glory of the sunrise when she reached a low ridge from the slopes of which flowed the golden prairie lands. In the southeast she could see the dark spots, swarming like flies, which were part of the Crowell herds. The green band of the river's timbered banks led eastward to the pink buttes beyond Pondera.

The girl was alone with her thoughts even more than she would have been in her own room. And these thoughts were disturbing. She could not help resenting certain statements her father had made the night before; she could not shake off the conviction that Ricky Odell—whoever and whatever he was— was being discriminated against in favor of Ira Crowell, backed by wealth and prestige. Odell was backed only by his own words and personality. With nothing definitely charged against him, he was forbidden to visit the Campbell home, whereas Ira was welcome without having to explain the cause or result of his own personal dislike of Odell. And Adam Crowell loomed in the background with his complacent smile of confidence, trailing his whip of power.

For a wild minute, as Hope sat her horse there at the prairie's end, she struggled with the impulse to send Bismarck fast as the wind into town where she could tell Ricky what had happened, ask him for the truth about himself at once, and ride back with him in triumph. But she soon saw such an act in its true light— that of a schoolgirl's daydream. And she had reason enough to know she no longer was a schoolgirl. In a matter of a week had come an intangible change. She only knew that she had suddenly been thrown into life, had been precipitated into it with much the initial casualness that a stone is tossed into a pool.

But, like the stone, her plunge was making ripples that were widening and encompassing the lives of others, and. . . .

She gave up trying to solve her dilemma and became angrier. She rode back slowly, and when she finally reached the hitching rail and turned in toward the barn, the obsession uppermost in her mind was to the effect that, since men wanted her, she was no longer a child. Within the week, then, she had become a woman. She smiled to herself at this decision, which she thought smacked of adolescence, but she was to learn that it was warranted.

Her father appeared uneasy at breakfast and he looked at her thoughtfully from time to time while her mother talked of everything except what was in her mind. Already John Campbell was dubious as to whether he had taken the proper course in meddling with his daughter's personal affairs. He had to confess to himself that he had taken what looked like a definite side in the matter. Perhaps such a course was more dangerous than he had suspected.

"Oh, there's one thing I'd like to ask you about, Father," said Hope, after she had told her mother about Bismarck's complete recovery from his sprain. "Why is it that Vagle keeps wandering about the house and yard every night, armed with a pistol, and talking and trying to sing to himself?"

"He always was a night hawk," her father answered briefly.

"Last night he woke me up with his crooning and groaning, and I got up and looked out the window," said the girl in a nettled tone. "There he was, slinking around the trees like a big cat. I don't like it. It interferes with my rest. I told him about it this morning and he said he had to keep watch, whatever that means, and if I didn't like it, I could talk to you. He has no business to speak to me like that, and I won't have it, even if he is a half-wit."

Campbell frowned heavily. "He had no business to say that,"

he told her. "I'll speak to him about it."

But Hope had no intention of letting the matter drop with a casual promise. "I asked him if he expected somebody to come here in the night," she said. "He mumbled that somebody might come or might not come and blinked his fishy eyes and put on that yellow grin that is sickening. I asked him what he would do if someone did come, and he said he would stop him. Is anyone expected to come here in the night to do us harm, Father?" She put the question pointblank, and John Campbell put down his knife and fork with a startled look.

"Of course not," he answered with a quick glance at his wife.

"Well, you better tell him. He patted his gun in front of me and I asked him if he would shoot. He said if it was the right one, he would shoot if he didn't go away. Imagine. Why the first thing we know, someone will be killed here because he happened along after dark. A lunatic has no business with a gun."

Her father looked at her steadily, but he remained speechless. There was nothing he could say. He realized more painfully than ever that there were some things—some parts of his past life—about which he couldn't take his daughter into his confidence. He could not tell her that there was one for whom Vagle had reason to watch, from whom he himself had reason to fear. But he would not have Vagle exciting Hope and spurring her into asking questions that he could not answer.

When her father made no comment, Hope resumed in a modulated tone. "I asked if he would shoot Mister Odell or Slim, who were here, and he said he didn't know. He might even take a shot at Ira, for that matter," she added with a hint of sarcasm. "I want to be able to sleep peacefully in my own home without that man sneaking about during the night with a loaded gun and his defective mind filled with thoughts of using it. It's downright dangerous. That man, Father, isn't merely queer. I've seen madness blaze in his eyes."

"I'll put a stop to it at once," Campbell declared. "I've not been in the habit of letting him carry a gun, but I got lax when you and your mother were here alone. I'll take it away from him and stop his prowling around. I don't think he's as . . . as crazy as you think, but if he gets any worse, I'll send him away."

"I think you had better talk to him, John," his wife put in.

"Yes, he'll listen to you when he won't pay any attention to anyone else," said Hope. "I didn't mean I . . . that he should be sent away. He's not so bad when he obeys you, as he always has before."

"There's nothing to be afraid of around here, Hope," Campbell told his daughter. "This is your home, where you can have peace and comfort and everything that our love for you can give you."

But deep in his heart Campbell wondered if this were true. He also was struck by a new dignity and spirit that Hope had shown. If she could assert herself so plainly in a matter such as this, and with such reason, she was perfectly competent to deal with more important emergencies. He could not keep a gleam of admiration out of his worried eyes.

Meanwhile, Hope had told her mother of Ira Crowell's expressed intention the day before of visiting her this night. And what Jane told him after breakfast caused him to decide to prevent that visit.

Campbell's orders to Vagle were explicit. He was not to roam about the place at night, singing or making any other kind of noise. If he did have to go out for a walk in the night, as he contended, and had always been in the habit of doing so, he was to keep out of sight of anyone in the house and under no circumstances to walk near the side of the house where the windows of Hope's bedroom were located. And he was not to carry his gun or shoot at anyone. If anything should happen, he was to wake Campbell with as little disturbance as possible.

When Campbell was through, Vagle understood his orders perfectly and agreed to obey them. But Campbell did not take his gun.

Hope went riding again in the afternoon and they had an early supper at her father's request. He rode off after supper and the girl suspected that he was going to the Crowell Ranch but said nothing. However, Campbell's intention was to meet Ira on his way up and persuade him not to come that night. In this he was thwarted by the appearance of both Ira and his father. They met on the trail just below the house and Campbell rode up with them.

"Ira said he was coming up tonight and I thought I would ride along," Adam Crowell said in a pleasant, rumbling voice. "You and me can have a little talk while the young people are together. Makes me feel old to see our youngsters growed up and . . . and interested in each other, John. How about you?"

"I'm . . . not used to it yet," replied Campbell. "I haven't been home so much and Hope is just back from school to stay. I'll stay home from now on, I reckon."

When they reached the house, they rode to the barn while Ira turned his mount over to Vagle at Campbell's bidding.

Ira hastened to the porch where Hope and her mother were sitting and Campbell and Crowell sat on the bench in the yard after the latter had greeted Jane and the girl in his amiable, booming voice.

"Ira was telling me something today that made me sit up and listen, after what I heard from you and others in town," Crowell told Campbell, when they were settled and smoking. "It was about those young fellers who were mixed up in the shooting. I suppose you know they were up here yesterday, and on my range?"

"So I heard, but that's all I do know about it," said Campbell.

"I'm not going to say anything about the shooting scrape,"

said Crowell, frowning, "but I'm wondering what they were doing roaming around this corner of the range. If I'm not
mistaken, Campbell, there are two or three, maybe more,
quarter-sections up this way that ain't filed on. I ran out of
men, you took up what you could, but . . . well, I'd have to look
at the plat to make sure." He paused and looked closely at the
face of Campbell. "You don't suppose they could be so rattle-
brained as to try to file on land in here, do you?"

Campbell had almost forgotten that Odell had announced
just such an intention. And, if he still had the idea in his head, it
would explain why he and Slim had come up there the day
before. He swore softly but Crowell heard him.

"I see you're wondering about the same thing," said the H
Square owner. "Well, John, it looks to me as if your first job as
general agent would be to find out these fellows' intentions, and
if they've got any such idea in their heads, knock it out of 'em."

"I'll certainly find out," Campbell promised, meaning just
what he said. "I thought maybe Odell had another reason for
sneaking up this way, but. . . ."

"You mean Hope?" Crowell broke in. "That's nonsense. Your
girl has too much sense to take up with a tramp of a gunfighter.
And I think she likes Ira too well, anyway. They've run around
together since they were kids and . . . well, I have no objection,
have you?"

"No," said Campbell reluctantly. "Of course, it's up to Hope."

"Of course," Crowell agreed heartily, "and if I know her at
all, she has plenty of common sense. She'd get that from you,
and her mother is a smart woman. If I was you, John, I'd sort of
tip that pair off that they're not wanted around here and I'd
make it strong enough so it'd stick. Then, if they've got to be
convinced, slip the word to me." There was a sinister promise in
Crowell's speech.

They saw Hope and Ira walking in the yard, saw them stop

and face each other, and walk on, but the two were never out of sight of the porch where Jane was sitting, or of the bench where Campbell and Crowell talked of range conditions and of Campbell's future. Link by link, Crowell was forging a chain that he thought would bring Campbell to his way of thinking. But he was not taking Hope into the reckoning.

Hope had been reluctant to leave the porch where she had been sitting with her mother. This had irritated Ira, who had been warmly welcomed by Hope's mother. The girl had appeared a trifle cold toward him and this annoyed him, also. He had something very important to say to Hope this evening, for he had learned considerable from his father after the latter's return from town the day before.

"You know I'm awfully sorry for what happened yesterday morning," he told her when they were in the yard. "I really couldn't help you being there, though. But I tried to make it as easy as I could."

"Oh, it was all very interesting," said Hope, tossing her head. "I didn't know such feeling could develop on such short notice."

"Well, you know why it developed, don't you, Hope? It came about through my sending that note to you by that pair. And when this Odell came down the trail calling you by your first name, I couldn't very well not resent his insolence, could I?"

"Why did you judge it to be insolence?" asked the girl quietly.

Ira halted and looked at her. "Why . . . why, it was insolence, wasn't it?" he demanded, showing genuine surprise.

"Not necessarily," replied Hope coolly.

"Hope, I don't understand you. Here you are the same as telling me to my face that this tramp, this nobody from nowhere, this gunman and gambler has a right to. . . ."

"You're forgetting yourself," Hope interrupted haughtily. "At present Ricky Odell happens to be a friend of mine. Whether he continues to remain so will depend upon him and not upon anything you can say against him. He at least refused to talk about you behind your back."

"And with darn' good reason!" Ira exploded. "He knows who I am and he couldn't say anything against me if he wanted to, unless he lied. Surely you are not placing him in the same position as me?"

"Slim Olsen dared you yesterday to tell me all the truth, Ira," flared the girl. "Now, suppose you do that before I go back to the porch." She walked on and he quickly gained her side.

"There was nothing to it," Ira said, anger swelling within him. "I suppose you know this Odell shot a man down and killed him in town the other night?"

"I knew all about it before you did," answered Hope calmly.

"And you receive him at your home?" he asked incredulously. "Don't you know he's a common killer?"

"No, I don't know that," replied Hope, her lips tightening. "And you don't know it, either. It seems to be that you should know more about him before condemning him. Incidentally, I have his promise to tell me all about himself on the night of the rodeo ball. I think we can let further conversation in the matter rest until then."

"You don't mean to tell me that he's going to the big dance!" exclaimed Ira. "Why, he might even have the audacity to ask you to dance with him."

"He already has asked me that, and I'm saving a dance for him, of course," said the girl sweetly.

"Well, I object to that," said Ira stoutly. "And you can't blame me, Hope, one bit. After all, I'm to be your escort."

"But you don't have to be unless you want to," said Hope.

Ira fumed. "Of course I want to be!" he blurted. "I wouldn't let any man on earth cheat me of that pleasure and privilege. Why, Hope, I love you."

Both stopped and both of them looked startled. It was the

first time that Ira had told her straight out. She saw his eyes were serious and turned her own away. She could not berate him in the face of his declaration, nor could she resist the thrill she felt at his next words.

"You must have known that, Hope. It came out sudden-like and unexpected, but I should have told you long ago. Like a ninny, I thought you would take it for granted until I told you at a better time and in a different way. I not only love you, Hope, but I want to marry you."

"I . . . don't want to appear old-fashioned, Ira, but this is sort of sudden," said the bewildered girl in a low voice. "I suspected, of course, that you . . . had some intentions, but you never came right out and said as much, and . . . this puts me in a queer position."

"It's my fault," said Ira quickly. "I should have told you before this. After all, I didn't have the right to question you so closely about Odell. But you can see now why I thought I had the right. Naturally I hated Odell the moment he spoke your name. I feel that our happiness is at stake. I can give you a good home, everything you want. Since we were kids I never thought of any other girl the way I thought of you. I never knew how much I wanted you till now. Life would be a dead thing without you. Will you marry me, Hope?"

The girl stood still, her face the cool color of marble. But she did not take her eyes from his. "I cannot answer that question now, Ira," she said slowly. "You have waited, and now you must not expect me to answer on the spur of the moment. It's dark. Let's go to the porch. I . . . I have so much to think about."

Ira hesitated. Then he took her in his arms quickly and kissed her. In another moment he was leading her by the hand to the porch where her mother and father and Adam Crowell were talking.

"Well, are you ready to go home, Son?" boomed the elder

Crowell. "I was just about to ride off and leave you. What's the matter with you two kids? Lost your tongues with grown-ups around?"

Ira and his father rode away shortly afterward. Hope stood at the porch railing while John Campbell and his wife sat in chairs,

"What's the matter, Daughter?" asked Campbell quizzically. "You're thinking so hard it breaks right out on you like a rash."

"The world is tumbling down," said the girl. "Ira Crowell has asked me to marry him." Then she spied Vagle coming back from the hitching rail where he had earlier brought the horses. She called to him sharply. "Vagle, don't you go snooping around tonight, do you hear me? You're a jinx, that's what you are!" With this she flung herself inside and her father and mother heard her running up the stairs to her room.

CHAPTER TWENTY-TWO

John Campbell and his wife Jane were more in a quandary next day than ever, for overnight Hope's behavior had undergone a complete change from one extreme to the other. She was no longer moody, petulant, or capricious. She was sweet and pleasant in a determined way, radiating confidence, her head high. Her manner was altogether different from any they ever had seen her employ before.

Neither Campbell nor Jane could account for the transition. It was not due to Ira's proposal, as Jane learned before breakfast. Indeed, as she told John, Hope had said Ira wasn't the only man that loved her. But Hope would not comment on the possibility of Ricky Odell being in her thoughts. She laughed and assigned no reason for her apparent happiness and good cheer.

After breakfast, Campbell tried his own hand with the girl. "You seem more cheerful today," he observed. "I suppose what Ira told you last night has something to do with it. Well, Ira is a good, steady sort, so far as I know, and one of these days he'll be a big rancher . . . bigger than you think." What he had said didn't satisfy him exactly, but he told himself it was a feeler.

"He's got to prove himself before he gets any answer from me, Daddy," said the girl gaily. "I'm not going to marry any horrid old ranch, if that's the way he thinks about it. You know, Ira wouldn't have to try hard to be a bore. He lacks a sense of humor, for one thing. I won't see him again till the rodeo, and then I'll look him over again and maybe tickle his brain to see how it ticks."

"Of course," grunted Campbell stupidly. He looked at her rosy cheeks and sparkling eyes. "Well, it's all past me," he said truthfully. "But your mother wasn't like that. I guess they're teaching a different system in the schools these days." His tone was rich with sarcasm when he finished.

Hope merely laughed delightedly, and annoyed her father by not continuing the conversation. He went out and ordered Vagle to saddle his horse. He told Jane he was going into town in con-nection with his new range duties and his frown and tone convinced her. It really was his intention to see Odell and Olsen and warn them again against any idea they might have of filing on any open homesteads.

He rode fast this morning and made town well before noon. He put up his horse and inquired at the hotel, but neither Odell nor Olsen was there. With his face set in a frown he made the round of the various places where visitors to town were wont to congregate for refreshment and games of chance. He saw no sign of them. "Haven't seen 'em for a day or two," Mike told him at the Board of Trade. "Maybe they've beat it."

But Campbell decided this would be too good to be true. Then he bethought himself of the place he should have gone to first—the livery. He went back there and inquired. Thus he learned that the pair he was looking for had left the very night after they had been on the H Square range and had now been gone two nights and a day.

"Time enough for a long ride," Campbell told the liveryman.

"Yes, and they've got a couple of fine horses to do it with," was the man's rejoinder. "It ain't often that horses like them get into this barn."

"Did you notice the brand on 'em?" asked Campbell curi-ously.

"Didn't wear any iron, either of 'em. Brands are the first

thing I look for by habit. But those horses were thoroughbreds."

"I saw 'em," grumbled Campbell as he went out.

With his trip to town fruitless so far as its real purpose was concerned, Campbell decided to look in on Sheriff Tom Lane. The sheriff might have something to tell him affecting his position with the Cattlemen's Association. Anyway, Lane usually was a cure for grouchiness, and Campbell was not in any too pleasant frame of mind.

"Why, hello, John," the sheriff greeted in a sprightly voice. "You in town again so soon? Something on your mind, too."

Campbell's look was indeed glum. Everybody seemed to be so extraordinarily cheerful this particular morning. Either that or he was taking more than his usual notice of a display of high spirits. "You must have made a winning streak last night," was his comment.

"No, John, I haven't played any cards lately," said Lane in a matter-of-fact tone, fussing with some papers on his desk and looking up suddenly. "I'm too busy. I have to have some sleep now and then. Besides, there's no sense in a small-money man like me gambling."

"That's a sweet lie, too," grunted Campbell as he sat down. "I've known the time when you'd crawl on your hands and knees till you wore out a pair of chaps to get to a green-topped table, and once a gambler, always a gambler . . . at heart, anyway. Besides, you haven't got so all-fired much business on hand that I know of."

"Well, just because you're a deputy now is no sign you know all about everything that's going on in this office," said Lane with a nod. "I'm always busy, and when I don't show it, I'm thinking."

"I see," said Campbell, unable to resist a feeble grin. "I suppose you've got an awful lot of thinking to do. Well, I'm doing some this morning myself."

"That's good news," Lane said, brightening. "If there's anything I like to hear . . . even if I can't prove it . . . it's one of my deputies saying he's thinking. What're you thinking about, John?"

"I'm wondering where that young Odell and his pardner have gone to, and if they're coming back," said Campbell, scowling.

"I can't answer the first question, John, but I can answer the second . . . if they're not putting a joke over on us," said Lane. "I heard they'd left town, which didn't worry me none, but before they left they entered in several of the rodeo contests. So I figure they'll be back to try and grab some of the prize money, which will be only about two weeks from now."

Campbell came very near telling the sheriff what he feared. He suspected that Odell and Olsen had gone to Great Falls to file on the vacant homesteads near the foothills. What their purpose in doing so could be, he could only guess. But he didn't want to express his suspicion to Lane. After all it was Association business.

Shortly afterward Campbell left with the announcement that he was going home. "You needn't look for me again before the rodeo," he told Lane.

"And I want a word with you about the celebration, whether you like it or not," Lane responded seriously. "The rodeo is going to bring a big crowd into town. It's well known all over the state and beyond that we put up a mighty good show and wink at the hard stuff if it isn't too rough. Somebody might come along that you don't want to see. Are you going to bring your family in?"

"Of course," said Campbell. "We'll be in for the whole three days, I reckon. I've already promised them." He was looking straight at Lane, reading the question in his eyes.

"You're taking a chance, John," said the sheriff quietly.

"I've got to take it sooner or later," Campbell snapped. "I'd rather it would happen here in town, if it has to happen, than up at the place. I know what you mean, Tom, you mean Brackett. Well, we both know too much, him and me, to live in the same place. I don't think he'll come, and if he doesn't show up at the rodeo, I never expect to see him again. He's the last link, and I'm thinking he pulled out for distant parts long ago."

With this, John Campbell went out of the office, his face gray, and his eyes cold and hard.

A week went by with the weather holding fair and the beef stock being shipped daily. Campbell went down and had a talk with Crowell and spoke, also, to Ira. He advised the youth to remain away from Hope until the rodeo to give her time to think, and made it clear that he would not attempt to interfere with her affairs in any way. Ira was welcome to such comfort as he could derive from their talk and Campbell's encouragement was veiled and scant, but left the youth hopeful. Adam Crowell moved his beeves toward Pondera to ship the first of the week before the celebration. He was shipping to the Chicago market and was going with the cattle himself, due to return the Monday of rodeo week.

Hope took her morning and evening rides on Bismarck and the horse streaked like the wind across the plain while her thoughts kept pace. She was waiting, and this thought gave her a thrill. At the end of the week her piano came, and then there was music in the Campbell home, with her father before the fireplace smoking his pipe, and her mother sewing quietly. A tang came into the air and the nights were cooler. The leaves began to turn, and already the wild cherry trees were bursts of crimson on the hillsides. Prospectors began to trek down the trail from the high hills to make carnival at the rodeo, later to return with their winter's supplies of provisions and powder.

Then came the Sunday morning, of the week before the rodeo, when Hope rose earlier than usual, slipped down the stairs, and out for her ride with the bloom of the dawn. The air was crisp and a light frost sparkled on the grass. Bismarck was full of life and pranced down the trail to the prairie like a show horse, every line and move stamping him as a thoroughbred. The sun came up like the golden standard of a galleon in a sea of blazing red, which quickly shaded to pink and turquoise, finally to float like a silver river along the horizon's rim. The wind from the west rippled in the grass and flocks of blackbirds, dallying on their southward flight, swung in erratic circles over the trees by the creek. The air, the land, the sun—all were reflected in the sparkle of the girl's eyes. But it was too wonderful a world for just one to enjoy. From amber-tinted trees and bushes another rider came racing to meet her, and Ricky Odell, his eyes flashing with a dancing, mischievous light, swept his hat low and pulled up in the trail squarely in front of her.

"The fairy of the dawn!" he greeted her. "There's dew on your eyelashes, girl, and the sun's rising in your eyes. I told you I'd get word to you before the great annual powwow, and . . . are you glad?"

"I'm surprised," said Hope, but the luster in her gaze belied her and they laughed.

"Nothing of the kind," he said confidently. "You've been riding out every morning expecting, or half expecting, that this young son of Erin and nephew of the goddess of fortune would show up. 'Tis a morning for the truth, Hope, girl, and I bring it to you myself. I haven't seen you in more'n a week and I reckon I've thought of you about every minute in that time 'cept when I was sleeping . . . then I dreamed."

"I . . . I had decided not to see you again until the rodeo," she said, her brows tightening. She was looking at him closely and saw the unmistakable signs of travel on man and horse. He looked tired this morning and she suspected that he had been up all night, perhaps riding. "I told Ira Crowell the same thing

. . . concerning him, I mean," she confessed frankly. "It seems so much has happened since you've been away, but now that you're back, it doesn't seem very important." As she realized what she was saying, she flushed.

"I knew you'd play square, Hope," he declared. "I'll have much to tell you. Will you keep a secret until the rodeo dance?"

Hope hesitated. It didn't seem right that she accept any confidences at this time, but her interest and curiosity got the better of her judgment. "If it isn't too important," she said evasively.

"I thought maybe you'd want to know where I'd been," he said. "I feel that you are entitled to know. Oh, I'm not taking too much for granted, Hope, but I want to tell you. I've been down to the Falls with Slim, and I've been home." He looked away toward the gleaming minarets of the mountains as he spoke the last words, and Hope sensed at once that what he had told her was far more important than his tone had conveyed.

"I won't ask you anything more and I won't tell anyone," she said hastily. "You look tired, Ricky. I'll bet you didn't have any sleep last night but rode straight here and waited. Did Slim come back with you?"

"Sure," replied Ricky, his eyes brightening. "He's gone on into town. I couldn't go in till I'd seen you. 'Course, I'm a bit tired, and so is Soldier, here." He patted his horse on its neck. "They make a great pair," he said, smiling, "Bismarck and Soldier."

"Yes, and I'm not so sure Bismarck could run away from you," she returned with a critical look at the magnificent animal Ricky was astride. "But, Ricky, we mustn't stay here together because . . . some folks . . . somebody might see us. Oh, it isn't that I care, but. . . ." She ceased with a hopeless gesture.

Ricky's smile was flashing again, dazzling her. "The opposition!" he exclaimed, straightening in the saddle and putting on his hat at its impudent angle. "Good! I like a contest, especially when there's so much at stake, dear. Why, Slim and me have gone in for all the riding contests at the rodeo, with bull-dogging and roping as extras. But that's just for sport. This . . . is different." He paused, and Hope looked away to hide the happy thrill in her heart. "I'll be going," he said, holding out his hand, which Hope took quickly and pressed. "So long, girl!"

He whirled his horse and threw a kiss back to her on the fragrant wind. Hope watched him almost out of sight. And on the ridge above her, a small, beetle-eyed man also watched, his tongue slightly outthrust between his lips, his fingers snapping softly. Vagle.

CHAPTER TWENTY-THREE

Ricky Odell rode on to Pondera at a moderate pace, saving his mount as much as possible, although the splendid horse was by no means nearing the limit of its power of endurance. He entered the town quietly, by a back street, and made his way to the livery where he put up his horse. He tarried there to be certain Soldier was properly cared for, and then went into the hotel by the rear door and up to the room where he found Slim asleep.

Slim woke as his partner was undressing. "Everything all right?" he asked sleepily.

"Everything top of the world," Ricky answered, pressing his lips. "I'm going to sleep straight through till tomorrow morning if anyone should ask."

This was exactly what both of them did, and when they went out on the street early the next morning, Monday, they found half the town already stirring. With the rodeo about a week away, Pondera officially began its preparations for the annual celebration that attracted patronage from the whole of the north range and from all surrounding states. For the Pondera Rodeo was famous. Already strangers were coming into town. Many of these were gamblers and hangers-on who hoped to profit at the gaming tables and in diverse other ways. Then there were those who had small tent concessions where rings would be thrown at canes and balls would roll into the wrong holes, and keno would be played, and other inducements offered for the entertainment of the throngs. Wild broncos already in corrals at the fair ground and the racetrack were receiving a semi-annual combing and rolling and sprinkling. It was to be a big show.

Ricky and Slim both caught the excitement that was rife. They dropped into the Board of Trade and found Mike glad to see them again.

"I see you're making a bid for some of the prize money," he told them. "I hope c wins. There'll be some hard nuts drifting in before this week is up and I'll point 'em out to you so you can steer around 'em."

"Much obliged," said Ricky, "and if there's one thing we don't want and won't have, it's trouble during this rodeo. That goes flat and I'm wearing my gun inside. Any news, Mike?"

"Not much," was the answer. "Your trouble has blown over, although none of the regulars has forgotten you. You've got a big rep here, and that's why you've got to be careful. I was sort of glad you didn't enter for any of the sharp-shooting money. Campbell was asking for you, and the home boys always talk, but that's all since you left. Have a drink?"

"Too early," said Ricky cheerfully. "Fact is, Mike, Slim and me go light on the drinking. You're a regular bartender and you'll understand."

Mike nodded. "Don't hurt my feelings any," he said. "I know too many of 'em who should do the same thing."

"Oh, we'll take a few beers now and then, Mike," drawled Slim. "I ain't got no angel wings pricking my back, and we sort of look to you for a bit of information if any's being passed out. You're in a position to grab any whispering that goes around."

Both Mike and Ricky laughed. "He's the lawyer of the firm," Ricky remarked. "But he doesn't use such language in court."

"Did the sheriff act like he was missing us?" asked Slim.

"Dropped in regularly," Mike said, grinning, "but he didn't

say a word to me. Tom Lane's not a bad sort when he isn't crossed."

"Did you get that last?" Ricky asked Slim as they went out. "He said Lane wasn't bad when he wasn't crossed. I've always had a notion that sheriff could be mean if the occasion warranted it, and he's smarter than a whip."

"You don't know the half of it," Slim remarked. "I had to battle that boy with words. I suppose we ought to report that we're back in town, and here he comes to take the words right out of my mouth."

Ricky looked and saw, true enough, that the sheriff was walking down the street leisurely in the direction of the saloon. They both headed out and walked toward him to make sure of the meeting.

"Hello, boys," Lane greeted. "Back in plenty of time for the big doings, I see. Have a pleasant trip?"

"All our trips are pleasant, Mister Sheriff." Ricky smiled. "We hope our second trip to Pondera will be more pleasant than our first."

"That's up to you," said Lane. "There'll be some tough lads here, if the record holds good, and some trouble. We've had it before and taken care of it, and I'm thinking we can take care of it again. Did you stop at the Campbells' on the way in?"

"We didn't come over the mountains," Slim drawled, "and the Campbell place was out of our way. I suppose you know where we've been, so there's no use telling you."

"No, I can't say I do," said Lane. "And I can't say I care much. But I am interested in what you do around here. Your friend, Campbell, is now a deputy, by the way. General agent for the Cattlemen's Association. I guess that's all the news. So long."

Ricky stared after him as he walked on down the street. Then he looked at Slim whose eyes also were a bit wide. "That's news," said Ricky, "and he seemed to want us to know it right straight off. I wonder why, Slim? Didn't I tell you he had his sleeve full of tricks?"

"He's just throwing a mild scare into us, so he thinks," Slim decided. "But I don't see why. I had a feeling that he was talking for your benefit. Maybe it's because you're sweet on Hope."

"Well, if he thinks it's going to scare me because her dad has been given that job. . . ." Ricky paused and looked at Slim in a startled way. "Listen, that job pays money and don't you forget it, and, unless I miss my guess, it puts Campbell in charge of the range. Now, who's the biggest cattleman hereabouts that would have a hand in that business? Crowell, of course. And Crowell is Ira's father."

Ricky laughed loudly and his merriment died as suddenly as it had come. They were nearly opposite the hotel, and walking jauntily down the steps was Ira Crowell.

There was no question but that he had seen them. "Careful," said Slim in a low voice. "If we ever had to use our heads it's not been so much as now. If he starts something. . . ."

"Keep still," said Ricky. "Look. He's coming across the street."

Ira did cross the street and turned in their direction. He was dressed in town clothes and made an excellent appearance in them. His head was up and he nodded affably to several who spoke to him. When he was nearly in front of Ricky and Slim, he gave them one quick, keen, cold glance, shifted his gaze straight ahead, and walked past them without any further notice of their presence.

"Slim," breathed Ricky, "we were wrong. That boy's got sense . . . or else he's been well coached. That was the sweetest piece of work of its kind I ever saw."

"Well, he knows he can't insult us by snubbing us after that last play he made," said Slim. "Just the same as told us in front of the others that he would tackle us here at sight, and since he's seen us and passed us up, his position doesn't look so good."

"Shucks," said Ricky, "I don't think he's putting up any bluff. I think he's waiting till he can catch us alone, that is one at a time apart from each. Or else he wants to catch us in a crowded place where someone will come in and help him."

Slim shook his head. "If he wants to have some friends around, he'll wait for the rodeo, when the H Square outfit is here full force. Of course, there is a chance some of the Crowell men are in with the beef shipment, but they won't have time to bother with little Ira's plans."

"Well, I'm not going to hang around this town dodging behind barrels and into alleys for fear that I'll meet up with Ira Crowell. I propose to make him snub me in a public place with folks around to see it. Then he can't go back to the ranch and tell his 'punchers that he didn't see us or that we ran away from him."

Slim shrugged his shoulders. "Well, unless my guess was a poor one, he's in the Board of Trade this minute, and there's usually plenty of customers there. But listen to me, Ricky, it's up to you, and me, too, not to notice Ira until he notices us. If he does notice us or starts making wisecracks, ignore him. That'll probably make him mad and start him talking straight to us in rough fashion. Then, if we want to notice him and any more talk goes on, or if there should be trouble, the whole bunch present will know Ira started it. He would be asked questions he would find it hard to answer. Ridicule would kill that bird quicker'n a gun."

Ricky threw up a hand in impatience.

"If you start it alone," Slim warned, "you'll end it alone."

Ricky stopped short with an angry light in his eyes. "If you're going to . . . if you're thinking of quitting and us two busting up, Slim, the time to do it is before we get into another ruckus. I'm not thinking of another ruckus, but I've had trouble come when I didn't want it."

"That may all be, and I didn't want it, either, but I was in it just the same and I've a right to ask you to take more than usual stock in what I'm thinking now," said Slim firmly. "I'm telling you that an open run-in with this Ira will be bad medicine. We got away with that other trouble, all well and good, but don't forget that Pearlman was a stranger and a gambler, and, in a way, we had Campbell behind us, and the sheriff, too, I guess. If you have more trouble with Ira, it will bring Miss Hope's name into it and she won't like that, nor will Campbell and Crowell. And it's a cinch the sheriff will be on us. It will ruin your chances in the direction where you want 'em to be the best. If you don't go slow, you're going to lose out all around, and I'm just a good enough friend to tell you and tell you why. If that lets me out, I've a horse and saddle."

"Now, just wait a minute, Slim," said Ricky earnestly. "There isn't anything short of murder that can let you out, and there won't be any such thing as murder. You've traveled with me since I was a kid. I know this business has got to be handled with gloves, and I'm going to take your advice. I've taken it more'n once. So, there."

"You know it's jake with me, Ricky, but be mighty slow in this case," said Slim determinedly. "I think you stand right with the girl, but if you get in bad with Campbell, it'll be none too good. As you say, old man Crowell has put Campbell in a good job, and he can help him a lot if Ira gets free running with the girl. We'll have a hard enough time to get through the rodeo."

"That's just it. If they set the H Square gang on us, we're bound to be crossed," said Ricky dolefully. "We've a bunch of the town crowd with us, but they'd be nothing to run against a cow outfit. Slim, I'm beginning to think this is the toughest proposition we've ever run up against, and if you want to blame the girl, as usual, go right ahead."

"I'm not blaming the girl, nor you," said Slim gruffly. "If anything, I could blame myself for promoting this trip north. You left it to me and I had three different directions than this to choose."

"When you start blaming yourself, you're getting in good humor again." Ricky laughed. "Well, here's the Board of Trade, let's go in."

The big saloon was crowded with the line at the bar three deep. A place, however, was immediately made for Ricky and Slim because of their fame, which had swept the town and had been told to newcomers. Mike was before them in a moment with a smile. It seemed that the pair's presence already was a trade bringer.

"Two beers, Mike," Ricky ordered. "We can't stand here and just talk without a reason for doing so. Hustle 'em up while we look around."

Both Ricky and Slim were looking stealthily about and glancing at the faces reflected in the mirror behind the bar. Both saw Ira Crowell at the lower bar talking with a man who was distinguished by a point of a silver star protruding from beneath his coat. Mike had hardly arrived with the drinks when the man with the star left hurriedly.

"Anybody talking about us today, Mike?" Ricky asked with a quick look toward the lower bar.

The bartender caught the significance of Ricky's look at once. "That's an extra deputy. I don't know where he comes from, but they always bring in a few to help handle the crowds at the rodeo. Don't believe he knows you."

"Fine, although we're not scared of any of them. I thought maybe young Crowell had heard about us, and so on. . . ." He left the sentence unfinished and winked. When Mike shook his head, Slim spoke. "Don't forget, Mike, we absolutely want no trouble during the celebration. We'd rather not be here, for that matter, except that we've entered for some prize money and we'll likely spend any we rake in. If one of these tough *hombres* tries to pick trouble, we'll tell 'em we won't have it and let 'em get away with it. The crowd can think what they please."

"And I'll tell you both something," said Mike, leaning across the bar and speaking in an undertone. "I'm with you. A man who can handle a gun like you can, Ricky, don't have to be afraid of trouble. And I reckon your partner isn't so slow, either. I'm going to tip off the boss and all the regulars and I'll guarantee there'll be nothing started in here." He nodded several times for emphasis.

After he had gone away, Ricky and Slim noted that Ira Crowell apparently had left. They drank the mild beer and walked casually to a roulette wheel, playing some loose change. There Ricky was tapped on the arm and turned casually to see the special deputy. The man pointed toward the side door.

"What's it about?" Ricky asked in a low voice.

"The sheriff wants to see you," was the answer, "but I don't think it amounts to much."

"Shouldn't." Ricky shrugged. "But we'll go over. C'mon, Slim."

Ricky led the way with Slim and the deputy. When they walked into the sheriff's office, Lane was sitting at his desk, and Ira Crowell and another were there. Both Ricky and Slim smiled and chuckled, Ira frowned, and the man with him looked curious.

"What's the trouble now, Sheriff?" asked Ricky pleasantly.

"For once, there's no trouble, Odell, but I called you two in with Ira Crowell and Jake Lake from the H Square to prevent any trouble."

"If that's the case, Slim and me already have declared

ourselves as wanting no trouble of any kind." Ricky scowled.

"I'm inclined to believe you boys," said Lane, nodding, "but I happen to know from a positive source that there is bad blood between you and Ira."

"I don't see how I enter into it," Ira snapped.

"I'm just about to show you that, and I want Jake . . . and order him . . . to carry the word to Adam Crowell himself, although it's no fault of his. There is liable to be trouble between you and Odell and Olsen, and you know it."

"If there is, they'll naturally start it," said Ira with heat.

"I'm looking for it to come about the other way," said Lane in a strong voice. "I happen to know that you, Ira, threatened to make trouble the first time you met 'em in town. Now don't deny it for I know it. And your face would show you know it too well. Don't interrupt me. You're going to have a crowd of H Square men in town next week for the rodeo. With my office rodeo starts ahead of time. It's rodeo right now, and what I say goes from this minute."

Ira half rose from his chair, his face a thundercloud as he glared at Ricky Odell. "So you came in and squawked to save yourself so you could start something, you tramp!" he cried.

"And you stop!" commanded Lane. "As sheriff of this county, I'm bidding you to keep the peace as well as Odell and Olsen. Don't get any false notions. The unquestioned word, as I've passed on to you, came in this envelope." He held up an envelope. "The sender asked to stop any more trouble. If you can guess who the sender was, you'll keep it to yourself. Understand, you four, that there's to be no direct or indirect trouble caused by you or your friends. Now you can go. Jake, you'll explain this to the old man."

Ira's face was livid with rage and suspicion as he strode out.

Slim and Ricky left more leisurely.

"That's a game kid," said Ricky to Slim.

"You mean, who wrote the letter?" asked Slim. "I'll say so."

"It was Hope Campbell and nobody else," Ricky whispered.

CHAPTER TWENTY-FOUR

Ricky Odell and Slim Olsen met Ira Crowell again that day. They had been craftily avoiding such a chance meeting since the trio and the H Square hand had talked and received their orders from the sheriff. Thinking Ira and the hand had left town, they had gone to the livery to inspect their horses, as was their custom each evening. They ran into the pair just inside the door, talking with the owner and a barn man. They passed without a glance at Ira and his companion.

"Hey, you two! Don't think because you fixed it with Lane that you're going to get out of it so easy!"

Ricky whirled and looked straight at the liveryman. "Did you hear that?" he asked in a drawling voice.

"Why, yes," replied the liveryman, his eyes widening in surprise.

"You, too, eh?" Ricky demanded of the open-mouthed barn man.

"Sure." The barn man grinned.

Ricky stepped squarely in front of Ira with Slim at his back. "Now, listen, Crowell, two men here and Slim heard what you said distinctly, and the sheriff would take our word against yours in a pinch. That was an outright threat, enough to start an argument that would result in a fight in which you would get hurt. You heard the sheriff's orders, and I heard 'em, but neither Slim nor I propose to take anything from you. If you want trouble, you can have it here and now. But don't forget you're starting it, and you'll be in jail when it's over, for the sheriff is a man of his word."

Ira turned to the liveryman. "Did you hear that?" he asked.

"I did," the man answered promptly, "and I heard what you said first. I don't know your deal with Tom Lane, but don't think for a minute that I would perjure myself for any man. I don't want anything to do with this affair, but if Lane asks me, I'll tell him to the letter what was said and I'll have my man back me up. I'll have nothing further to do with this, but you can't start any rough stuff in this place, even if you are Ira Crowell."

"And there, if anybody inquires, is one square-shooter," stated Slim.

Ira turned furiously, his eyes red, confronting the two he hated. But the man with him was holding his arm and speaking in his ear. "All right!" Ira snarled. "Get our horses, barn man!"

Ricky and Slim started down the length of the barn with the liveryman following them. "Want me to get your hosses out?" he asked.

"No, thanks," said Ricky brightly. "We just drop in every night to see they're taken care of all right. Always found 'em fine."

"Don't blame you for looking 'em over, frequent," said the liveryman. "They're as fine a pair as I've ever had in my barn."

"Now that's something to thank you for." Ricky smiled. They inspected the horses and started out.

Ira and his companion had mounted and were about to pass them.

"Look out!" Ricky cried to Slim. "Jump clear!"

As the two leaped aside, Ira's quirt cut through the air, missing them by inches. Then he gave his horse the steel and dashed out the rear. Slim swore, but Ricky merely smiled at the barn man. "I looked for a dirty trick like that," he drawled, "but don't mention it to anybody. The kid was mad and forgot himself, that's all."

But in the courtyard on their way to the street, Ricky told his companion something in a different vein. "We've got to watch little Ira more'n I thought. He's sneaky and mean. He'll probably kick Lane's warning into the street and try something, thinking that his old man can get him off. And maybe his old man can, for that matter."

"I don't know if you ever saw me take a dislike to a man on first sight, Ricky," said Slim slowly. "I'm a tolerant cuss, and I'll always give a man a chance to make me dislike him. I didn't have the time to give this fellow a chance when we first met him. I didn't like Ira at first sight. I reckon it was his look that did it, but I've got him down as no good. For which his dad is partly to blame. He's been petted and pampered, and they've never let him forget he's heir to the H Square. But every man should have some common sense."

It was cool, quiet declarations such as this that made Ricky Odell respect and admire Slim. He had more than common sense; he had horse sense and a calculating mind that enabled him to determine to a fine point between right and wrong, a keen brain by which he could form a decision and act in a flash, and be right nine times in ten. All told, Ricky loved him most because they had trailed together so long, and in the big pinches it had been Slim Olsen who had found the way to act in the emergencies.

"You're a good scout," said Ricky with affection in his voice.

"Why . . . why," Slim floundered with a blush, "are you just finding that out? I'm better than that with you, Ricky. I'm your pal."

Out on the sweep of plain west of town a conversation of another and more drastic turn was being carried on between two riders, headed southwest with the purple twilight racing with them, the first stars beckoning them on, and the silver robe of the sunset's end trailing the high peaks.

"He wanted a fight, I tell you!" cried Ira in self-defense.

"He kept you from starting one, just the same," Jake, the H Square hand, said wryly.

"What's this?" demanded Ira, bringing his voice under control. "I suppose you're taking sides with him."

Jake waited a full minute before he spoke. "I reckon, Ira, that you haven't lived long enough on the ranch in the past years to get acquainted with us old-time cowhands. We're old-fashioned enough to want to see a fellow get a square deal. You're not giving that pair a square deal. It's just possible that you might not pay any attention to what the sheriff said, and get away with it with your dad's help. But it wouldn't be square just the same, and I'm one that wouldn't like to see it."

"No? Well, you will see it, or get off the ranch!"

"Why would I get off the ranch, after working there for fifteen years straight with a clean record? I don't want to leave the ranch, boy. I like it there."

"You'd get off because you'd get fired, that's why!"

"Why, I couldn't be fired off that ranch unless I was proved to be disloyal, Ira," said Jake softly. "Nothing you could do and say would get me fired from the H Square. If you don't believe me, ask your dad."

"You're still living fifteen years back," Ira snapped. "And things have been changing right under your eyes you haven't seen. Employers require something more than loyalty these days. They require their employees to do and think as they're told, for one thing. They. . . ."

"Stop right where you are, Ira," Jake interrupted sharply. "The cow business is run about the same today as it was fifteen or thirty years ago. I haven't seen any machines yet that can take the humps out of a mustang afore daylight. I haven't seen any machines that can ride herd, or rope a calf and brand it, or calm a stampede, or shift cattle around the range, or a dozen and ten other things you've got to do to work cattle. As for 'punchers doing what they're told, that's all right so long as it's clean work and not getting mixed up with another herd in queer fashion, but no stockman on earth can tell a cowpuncher what he must think, Ira. I'm reckoning a whole lot of things about you this minute, none of 'em vicious or what you might imagine, but I'm not telling you, and you're not telling me what I think. Wait a minute! Us boys have taken a lot of high-brow junk off you, and a lot of fool orders that we've covered up for you, and you've got a lot to learn, but don't forget that in your position one of the first things you've got to learn is how to handle men, because someday that's going to be your job."

Jake's last words halted the hot, sarcastic reply that was on Ira's tongue. The sharp spear of truth hurled bluntly by Jake had hit home. He was wise enough to see there were some items of advice in what the older man had said. He must not only learn how to handle men, but he must learn men themselves. Jake had hinted that the ranch hands despised him or were amused with him for "high-brow junk", as he put it. But they had been loyal to him, took his orders, and covered up his errors. And this was a real cowman riding beside him. He could not be overbearing.

"All right, Jake," he said easily. "I guess there's a lot about the game I'm trying to learn. But I reckon I'm entitled to consideration in this . . . er . . . particular business. I've got more at stake than you think. And if trouble should come about, I'd like to think the boys were behind me on . . . on general principles."

"Yes," Jake assented. "You've got too much at stake to start any trouble. And the boys would have to be behind you, right or wrong. That may sound funny after what I said before, but it's also a matter of ranch code."

"Are you really going to tell Dad what the sheriff said?"

"Every word of it. I've got to, because the sheriff will ask your dad, and if he finds out I didn't tell him, the sheriff will be dog-goned sore and your dad will have reason to fire me."

"But how about what happened in the livery?" Ira asked anxiously.

"It's up to you to tell him that, if you want to," replied Jake quietly. "I don't see any need of me saying anything, and don't expect to, anyway. But that cut at 'em with your quirt was awful bad business, Ira."

"I regret I did that," said Ira. "Something snapped in my head and I saw red for a moment. He could have come back at me in a flash with his gun, but he didn't. I reckon he intends to hold to his bargain with Lane."

"I'd gamble on that," said Jake dryly. "And whatever you do, don't get mixed up in a gun play with him. You could draw and aim, and he'd beat you to it. You don't suspect how fast he is. Those who've seen him in action say that his right hand must be a gun in disguise. He's been seen with a glass in his hand and next instant there's a shot, and only a little smoke at his hip, maybe, to show he did it."

Ira Crowell spoke no more as they entered the H Square road. The moon was up and the dying leaves of the trees along the river shivered in the cool night wind. An owl moaned in the cottonwood windbreak north of the ranch buildings. The lights in the windows of the ranch house gleamed like pale candles. Horses nickered from the pasture. The air became slightly warmer and smelled of dry grass.

"I think I better go in the house with you, Jake, when you go to tell Dad," said Ira. "I don't want him to think I hid out."

"Good idea," said Jake cheerily. "I won't say more'n I have to!"

They went into the living room of the house, leaving their horses with a hand at the barn.

Back in Pondera, yellow and orange lamplight shone like toy balloons in the windows, giving depth to the shadows in the dusty street. Encircling the town and the brooding plain, rising gently upward, was the arch of a black satin sky, with stars winking saucily and a cold, haughty moon mounting to her throne at the zenith. Ricky and Slim were standing in the middle of the street, saying nothing, frankly enjoying the night. Thus Sheriff Lane found it easy to spot them and join them.

"Nice night for a ride," he said in a friendly voice. "I wish I was young again, for I'd be in the saddle on a night like this."

"You wouldn't be admiring the night," said Ricky dryly. "You'd probably be hot-hoofing it to some sweetie's house."

"And coming in on a lathered horse late for chores in the morning," added Slim in such a pleasant voice that it was almost sweet.

Sheriff Tom Lane laughed heartily. "I suppose that's about what I'd be doing," he confessed, "and if so, I've got the same sweetie yet . . . and a brood of five."

"We didn't mean to be smart," Ricky remarked.

"If I thought that, I'd have slammed you on the chin," the sheriff reflected.

"And I thought you wanted peace in this town?" Slim complained.

"That reminds me," said Lane briskly. "I hear you met up again with Ira and Jake before they left."

"Couldn't help it," said Ricky. "We let 'em have the town to themselves all day, and then met 'em when we went to look at our horses. Just a natural meeting. I suppose you heard all about it."

"Yes, I was talking with the liveryman. You seem to have acted very wisely. But . . . how about that last?"

Ricky knew the sheriff was aware of Ira's attempt to lash them when he rode out of the barn. "I don't know anything 'cept the gentle exchange of remarks we had. There! Look at that shooting star. Now it's gone and I didn't have a chance to make a wish, dog-gone."

"*Humph,* I reckon I know what you'd have wished, but don't let any shooting stars bother you so long as they're not too close to earth. I'm going home. Good night, boys."

"Good night, Sheriff."

"You know, Rick," said Slim, "I've got a hunch we stand high with his nibs, but I don't know why."

"If that's all you've got on your mind, don't bother," said Ricky. "Come on. We haven't caught up on sleep. Let's go to bed, and tomorrow we'll help the committee on decorations."

The next day the offer of the pair was readily accepted, and they worked the rest of the week helping Pondera's citizens to decorate the town with pine and fir trees, brought from the foothills, with bunting and flags and streamers hung across the main street. During the week they won many friends among the townsfolk and became popular.

The H Square cattle were shipped to Chicago. Adam Crowell went along and took Ira with him. The ranch cowpunchers were ordered to stay out of town and remain at the ranch for the pay-off the next Monday before the celebration.

Sunday and Monday found Ricky and Slim practicing their horsemanship. A special saddle had arrived for Slim that he intended to use. Scores of contestants who arrived recognized Slim as the winner two times straight of the big event at the Miles City Rodeo, and once at Missoula, and he became a personage. The town was filled with strangers of all sorts; resorts were crowded; there were a number of first-class fights and a few minor ones. The big dance pavilion was the talk of everyone. A band and orchestra arrived from Great Falls. Then came Wednesday morning and—the rodeo.

CHAPTER TWENTY-FIVE

Rodeo! There comes a time in the big range country when an intangible stir comes into the keen air, and, as it sweeps over the golden sea of plain, growing in the strength of the wind, it throws off subtle breezes in which are thrill and excitement and a devilish dare to do. It is a period of prosperous satisfaction to elder folk, of prancing and dancing to the sun by the young, of wild and gentle passions, of the final lilting of the meadowlarks, the assembling of the wild flocks of blackbirds and ducks, harbinger of the migration to the south—of the flying V of wild geese, sure symbol of Old Man Winter, herding his elements in the north for the great onslaught. Nature opens her color pots and taps gently here and there, then with great sweeps of her magic brush showers the hills with brilliant reds, and bronze, and blue, deepening the purple robes of the mountains, painting the banks of the smiling rivers with flaming orange and yellow bands, and dips the pot to flow in a stream of gold over the restless plain. Prairie grouse do their sunrise dances in the shadow of blushing buttes. The air is cool at night, crisp in the early dawn, hot in midday. It is the soft, indolent, intermediate period of Indian summer. Then these mysterious convolutions of Nature at play with the universe strike at the hearts of men and women, and of youth. Their spirits shoot upward like a rocket's flight and burst into myriads of stars of dazzling happiness. The outlets for these spirits are in love, and action, and in carnival. Each region has its fashion of festival and its mode of revelry.

In the West it is rodeo, and at this September's going, Pondera proposed to show the range, the state—the world even—what it could do in the way of entertainment. And the show was on. The parade to town began early on the first day of the celebration. Although already crowded with visitors, the stockmen and their families would find accommodation reserved for them. Cowpunchers and other hands would have to look out for themselves, of which they were fully capable. The stockmen came in buckboards with a sprinkling of spring wagons; in some cases whole families rode in with the ranch outfit trailing, but generally the outfits chose to race into town in a single unit, sweeping through the street, waving their hats and yelling to let the throngs know ahead of time that the ranch owner and the family were following more leisurely.

Ricky and Slim had ascertained that both the Campbells and the Crowells would stop at The Cattlemen's Hotel, the largest in town, where they were stopping themselves. Ricky had suggested that they move to another hotel, less pretentious, during the show to avoid personal contacts at the larger place, and the proprietor of the small hotel they selected agreed instantly, and with some showing of pride, to the proposal.

With the arrival of other noted riders, the spirit of the show had taken hold of Slim. There had been other things in the box that contained the saddle. The saddle itself was rather worn, and bore the noted imprint of a Miles City saddler. Slim had won on it three times and he didn't count a win at Billings because he looked upon it as too easy. Now he blossomed forth in wide-hinged, white angora chaps, in a soft, black, satin shirt, a green scarf with red-striped border, and a prize black Stetson, which proved to be the largest hat in town.

"As big as his head," sneered a bronco competitor. "He wears it all right," was the rejoinder of a townsman.

Slim was entered in the leading event, the championship bronco-busting contest. He had withdrawn his other entries. Ricky was entered in the big horse race, and he, too, had withdrawn his other entries. Both were entered as from Pondera, and the citizens put up enough money to hold the betting to even money, finally backing Slim to win against the field, and coupling Ricky's Soldier and Hope Campbell's Bismarck against the field. Bismarck had been entered since the list was first opened and Ricky kept wondering who would ride the horse. Surely Hope wouldn't attempt to ride such a speedy, powerful horse in competition with a large field of fast horses and noted riders. The preliminaries were to be on Wednesday and Thursday afternoons, and the two crack events on Friday afternoon, with the rodeo to close with the grand ball in the dancing pavilion that night.

The crowded street of the old cow town was the greatest spectacle of the celebration. The cowpunchers, and particularly the contestants, wore their rodeo best, which was quite different from the drab dress worn in actual work on the range. They came and paraded in marvelous chaps, shining boots and silver spurs, red, pink, blue, green, brown, yellow, and purple shirts, scarves of contrasting colors that shrieked defiance to the town's gaudy decorations, and Nature's pictures on the hills and plains about them. Beaver-plush hats of incredible size with high crowns were dented in front, or four-pointed with three indentations. The round white tag of a cigarette tobacco bag dangled from every shirt pocket, with papers stuffed behind. Every stockman wore a white, soft shirt, open at the throat, or a stuffed shirt, buttoned but with no collar. They wore vests and heavy-linked gold watch chains, and stockmen's hats that curled at the brims and were medium of crown with rarely a dent. The women wore their silks and satins, with white laces and

embroideries, and the girls were bright in white or pink or blue
dresses, with flounces and ribbons, and gay little straw or satin
bonnets—but the youths looked only at the sparkle of their
eyes, their taunting smiles, and, in many cases, their shyness.

Slim was early to the barns and corrals at the show grounds
on Wednesday. His flaming figure was followed by scores. He
might have to ride Do-or-Die, or Shameless, the two outlaw
broncos that had never been ridden to a standstill, nor into the
straight-out that preceded it.

Ricky wore none of the gala attire affected by Slim. He was
simple in shining boots, blue serge trousers, soft gray shirt, and
big gray hat. He wore a coat of blue serge. Just an average visitor from another town, for all the crowd knew, distinguished
perhaps by his good looks, his wide shoulders, and the sparkle
in his eyes. Just the same, on this notable Wednesday morning,
he kept a position, screened by the moving crowds, that enabled
him to see the Crowells arrive in a double buckboard. Adam
drove up to the front of the hotel with a flourish. In the seat
with him was his wife; in the seat behind were two girls, his
daughter and a friend.

Ricky merely noted that Ira was not with him. The youth had
doubtless ridden in with the outfit. He resumed his vigil, and at
noon sharp was rewarded by seeing John Campbell drive up,
also in a double buckboard. At his side was the weasel-faced,
diminutive figure of Vagle. Behind were Jane Campbell and
Hope. His eyes were for Hope. She was not dressed like most of
the other girls. Ricky only knew it was something soft of a lemon
shade and a hat like a rosebud. His heart leaped as he caught a
glimpse of her dancing eyes as she slipped down from the
buckboard to help her mother alight. Jane Campbell looked
years younger in a fitting dress of gray with a brooch at the
throat and a black hat. Ricky watched Hope lead her mother
into the hotel. It would be different here in town, he was think-

ing, and his eyes were glistening with conquest. A porter came out of the hotel and took the two bags. A swarm of stockmen surrounded Campbell, including Adam Crowell. Vagle drove away. Ricky decided to ride out to the show grounds. His horse was quartered there under guards furnished by Mike of the Board of Trade.

Both Slim and Ricky had to go through the form of perfunctorily clearing the first day's qualifying round that afternoon. Hope Campbell rode Bismarck to Ricky's dismay. Did she intend to go through with it and ride in the final? It wasn't that she couldn't ride, for she rode and handled her mount splendidly. She wore a smart riding habit and looked like the jewel of his dreams in it. He hadn't looked at her directly. He wanted of all things to speak to her alone, just for a moment, but it would have to be some chance meeting. He was waiting for the night of the big dance.

Slim broke his bronco down in less than a minute and walked off the field getting the biggest cheer of the day. He waved his hat gaily. Ricky had seen his partner in this rôle before and knew he was thoroughly enjoying himself. First prize in the bronco-busting contest was $1,000 in cash, a hand-made saddle with the leather finely worked, a medal, a bridle, and a quirt. Ricky stood to win $1,000 cash in the racing final. And both youths felt confident of annexing the prizes.

"Watch out that some of those sleepy-looking dogs don't wake up and toss you," Ricky warned. "Remember, I've got a bunch of dough planted on you."

"Them ain't dogs, they're sheep." Slim grinned. "Didja hear the hand warming I got?"

Before Ricky could reply, Hope Campbell was before them. If Ricky had thought her beautiful up there in the foothills, then, here in town, surrounded by the gaiety of the rodeo crowd, dressed as she was, she was an angel. He was tongue-tied. He couldn't think of anything to say. But he didn't have to, for Hope, her eyes sparkling, was looking at Slim and smiling.

"Slim, you've got 'em knocked dead with that outfit. That white and black effect with the green scarf and the size of your hat puts you right in the front row. Why didn't you tell me you were a bronco buster with a string of notches in your saddle?"

Slim grinned and was unabashed. "I'm glad, lady, that you recognize a real buckaroo when you see one. But I'm worried. I'm awfully worried. I hope I haven't gone to all this trouble for nothing?"

"Why, I don't believe I know what you mean," she said with a smiling glance at Ricky, who looked astonished.

"It's this way, lady," said Slim in a confidential tone. "I've gone to the trouble to get my real bucking saddle up here and decorate myself in the spirit of the occasion, and . . . and I'm afraid these tough horses they're raving about will be too tame for me to give a decent exhibition."

At his woebegone expression both Ricky and the girl laughed heartily.

"But I'm going to do the best I can on whatever they've got," he said, brightening. Then he walked away abruptly, leaving Hope and Ricky facing each other.

"Gee, I wanted to see you," said Ricky, regaining his old poise alone with her, "but with all these people around, I'm sort of flustered."

"You look fine, Ricky. Have you got anything to tell me today?"

"Well, no," he said with a squint, "except that you're the most beautiful thing that ever had the nerve to come around near a man."

"That doesn't ring the bell, Ricky. It isn't the old blarney, and the light in your eyes isn't bright. What are you worrying about?"

"Hope, are you going to ride Bismarck in the finals?" he asked.

"Why not?" she asked saucily. "Didn't I do all right today?"

"Yes, but all of us that had good horses were merely sitting in our saddles," he answered. "Half that were in were disqualified."

"I know it wasn't much, but maybe we'll have harder work later," she taunted him.

"From what I've seen of these other horses, the big race will be between Bismarck and Soldier, Hope," he said earnestly. "If you ride in the race Friday, it'll be dangerous for you. That race will be for blood, as they say. These outside riders will pull tricks. I can't withdraw because that will . . . that would look funny. And if Soldier can beat Bismarck, I don't think I'd be able to let him do it with you in the saddle ahead of me."

"I know," said Hope. "I'm going to ride tomorrow for fun, but I'll not be in the saddle Friday. Bismarck will carry a rider who'll give you a test, and don't sneer at that."

"I wouldn't . . . oh, here comes our friend Ira. Looks mad, too. Is he your escort?"

"I have to humor him, same as you." Hope laughed. "But don't forget our date for the dance, Friday night, Ricky."

"I'm just living till then," said Ricky, looking inquiringly at Ira.

"Are you ready, Hope?" Ira asked stiffly, ignoring Ricky.

"She's quite ready, Ira," said Ricky gravely, winking at Hope.

Ira's eyes blazed. "If it were not for your ignorance of the principles of common politeness. . . ."

"Oh, come on and don't be silly," said Hope, dragging him away.

When the preliminary contests were completed next afternoon, nine remained eligible to enter the bronco-busting feature, and six horses remained on the list for the final race.

Among the first nine was Slim, and Bismarck and Soldier were two of the six horses to run what was predicted to be the best race the north range ever had seen.

Ricky and Slim went home early for a good rest before the finals. Both were nervous and Ricky was actually handicapped by worry. He kept thinking of Hope, too. Strange enough, he hardly thought of Ira Crowell at all.

"Listen, Rick," said Slim sleepily, when they were in bed. "You've got to quit thinking of that girl till after the race tomorrow or you'll make a mess of it."

"I wouldn't care if I only knew who was going to ride Bismarck," Ricky complained. "Hope may spring a ringer on me and ride after all."

They were out early in the morning and several other contests were decided before noon. At 1:30 p.m. the stands and enclosures were crowded. The band was playing. Three finals were scheduled: the steer-roping and hog-tying, the bronco-busting, and the horse race.

Slim and Ricky didn't even bother to watch the first contest. At 2:30, Slim, dressed in worn riding clothes, carried out his saddle, blanket, and bridle. Ricky watched anxiously. It was hot with a haze on the horizon. He watched while Slim broke a wild one in less than two minutes. He saw the great Colman, who had come all the way from Pendleton, do the same on a tougher bronco. One by one he watched seven of the nine to ride eliminated. There remained but Slim and Colman. They drew lots for the most vicious of the buckers. If each stayed on, the ride each made was to count. Colman drew Do-or-Die and Slim drew Shameless, considered, even by himself, as the worst of the two outlaws.

Colman came out of the chute a tangle of leather and flying hoofs, his right hand high in the air. Do-or-Die flung himself onto the field in a succession of straight bucks, with his head between his front legs, as the crowd roared. He came down stiff-legged and paused. It was the roar of the spectators he listened to, and Colman raked him with his spurs. The horse lunged ahead and swapped ends like lightning; he sunfished and rolled, then reared straight in the air with what appeared to be all four legs off the ground.

Colman drew his right foot from the stirrup, slipped off to save himself, hitting the ground lightly, holding the rope in his left hand. But the horse came down on his hoofs and Colman made a flying leap that landed him back in the saddle. He caught his right stirrup, but before he could get the other, the outlaw was in the air whirling, and Colman went spinning in a somersault to the ground. Do-or-Die raced away to be caught by the hazers.

Fully twenty minutes elapsed before Slim Olsen came out on Shameless like a burst of fury. A tremendous roar swelled from the throng but it didn't bother this wild, ruthless fighter, who had been saddled for but the third time in his tempestuous career. He made it across the enclosure with a series of heartbreaking twisters, sunfished until the stirrups brushed the ground, humped his back and went into the air as if jerked up by an invisible wire, came down with his forehoofs straight, his head between his legs, and from that position lunged as if to turn over headfirst. But Slim stuck with blood oozing from his mouth. The crowd was yelling like mad. Shameless came out of it with a shudder, made a snap with white teeth flashing at Slim's left leg. Then more twisters and those terrific, humped, straight-legged bucks, when his four hoofs off the ground seemed sewed together. He broke into a mad run, ordinarily a sure sign of victory for the rider. But not with Shameless. He stopped short, his forehoofs plunging into the soft earth. But he hadn't caught Slim napping. He shook himself as if to make sure his rider was still seated. Then he went straight into the air with his nose to the sky, his forelegs bowed. And still Slim stuck. The crowd held its breath. Would Shameless go over, crushing his rider rather than be defeated? None breathed as this man-eater reared straight as an arrow with Slim's face hugging his neck, the hand with the rope outflung, the other held aloft. Then Shameless came down, headfirst, and stood quivering as the hazers closed in, and Slim slipped from the saddle, the victor. He leaned on the shoulder of a man who had dismounted and waved weakly to the thundering throngs.

Ricky turned away with unknowing tears in his eyes and bathed in sweat. "And that was some ride," he said over and over as he waited for Slim to come in.

The mob or such as could manage to get through the ropes, which were guarded by cowpunchers at the entrance to the corrals and contestants' quarters, surged about Slim as he came in off the field, a man following with his saddle. But Slim swept away the outstretched hands and the crowd, and, guarded by other riders, made his way into a barn. The throng was chased away.

Slim found Ricky, who took his hand a moment. "Nice ride," said Ricky casually.

But Slim knew this was high praise. "Ricky," he said slowly, wiping the blood from his lips and looking toward the wash stand, "that was the hardest ride I ever had. I've a notion to buy that horse, so he can stay. . . ."

He was interrupted by a slap on the back. It was the president of the Rodeo Association. "Boy," he boomed, "the prize money and saddle wasn't enough for that ride you gave us. I've a notion to add a thousand to the prize out of my own pocket."

"You can do something better'n that," Slim said curtly.

"Name it and it's yours," said the other, rising to his full height.

"Let that horse loose and let him run for the rest of his life," said Slim.

"We'll do it," came the promise instantly.

Slim turned to the wash stand. He was doing great work with the soap and water when he heard John Campbell speaking. "So you boys did come here for the rodeo," he said. "And no wonder. That ride was the best I ever saw." He turned to Ricky. "But you'll have to go some to beat out Bismarck. Maybe you'll have to take second or third money." His smile was pleasant.

"I didn't stay just for the horse race," drawled Ricky. "But as long as it was coming off, I thought I'd take it in."

Campbell frowned slightly and cleared his throat. It was plain he was somewhat embarrassed. "You haven't seen much of Hope this week, have you?" he asked, uneasily.

"I've seen plenty of her but have spoken to her but once," replied Ricky coolly, meeting Campbell's gaze squarely. "But tonight I'm going to see her, and dance with her, and talk with her."

"No doubt, no doubt," said Campbell, and then he walked away.

The horse race was scheduled for 4:30 p.m. At a quarter of an hour before that time, the six horses were in the paddock. Of this number, three stood out as favorites, Hope Campbell's Bismarck, Ricky Odell's Soldier, and a chestnut, Square Deal, owned by Adam Crowell, which was to be ridden by none other than Jake.

Crowell was there with Ira, his wife, and his daughter and her friend. They stayed only a few minutes and left. Then came John Campbell and Hope. Ricky looked quickly at the Campbell horse and his eyes bulged as he saw the small Vagle standing ready to take the mount. They talked with Vagle and the tall cowpuncher who was ready to give the little man the leg up. Then Hope walked quickly to Ricky, with her father following.

"I'll bet you a hundred, Ricky Odell, that Bismarck wins," she said with a toss of her head.

"Taken," said Ricky instantly as he saw the dare in her eyes.

"And a hundred to you, Mister Campbell?" said Slim, who was holding Ricky's horse. "I need money, too."

"Why . . . of course," stammered Campbell. "Yes, of course."

"Come on, Daddy, we'll go join Mother and watch the race just for the fun of it."

"Well, I reckon you're going to have to ride a horse race," said Slim dryly as the Campbells moved away.

Ricky didn't answer. He was looking over his mount and what he saw was an animal in the very perfection of form—ready to run. But Bismarck was in excellent form, also, and so was Crowell's Square Deal; the other horses were all too plainly running for a try at third and possibly second money.

Ricky was up at the whistle. "G'wan out and come back the way you oughta," was Slim's frowning instruction as Ricky rode out and joined the parade to the post. Bismarck was on the outside, Square Deal had the rail, Soldier was third from the inside. There was little trouble getting lined up, and they shot ahead as the starter's flag swept down.

As a race there was no doubt as to the outcome from the first furlong of the eight to go. Square Deal, Soldier, and Bismarck shot ahead, leaving the others to trail around the course. Soldier closed in on Square Deal, with Bismarck streaking for the lead in the center of the track. One look showed Ricky that a master rider was astride the Campbell horse. Neither he nor Vagle carried a whip. It was to be a battle with hand-riding only. At the first furlong Jake resorted to the whip, Square Deal spurting ahead. Both Ricky and Vagle were left a bit behind for the moment. Then Square Deal slowed, suddenly crowding Soldier, and Bismarck swept across them to the inside.

Ricky swore as he realized the trick Jake had played. But he wouldn't claim a foul in a million years. The thought flashed through his mind that Square Deal, a late entry, had been entered solely by Crowell—perhaps at Ira's instigation—to race to the advantage of Bismarck. Ricky let Soldier out a bit and at the quarter he was a half-length behind Bismarck with Square Deal two lengths behind, never to be a contender in the race again.

As they rounded into the backstretch, Soldier began to creep up, inch by inch, it seemed, to the frantic spectators, until at the half he had caught Bismarck. Square Deal was several lengths behind, but Jake was riding him easy, holding him for a last mighty spurt.

The stands were a bedlam as Soldier continued to gain slowly as the horses clicked off three-quarters and rounded the turn. They came into the stretch neck and neck with Bismarck hugging the rail and Soldier closing in smartly to lose no ground. All thought of anything but the race in hand had long since left Ricky Odell's mind. Soldier was racing a true thoroughbred that liked it. Just once he wondered where Campbell had picked up such a horse. The thought was gone in an instant and forgotten.

In the distance Ricky heard a rumbling roar. Soldier was a nose ahead, now half a head. He caught a look of stark terror from Vagle. It startled him so that he let Soldier drop back a fraction. But Soldier was not to be stopped. He made up the distance and ran a full head in the lead. A great, throbbing thrill ran through Ricky. In the short intervening distance to the wire he could run to win by half, maybe a whole length!

He caught Vagle looking at him again in agony. Tears were spurting from his eyes and he was riding Bismarck to the uttermost limit of his speed and calling on him for the impossible. Bismarck was beaten. Had it not been for Jake's trick at the start, Ricky never would have seen that look; he would have left

Bismarck three lengths behind at the finish.

Vagle knew he could not win. His thoughts were as clear to Ricky as if they had been written in thunderclouds athwart the sky. He wanted to win because he had ridden masterly on a splendid horse. He wanted to win because the horse belonged to Hope, and he had promised her. Soldier was pulling for his head. It was all Ricky could do to hold him. Another look at the anguish, pain, and suffering in those faded blue eyes, and Ricky began the best exhibition of horsemanship the howling mass of spectators ever had seen—had they but known it. Slowly Soldier began to lose ground. Ricky was using all the strength in his arms and shoulders, checking Soldier so that none could see he was doing so purposely. The end was yards ahead, and then—with the roar of crashing avalanches in their ears, Bismarck and Soldier flashed past the finish nose to nose!

Vagle topped from the saddle in a faint when he had brought his mount to a stop. Ricky waited until he had revived sufficiently to be lifted into the saddle to ride back with him to the cheers of what seemed a multitude.

They saluted in front of the judges' stand. "A dead heat!" As they dismounted, Ricky turned Soldier over to the white-faced Slim. John Campbell himself led Bismarck and Vagle trudged behind.

Near the stables, Hope Campbell joined them. Her eyes were for Ricky, who looked at her grimly. "Why did you do it?" she asked angrily, as her father looked on. "It was a race, and you could have beaten Bismarck by a length! You held Soldier, Ricky Odell, you wouldn't let him win. He deserved it. I suppose you thought it would please me not to win from Bismarck. I don't want to win that kind of a race!" She stamped her foot. "Oh, why did you do it?" There were almost tears in her eyes.

"If I hadn't done it, it would have broken your spider-man's heart," he said sternly.

Chapter Twenty-Six

Ricky and Slim met Jake as they left the barn by a roundabout way to avoid the crowds. Both stopped short when they saw the H Square hand, who had finished second on Square Deal. He walked up to Ricky and confronted him.

"That little incident at the start was my fault and not intended," he declared earnestly. "I . . . haven't rode in such a race in a long time and guess I was careless. Anyway, you could have won at a gallop if you'd wanted to, so I didn't do you any harm."

"All right," said Ricky, his lips compressed, "if that's the way you look at it."

He and Slim slipped along a back street until they reached their obscure hotel. There they managed a bath each in clear, cool water, and rubbed themselves down with the rough towels the proprietor had given them for the purpose. Their skin glowed a rough pink. Then they proceeded to tog out for the night, which was expected to be a glorious end to the famous Pondera Rodeo.

Slim Olsen shed his magnificent white angora chaps and black shirt that he had worn all week, except when riding, and donned a modest gray suit with a white shirt and a blue bow tie. He clung to his handmade boots, however, shining them till they looked like patent leather, and put on the great white hat that at once set him apart from other men. He spent much time at the mirror, fussing with his bowtie to get the wings right.

"Going to step out at the dance, Slim?" asked Ricky curiously.

"I intend to dance with a little red-headed girl from the Knees Butte country, if it's any of your business, which it isn't," replied Slim, while Ricky chuckled.

Ricky donned a double-breasted dark blue suit, with white shirt and dark red four-in-hand, polished black town shoes, and a gray Stetson. He sat on the bed looking down at his blue socks with the red dots a long time.

"Well, what is it now?" asked Slim, putting a green handkerchief in his breast coat pocket, and arranging it with care. "Think the girl is fussed, eh? Well, don't worry. I saw her look when you answered her. And was it the truth you told her, Rick?"

"Yes," replied Rick dully. He straightened up. "Slim, do you think we should wear our guns inside or anywhere?"

"Haven't seen any of the boys packing 'em much," said Slim. " 'Spect we better leave 'em home tonight. This is a social affair, isn't it?"

For answer Ricky dropped his weapon into the top drawer of the bureau. At this moment there came a tapping at the door. Ricky put a finger to his lips to caution Slim, stepped lightly as a cat, and opened the door suddenly.

Sheriff Lane stood outside. "Always best to be careful, boys," he said, entering. "There's always them as will be after the money and general trade goods you won today. I want to congratulate you on the two best exhibitions we've seen here in years." He surveyed them with a critical eye, cocking his head. "All dolled up. Fit to dance with the best of 'em. But that isn't what I came here to say," he added hastily, closing the door.

"What's wrong now?" growled Ricky. "You always seem to be following us around, Sheriff, and I'm sick of it and ask you to cut it out."

"That goes with me, too," Slim chimed in with a convincing nod.

"Then I suppose I can't ask you to do me a favor?" said Lane.

"That depends on what the favor is," Ricky snapped back.

Tom Lane sat in one of the two chairs in the room. "I'm going to tell you, too, Slim," he announced.

"That tickles me all over," Slim remarked. "Shoot ahead, Sheriff. I've got a hunch you're not here to pepper us with jokes."

"There is only one other man in this town tonight who knows about this," said Lane impressively, "and it's because of a little deal you figured in with that man that I'm going to confide in you."

Slim had sat down in the other chair and Ricky was sitting on the edge of the bed. "You mean Campbell?" Ricky asked quickly.

Lane nodded, took out a cigar and lit it, and after a look at the door he spoke in a much lower voice, leaning forward in his chair. "That man, Pearlman, who passed out here a little time ago, knew John Campbell some years ago. He didn't have anything on John to speak of, but he could have made it nasty by telling around what he did know. He won't be missed." He looked straight at Ricky. "You know, of course, that Pearlman's exit did no harm."

Ricky shrugged but made no comment.

Lane lowered his voice still more. "There's another man who knows too much," he said slowly, "and I'll have to swear you boys to secrecy." He waited while both Ricky and Slim, intensely interested, nodded. "I've known for some time that he's been near here, and both John and me were on the look-out for him during the rodeo. I had also given his description, as best I could, to certain of my deputies. But we haven't seen him. Tonight will be a wild night in the drinking and gambling places and a swell night at the pavilion, where I reckon you boys are going."

"That's why we're all dolled up," said Slim. "Sure we're going."

"The man I'm telling you about might drop in tonight. If he does, he's sure to sneak a look in on the dance. He likes that sort of thing but never would go on the floor or enter into the light. He would try to look on from the outside. Now, I think quite a lot of you boys' judgment. I can't keep more than a man or two around the pavilion because I'll need my men in town. I know these last nights of rodeos. But I thought it was just possible that you two, being around up there, might keep your eyes peeled for this *hombre*."

"Sure thing," said Ricky heartily. "But you'll have to give us more information."

"I'll do that now," said Lane. "I'm even going to tell you this man's name, then there will be only four of us who know it . . . you boys, Campbell, and me. His name is Brackett." The sheriff paused, but neither of the youths appeared to have heard of him. "I guess he never worked near your territory," Lane went on. "He's a tall, burly man, with such tremendous muscles that his shirts and coats always look tight. His eyes are, well, a dirty brown, you might say, and set close. He has a big nose, thick lips, a full-moon face, and usually wears a stubble of black beard. Looking directly at him, a person would say his left eye slanted off lower than his right. That is the easiest identification. He wears range clothes and nobody ever saw him with a trim hat. His hats are . . . or always were . . . dilapidated. He's over six feet and sturdy as an oak. I think he wears a small black mustache." Lane paused, looking intently at the floor. His cigar had gone out unheeded. "The thing to remember about Brackett," he resumed, "is that he's a natural-born outlaw, dangerous as dynamite, treacherous, absolutely unafraid. If a deputy was to approach him, he'd probably shoot him down with one hand while picking his teeth with the other. He's so fast on the draw that those who know him never see the need of mentioning it. Now, if he does come here, it means no good to Campbell, or to me, or to the town. I haven't a thing on him, but I'd try to get him, just the same. Thought I'd tell you boys."

"Should we pack our guns?" Slim asked. "Suppose we see this terror, then what?"

"I wouldn't pack any guns tonight," said Lane. "If you see anybody that looks like the man I've told you about, keep him in sight and get word to me or Campbell. Maybe Campbell will be up there, too."

"All right, Sheriff, and thanks for telling us," said Ricky.

"I reckon I don't have to tell you to keep this under your hats, and I haven't even told Campbell I was going to put you wise," said Lane. He opened the door and left.

Rodeo night. Pondera's main street was crowded and the dust was thick. The same moon overhead, trailing the stars, the same subtle perfume in the cool breeze, the same shadows on the plains. But all these were forgotten in the activity confined to the small limits of the town itself. The saloons were crowded to the doors; endless fights started and ended as quickly, for lack of room. And the most beautiful sight was the big dance pavilion, its sides half open to the breeze, the benches along the walls crowded with women and girls in bright colors, the men crowding the entrances or standing talking between dances, and with Bill Steege's Grand Opera House Orchestra from Great Falls furnishing the music. The hanging lamps were festooned with twigs of fir and pine, streamers of bunting nearly concealing the roof. It was the biggest ball the Pondera Rodeo had ever experienced.

Mrs. Campbell was there with Hope, and nearby was Mrs.

Crowell, her daughter Rose, and Rose's friend. Ira had danced twice with Hope. Slim Olsen was there, the hero of the hour, dancing with a shy, red-haired girl from somewhere near Fort Benton. He was dancing every other dance with her, and he was dancing well.

Hope had an expectant look in her eyes. She constantly glanced toward the entrance, and as the night wore on became nervous. Had she offended Ricky Odell by what she had said after the big race? She had learned later that his explanation for holding Soldier to a neck-and-neck finish with Bismarck had been true. Vagle had admitted that Ricky could have beaten him; he admitted his fear and agony—all of it. And Hope had gone away with a sober, worried look in her eyes, while Campbell had patted him on the back and praised his ride.

As Ira was approaching to ask her for a third dance, Slim Olsen appeared suddenly, seemingly from nowhere.

"Would you consider me as a partner for this dance, Miss Hope?" he asked with a slight bow.

Hope caught Ira's frown. "Why, certainly," she said instantly, with a smile. "You're stepping out tonight, eh, Slim?"

"Rodeos are my meat." He grinned as they whirled away from the scowling Ira. "I love 'em. I ride 'em high, wide, and handsome, when I come across one. Your friend back there didn't seem to like it when we wiggled away. Looks snooty tonight, all dressed up."

"You shouldn't say that, Slim," Hope demurred. "He's my escort. Why, you're a good dancer as well as rider. Who is that pretty girl you're escorting tonight?"

"*Humph.* She's a sweet kid, and I believe she's honest. The most important thing about a girl, Miss Hope, is whether she's honest or not. I never would have permitted Ricky to have so much to do with you if I hadn't believed you're honest."

Hope could not control the flush that came into her cheeks.

"I suppose you're Ricky's guardian. Well, you would be a good one. He's sort of . . . impetuous, you know. By the way, Slim, where is Ricky tonight?" She tried to conceal her interest and failed miserably.

"I was expecting that," Slim announced cheerfully. "You see, in town like this, with so many girls around, Ricky gets bashful and sort of confused-like and. . . ."

"Now I know you're lying just as you do, Slim, so leave all the preliminaries out and answer my question."

"Gee, my little girl just gave you a nasty look," he whispered in her ear. "She doesn't dance herself, 'cept with me and some yap from over Fort Benton way, and she's jealous of me dancing with anybody else, especially a pretty girl like you. Don't look at her, Miss Hope, or she'll shoot daggers at you from both eyes."

Hope was momentarily diverted from the subject in hand, and she strained to get a look at Slim's girl. "Who is she and where's she from, Slim? Is she an old friend of yours? How did you meet her? I thought you had no use for girls."

"There's a lot of 'em, including Ricky, who would like to know just what you're asking, Miss Hope. But I'm not saying anything. How could she be an old friend of mine when she's so good-looking? I mean, when she's so young. As for me having no use for girls, well, I've been pretty bitter toward 'em, and there's one I'll never have any use for. Now, you take that little red-haired chip, who just cut you straight up and down the back with a look like a knife, she. . . ."

"Never mind her," Hope cut in with a testy touch to her tongue. "Answer my question about Ricky? Is he angry because of what I said to him after the race?"

"Of course not!" Slim exclaimed. "You don't think he's that small, do you? He told you the truth, knows you believe him, and he asked me . . . I'm in touch with him and can signal with my hand . . . to sound you out for the next dance. If everything is right, I'm to signal him."

"What's the signal?" asked Hope, partly suspicious.

"All I got to do is to brush my hand over my hair now and then." Slim grinned. "Just natural-like, so nobody'll notice it."

"Well, brush it," snapped Hope. "This dance isn't going to last all night, you know."

Slim brushed—and brushed again. And from his point of vantage outside, Ricky saw the movement the first time, and slipped around to the entrance with a grim smile on his face.

"So that's why you wanted to dance with me?" pouted Hope.

"Not at all," replied Slim sincerely. "But I had to tell you what I just told you the first time I danced with you, and I had to wait till Ricky thought the time was ripe. He wants to talk with you, and remember, Miss Hope, that Ricky Odell is one grand pal and a square-shooter. There. They've stopped. And they're not giving any encores . . . dog-gone!"

Ira had danced, but after Slim had left Hope at her place beside her mother, he quickly made his way to her.

"That fellow's not a very good dancer," he remarked. "But he sure can ride. I'll hand it to him for that."

"I think you're rather rude," said Hope primly. "Slim dances as well as most of them here and his talk is entertaining."

"Must have been," Ira observed, smiling in an effort to appear pleasant and not concerned with the incident. But he didn't like it. After all, he had definitely proposed to Hope and she hadn't given him an answer. It was rather a snub for her to dance with a rodeo performer when she might have known he had intended to ask her. And she was so dazzlingly lovely this night. All in white, with white stockings and white slippers set with buckles of brilliant. "I'm sorry if I said anything to offend you, Hope, dear," he said slowly, bending over to give her hand a pat.

"You've got a lot to learn about girls, Ira," said Jane Campbell with a sly smile at her daughter.

"And I'm beginning to believe it," said Ira ruefully. Just then a cheer rocked the pavilion. Men and youths shouted, and women and girls clapped their hands. Hope's heart leaped. She knew he was coming before she saw him.

Ricky was smiling—a splendid figure in his well-fitting clothes and polished shoes. But it was the way he walked, his graceful, upflung gesture with his right hand, and the way he held his head, with the lamplight glossing his hair to a deep auburn, and the dancing light in his eyes that distinguished him most. Almost all the men there liked him at first sight, and the feminine contingent clapped and whispered. For an aurora of mystery radiated from him, and it was whispered he had killed a man.

He signaled confidently to the orchestra as he reached a spot before Hope and the musicians responded like magic.

"I'm asking for this dance," Ira said in an undertone.

"Sorry, Ira, but it's taken, I guess," was his answer. Ira turned eyes that sparkled dark flames of hate at Ricky as the latter spoke.

"Are you ready, Hope?" he said with a smile at Jane Campbell. The mother could not resist the desire to smile back at him, and did. Ricky paid no attention whatever to Ira, who might have been part of the decorations so far as he was concerned.

"Did you think I wouldn't come?" asked Ricky, as they glided away, not knowing that John Campbell and Adam Crowell were watching them from the group about the entrance.

"Not . . . exactly, but I didn't expect a preliminary message. You didn't have to send Slim, Ricky." The girl spoke in a low, soft voice. "I was afraid maybe you felt . . . irritated because of what I said after the race this afternoon." She looked up at him but his lips were smiling down at her. She trembled a bit and felt afraid as she realized that here was the old Ricky Odell—the Ricky she first had met.

"You're a good sport, girl," was what he said. "I forgot about that thinking of this dance and tonight. I had to send word because I didn't want to take a chance on you being engaged for a dance and me having to wait around like a dummy. For, in that case, everybody would know that I had come to dance with you and was waiting my turn, and folks talk. It would center too much attention on me, and bring you into it, and . . . well, don't you think it was best?"

"Yes, it was good judgment on your part," she said. "I hadn't thought much about it in that way. And I know what you told me about the close finish with Bismarck is true. That was a noble thing to do, Ricky Odell."

"That's the girl!" he cheered. "This is one night I want to be a hero . . . to you, I mean."

Hope flushed. Neither of them was conscious of the others on the floor or standing in the rear, all with their eyes on them. And at this very moment, Hope knew in her heart of hearts that she was going to marry the knight who had ridden in on the first flush of the purple mist.

"Where did Slim get his girl?" she asked to mask her confusion.

"That son-of-a-gun!" Ricky laughed delightedly. "I've tried to find out and he won't tell me. But I've got a suspicion. The liveryman told me that she rode in with an elderly man, probably her father, and that Slim happened to be on hand when her horse got frisky at the corrals behind the barn. Who'd ever've thought the big stiff was such a fast worker? First time I really have seen or heard of him in such swift action. The big bum won't even introduce me to her!"

They both laughed as the music stopped. Ricky took her arm and led her to the refreshment balcony, from which steps led to the ground. Everyone saw them take two glasses of lemonade and descend the steps out of sight.

On the lower step Ricky paused and looked at the sky. "Hope, this is a night made to order," he stated. "Look at the stars leaning low for a look at us, look at the moon smiling . . . there. Hear it? Catch the notes he's giving us? The tinkling of the meadowlark, the happiest bird on the prairies. Let's walk out here on the grass between the trees."

She walked with him and they sipped their lemonade. He put down the empty glasses. The moonlight was filtering through the trees and an occasional leaf floated down upon them. Romance lingered in the scented breath of the wind.

"Hope, I've got to tell you first of all that you look more beautiful tonight than I've ever seen you. I thought you an angel before . . . now, I'm almost afraid of you. If it wasn't for the scent from your hair, your moving, smiling lips, your dancing eyes, I'd think you were a vision. For the first time in his life, Ricky Odell has found a girl he really loves . . . his mate, and he's going to win her here and now and for all."

He took her in his arms and kissed her, and the world swam in happiness before her eyes.

"I promised to tell you about myself tonight and I'm going to tell you the . . . the fundamentals. I'll fill in scores of details later. I'd have told you before, but I wanted to make sure that you believed me and trusted me. I held off, too, to give Ira an even break. I went so far as to file on a homestead up your way, and Slim did, too, so I could have a chance and an excuse to be near you, if I had to have the last. My name is Richard Odell, but I've been called Ricky since I was a kid. I was born on my father's ranch, the T-O down in the Musselshell country. Slim, whose real name was, or is, Tom Olsen, was adopted by my father when he was a kid. His father was one of our hands. Slim's mother died and Dad took him into the family. My mother died when I still was a kid." He paused, took her left hand in his, and patted it.

"My father was a noted gunman, Hope. He was too fast for a bad crowd that had it in for him, and they bombarded him from ambush one night and shattered his right arm and his gun hand. I was maybe nine years old then and could ride, of course. But from that time on, my father taught me the use of a pistol. He gave Slim and me guns to play with. He used to spend hours a day drilling me to draw and fire. It was his habit, so great a hobby that he let our foreman, Clayton, run the ranch while he taught me, made me practice, day after day, week after week, month after month. He seemed to think the day would come when I would have to meet his enemies. I was a good pupil. I had to be. Do you wonder that I'm so handy with a gun, sweet? They say down there that no man in the country can beat me. The only man I had to draw down on and shoot was Pearlman."

Hope had an arm about his shoulders now and her breath was coming fast.

"When I was twenty-one," he continued in a lowered voice, "an enemy of my dad's got him for keeps. Shot him down when he knew Dad was powerless to defend himself. I went after him, but before I could get him the sheriff had him. They hanged the murderer and I inherited the ranch. Slim is like a brother, for he's been close to me all these years. My father's will required that our foreman, Clayton, manage the ranch until I reached the age of twenty-five, when I'm to take charge. That will be next year. It's not as big a place as Crowell's, but it'll do . . . for us. Late in August, Slim suggested that we take a trip up north, and I agreed. We've taken trips every year. We had no intention of staying in Pondera any length of time until I saw you. There's the story, sweetheart, and papers proving it are being sent to Sheriff Lane, although I've a hunch he's inquired around and already knows. That's all for now, Hope, do you . . . believe me?"

"Yes," breathed Hope. Her eyes were like stars as she looked up at him, and he took her in his arms again.

"I love you, Hope," he said in a voice trembling with emotion. "And loving you as I do, I want you . . . your eyes and lips and hair, your body and your very soul I want to belong to me. Will you marry me, sweetheart?"

"Yes," she answered quickly. "I'd marry you anyway, regardless of anything, so long as I knew you were straight, because . . . I love you, Ricky Odell."

Their lips met in a long kiss and they heard someone running in the grass from the pavilion. Ricky turned, still with his arms about the girl, as Ira, his face pale, came up. Two other men were running, too. They were John Campbell and Adam Crowell.

Ricky's words were for Ira. "A kiss to the moon, Ira!" he said in a joyous tone, and he kissed Hope again.

Ira jerked him away. "What do you mean, you . . . you . . . ?" He could get out no further words. Campbell and Crowell were close.

"I mean that you've lost out, Ira," said Ricky evenly. "I'm going to marry Hope."

"You lie!" shouted Ira. He turned to Hope. "Have you let this rodeo performer fool you into promising to marry him?" he demanded.

Hope smiled happily and nodded.

Ira whirled on Ricky. "You skunk! You. . . ."

His hand went into his coat as Ricky swung the girl away and Crowell and Campbell leaped in. A shot split the night air, and John Campbell stumbled forward, his hand going to his face, with blood trickling through his fingers. Hope dropped with a little cry to his side as he fell, and Ricky Odell's right fist knocked Ira off his feet to the ground, where he lay, motionless.

In another moment those in the dance pavilion were pouring out all entrances, and Jane Campbell and Amy Crowell were holding each other with stark terror in their eyes.

CHAPTER TWENTY-SEVEN

As soon as the crowd from the dancing pavilion could get outside, and other crowds rush in from the street, Sheriff Tom Lane had the situation in hand with twenty deputies surrounding the spot where the shooting had taken place. Lane had rushed a messenger to Mrs. Campbell and Mrs. Crowell, with the latter's daughter, to hurry to the home of the doctor, where he had his office.

The doctor was at hand when several strong youths picked up the unconscious form of John Campbell to take him to the doctor's office. Hope went with them, but Sheriff Lane stopped Ricky Odell, the dazed Ira, and his father Adam Crowell. "I reckon you'll come with me," he said tartly. "No monkey business, now," he added sternly. "Step along smart. Close in here, boys, and rush these three with me to my office."

They moved forward with half a dozen men holding Ira and his father, who was speaking swiftly in an enraged manner, and Ricky, who followed willingly enough. The sheriff held Ira Crowell's gun in his hand, and dispatched another messenger to find County Attorney Berry and bring him to the jail office as soon as possible.

As they entered Lane's office, the sheriff assigned six men to guard the entrance. "No one is to come in or go out, without my consent," he ordered sharply.

"I reckon that doesn't include me," said Crowell the elder with a dark look.

Lane whirled on the men just without the door. "You heard me! What I said takes in everyone in this room and everybody outside it. Admit Berry as soon as he comes."

"Looks to me that you're kinda making a big fuss all of a sudden," remarked Crowell. "I reckon I'm entitled to more consideration than you. . . ."

"Than I think," Lane put in. "Well, Crowell, at the present you're entitled to just as much consideration as I think. Sit down in a chair or I'll have two men come and put you in one." He stepped to the door, but Crowell sat down immediately.

Then the sheriff turned to the pale, trembling Ira. "Sit down," he ordered. "You're under arrest."

"You can't arrest him for an accidental shooting!" yelled Crowell.

"I can't? Well, I have. And after the little talk we'll have here, I'm going to slam him into a cell. Every word you speak is going to be set down against you both."

Lane took the gun out of his pocket. "Ira, where did you get this gun?"

"I . . . it was lying around. . . ."

"Tell him you never saw it," his father commanded.

The sheriff turned to the stockman. His face was hard as he spoke. "There isn't a man on the range, Crowell, that carries a Derringer, except maybe some hard-boiled gamblers. I can identify this as your gun. It may be . . . I'm not saying it is . . . that you told Ira to pack this small gun, if he had to pack one, because it wouldn't show so much."

"I took the gun off the mantelpiece myself," said Ira stoutly. "My father had nothing to do with it."

"Now you're talking sense," agreed the sheriff. "It'll do you a whole lot of good to tell the straight truth."

"I demand that my lawyer be sent for!" exclaimed Crowell.

"Your lawyer cannot come in here," was Lane's sharp retort.

"I'm the boss here. Afterward you and your lawyer can talk. I expect he has already been stopped at the door. That's final."

Crowell glared at Ira who, apparently, had completely lost his nerve. His firm belief in his father's power was rapidly being shaken.

Lane confronted Ricky Odell. "Was this shooting accidental?" he demanded.

"If I was the only one concerned, I might say it was. But with three lives involved, I say absolutely that it wasn't. Ira, there, wanted to get me. You can see it in his face. When he whipped the gun out from under his coat, both his father and John Campbell leaped in. I just had time to toss Hope Campbell out of danger when the shot rang out and Campbell went down. Before Ira could shoot the second barrel, I knocked him flat. He drew on me, intending to kill me. That's how much of an accident it was."

Ira had lowered his eyes before Ricky's steady, accusing gaze.

"Why did he want to kill you?" Lane asked.

There were several moments of silence. "Because I was holding Hope in my arms. I had this right because Hope and I had just become engaged. I told him so, and when Hope affirmed it, he went for his gun."

There followed another silence during which the elder Crowell looked curiously at Ricky, and then spoke to Ira. "If she wanted to hook up with this show rider, I reckon it's a good thing you found it out."

"Providing it's not at the expense of John Campbell's life," the sheriff said. Crowell started and frowned. "I warned Ira and Odell and Olsen not to start any trouble during rodeo. I happen to know that on one occasion, at least, Odell prevented Ira from stepping into the syrup. There has been bad blood, particularly on account of Miss Campbell. There is no use beating around the bush. I happen to know that neither Odell nor Olsen carried a gun tonight. I happen to know that Odell had an appointment with the young lady to tell her about himself tonight."

"A bunch of romantic lies!" sneered Adam Crowell.

"On the other hand quite respectable," said Lane airily. He lifted a paper from his desk. "This is from a lawyer and the sheriff in a southern county in the state where both young men were brought up. Odell assumes the management of the ranch he inherited next year. They were up here on a trip and their show riding, as you call it, was done for the fun of the thing. Odell and Olsen stand all right with me and the contents of these papers will be made public tomorrow. These boys have quite as good a standing as your son."

Lane answered a knock at the door. "Come in, Berry," he invited cordially, as he opened the door, "and you, too, Slim."

Berry avoided Crowell's look, and the stockman's face grew blacker.

"Odell, suppose you tell the county attorney what happened tonight in as few words as possible," said the sheriff. "And you, Olsen, sit over there near your friend's chair."

Ricky repeated his story in short, terse sentences while Berry and the others listened. Berry was frowning and still avoided Crowell.

Then Lane asked Slim a number of questions, getting a direct answer to each. No, they hadn't carried any guns. He had danced with Hope Campbell, telling her Ricky wanted the next dance, if possible. Ricky and the girl had danced, gone to the lemonade booth, and then had slipped down the steps— in the best of spirits. Slim had seen Ira, his eyes flashing red, leave the pavilion and had hurried around to arrive at the scene of the shooting too late to take a hand in it. But he had seen Ira draw the gun. Yes, there had been trouble before, up on the foothill range. Ricky had told him what he intended to tell the girl. It was true—all of it. But, for that matter, it had been a case of love at first sight between the youth and the girl. That was all. The sheriff merely asked him to tell of the meeting at the livery.

"There you are, Berry," said Lane, walking around the desk to get a paper from a drawer of his desk. "I think we can agree on the charge."

"Certainly," snapped Berry. "Assault with intent to kill."

Adam Crowell leaped to his feet. "Why, you four-flushers!" he cried. "Do you think for a minute you can get away with that? All the testimony, so far, shows it was an accident."

Both Berry and Lane looked at him coolly. "You have heard the charge," said Lane. "No youth can carry a gun at the rodeo dance and shoot people promiscuously. Not even a Crowell can do that, Adam."

"Very well!" roared Adam, addressing Berry. "What's the bail? If you're afraid to take my check, I won't have any trouble getting cash!"

"That won't be necessary, Mister Crowell, and we'd take your check in an instant," replied Berry firmly. "But Sheriff Lane will have to hold Ira without bail until the full extent of John Campbell's injury is ascertained." He turned to Ricky and Slim. "Meanwhile, you fellows are held as material witnesses. You will not be confined nor put under bail so long as we have your assurance that you will not attempt to leave the jurisdiction of the sheriff."

"We'll stay," said Ricky as Slim nodded soberly.

"Come out with me," said Sheriff Lane to the two. When they were in the hall, he addressed himself to Ricky: "You'll remember the name and description of the desperado I told you about this evening? Brackett, that's right. I think you'd better keep a watch on John Campbell. This is mighty serious business. Go down to the doctor's office and I'll be over there as soon as I can. Our gunman, I believe, is close tonight."

After they left, Crowell, the officials, and Ira remained in the sheriff's office for some time. When Adam Crowell came out, he came alone. Some time later, Lane and Berry left, both going to ascertain Campbell's condition.

John Campbell was resting quietly in a stupor after regaining consciousness for a very short interval after being shot. The doctor still was working over him. He had been shot across the forehead just above his right eye. The bullet had plowed deep enough to render the wound dangerous, and a pinpoint more of depth would have been fatal. The doctor had stopped the flow of blood and was just finishing dressing and bandaging the ugly wound when Ricky Odell arrived.

He found Hope and her mother near Campbell's side. Mrs. Crowell was there, having sent her daughter and the latter's friend to the hotel at once. Amy Crowell was waiting for her husband and son. None of them knew much about what had happened except such information as Hope had told them hurriedly.

When Ricky was admitted (Slim remaining on guard outside), Hope went to him immediately. "I've told them of our engagement, Ricky," she said soberly. "Where . . . where are Ira and his father?"

"They're up to the sheriff's office," replied Ricky in a tone that just reached Mrs. Crowell's ears. "Some kind of a formality," he added hastily. "How's your father?"

"It was a grazing wound," answered the girl. "The doctor says he will be all right. He was hit hard and can't talk much as yet. You weren't hurt, Ricky?"

"Luckily no one else was hurt," he said grimly. "As it is, I wish it might be me instead of your father. But he has too good a constitution to let this bowl him over for very long."

Mrs. Crowell rose and came to them. "I'm sure Ira didn't intend to do it," she said in a sincere voice. "When he heard . . .

about you and Hope, he must have gone out of his head completely. You see, he thought so much of Hope."

"It was a poor way to show it," said Hope, "but I don't suppose we should bear him ill." She looked at her father's form. "I don't ever want to see your son again, Missus Crowell."

"Oh! I'm so sorry!" exclaimed the older woman.

Jane Campbell joined them. Her face was white, but she bore up with the hardihood of a pioneer prairie woman. "We mustn't say anything more about it," she told Hope, who was clinging to Ricky's hand. "Our duty is to nurse your father, keep him quiet and comfortable, and as soon as possible get him home." She turned to Mrs. Crowell. "I'm sure you understand, Amy?"

"Yes," said Mrs. Crowell faintly. "I'm waiting for Adam."

At this moment there came a rap on the door, and the doctor admitted Crowell, who stepped to his wife's side. He looked down upon the unconscious form of John Campbell, and pressed his lips tightly together. Then he looked at the other women. He spoke first to Jane Campbell: "It's hard for me to talk, Jane, but I'm . . . I'm clean knocked out about this."

"That's all right," said Jane. "It's a nasty wound in his forehead, but the doctor feels sure he will recover quickly."

Crowell looked directly at the physician. "How bad is it?" he asked.

"It's a bad nick over his right eye," the doctor answered. "Such a wound naturally would knock him out for a spell. Otherwise he's doing nicely with a good pulse. He must have quiet for some time."

"In that case, Amy, I guess it would be best for us to go," said Crowell. "We can't do anything here, much as we would like to."

As he turned away with his wife, he gave one sharp glance at Ricky, intended to cut him dead with scorn and ridicule.

Ricky stepped quickly and opened the door. Crowell led his

wife outside with a mumbled oath. It made the stockman frantic to realize to the fullest extent that he was undoubtedly in the wrong.

Ricky sat in a chair beside Hope. They looked at the motionless figure on the couch, and Ricky remembered the sheriff's warning. Lane had turned to him as the man he considered most able to meet the gunman, who was drawing near to see John Campbell.

As if in answer to Ricky's thought, Campbell moved restlessly. Then: "Brackett!" The single word came from the sick man's lips in a blunt tone that literally seemed to seep through the room.

Hope gripped Ricky's arm as her mother half rose, her hands flying to her breast. The doctor soothed her. "He'll be coming out of it soon. We'll keep him here in my house for the night and you really ought to go to the hotel and to bed, you and Hope."

"No," said Jane determinedly. "We'll stay here." She looked anxiously at Hope and Ricky. Ricky nodded to her softly. She came over to them. "We will stay here, Daughter," she said to Hope. Her voice wavered as she spoke to Ricky. "Do you . . . know . . . ?" But he was nodding significantly. "I recognized the name," he said in a low voice. "I know all about it. You can trust me, Missus Campbell."

A look of relief came into Jane's face. "He won't be able to take care of himself for a long time, Ricky," she said. "We'll have to depend on others."

"That means Slim and me," said Ricky, with a swift look at the girl. "Don't worry a single minute, either of you. We'll be near if that man comes to town." His tone was firm, reassuring.

Hope kissed him before he went outside.

When Ricky joined Slim on the walk, they met Sheriff Lane and Berry coming from the sheriff's office. "What's the news?" Lane asked.

Ricky told him briefly of Campbell's condition and of Jane's and Hope's decision to remain at the doctor's house with the patient all night. "He . . . spoke that name," he told the sheriff. "We figured to hang around here."

"Good," said the sheriff, "but keep out of sight. The crowd in town is acting up and I've got to keep an eye out the rest of the night."

"I've got to run up to the dance pavilion," Slim announced. "But it won't take me a minute."

"Well, take it around about," the sheriff ordered. "And don't stay to dance. I'll drop over to see you now and then. If I know John Campbell like I think I do, he'll be out from under before long and in the morning he'll want to be taken home. But that's up to the doctor. So long."

"Just a minute, Sheriff," said Ricky. "Remember I'm not making any complaint against Ira Crowell."

"That isn't bothering us any," said the sheriff, scowling. "We're holding him till Crowell sees the light and this thing has blown over. It was nasty work. If you hear anything, one of you get the word to me. I'll be over on Main Street. Ira's safe and Crowell is going to stay in the hotel, under guard. Feeling is running strong. That's all."

CHAPTER TWENTY-EIGHT

In the morning the town was astir with restless rumor and among the citizens, who had not celebrated so strenuously, the feeling over the shooting of John Campbell did run high. With the rodeo ended, ranchers and their families were leaving, the tinhorn gamblers and hangers-on were getting some sleep preparatory to departing. The town in general was cleaning up.

When Sheriff Lane told his deputies and Mike at the Board of Trade the truth about Ricky Odell and Slim Olsen, the tidings spread like wildfire. When it became definitely known that Ira had shot Campbell when trying to get Odell because the latter had won the hand of Hope, adverse feeling toward the Crowells intensified. More than one influential citizen expressed his sentiments regarding the matter in no uncertain terms. It was generally known—for everyone had the sheriff's word for it— that Ricky and his friend, Slim, had been unarmed the night before. Next, it was freely predicted that Adam Crowell would never again have the hold he had on the Cattlemen's Association. John Campbell was a favorite and Ricky was popular in Pondera, and the town was mad "clean through" in range parlance. It was perhaps best that Ira was in jail where he could not be harmed, for groups gathered and spoke in a threatening way.

Adam Crowell, ponderous and scowling, dominant as ever, received his first inkling of the change with regard to himself when he went down alone to an early breakfast. Every seat in the hotel dining room was taken. His frown increased.

"Here!" he called to a waitress. "Isn't there a place for me? There always is. I'm Crowell."

"We're crowded this morning," was the cool answer. "Maybe somebody will go out in a few minutes." She went about her duties.

Crowell stamped back to the lobby and addressed the clerk in a harsh tone. "I think I left an order that I'd want an early breakfast. The girl, or one of 'em, out there told me there was no place."

"Well, with all these people goin' away early, we can't stop 'em from goin' into the dinin' room, Mister Crowell."

Crowell swore under his breath and went out, ramming his big hat on his head. The first stockman he met turned away to avoid a meeting. Crowell was astounded. For the first time he felt a tinge of uncertainty, almost of fear. To make matters worse, the first two people who really noticed him were Odell and Olsen on their way to a café breakfast, having been relieved at their post by two deputies.

"How's Campbell?" growled Crowell.

"The best thing for you to do, in your position, would be to go over to the doctor's place and ask," said Slim Olsen coldly.

"Don't start to be fresh with me, you young. . . ."

"Stop doubling that right fist of yours," commanded Slim sharply. "Ira drew a gun on me and landed sitting on a prickly pear. If you try to take a whack at me, I'll lay you flat in the dust of the street."

Ricky restrained him as a little crowd gathered. "You better beat it back to the ranch," he advised, "till this thing blows over."

Crowell's face was nearly purple as he walked away. He forgot breakfast and routed out his attorney. "Go over there and get Ira out of jail," he instructed briefly. "You've always been a good lawyer and I guess you can handle this. I'll put up any bail they want."

"Being your attorney, I've always acted immediately in any case affecting your interests," was the lawyer's answer. "I can't get the boy out of jail or pull any strings in a case like this till the outcome of Campbell's injury is apparent. I suppose you know that if Campbell should die, the charge would be changed to murder, and I might have a better chance then than now. I'm going to get him out, but you've got to stop trying to intimidate the officials and let me handle the matter in my own way, or I'll resign the case at once."

Crowell sensed the attorney's tone was rather sharp. "All right," he snapped. "I suppose I might as well go home for a few days. I'd like my wife and myself to see Ira before we go."

"Sure thing. I'll go with you. But don't mess things up by making a scene. Just let the boy know the wheels are turning for him. Remember, there has been no charge by any of the principals in the . . . ah . . . accident."

It was Mrs. Crowell who went to the doctor's to find that John Campbell was conscious but wouldn't talk to anyone except the doctor and his wife. It was impossible to ascertain what they would do. So, after the visit to Ira, Adam Crowell, his wife, their daughter and her visitor, started back to the H Square in the buckboard, flanked by H Square riders, all of whom, for the time being, were retained. Ringing in Crowell's ears all the distance back to his ranch were the words Sheriff Lane had spoken to him in private before he left the jail office.

"There are two things you must remember and one you must forget," Lane had told Crowell. "You must remember why Berry and me, and Pete Lamont, president of the Association, and Alex Johnson and you engineered that business of making John Campbell the special agent of the Association. He will be of use there and we want it to stick, whether you like it or not. You don't stand too well now, Crowell, and if you kick over the traces, you're out."

Angered as he was, Crowell had withheld a sharp retort. He had observed certain evidences that morning that had convinced him that something was up, something which would not be to his advantage.

"Another thing you want to remember harder than anything you ever remembered in your life is that you deliberately went in with us and others of the Association for the benefit of Campbell, who returned voluntarily to make a come-back for the sake of his home and family. You're still going to help him do that."

The sheriff had paused once more. "The thing you're going to forget is any of Campbell's past you may know, or any names you may know connected with that past. You not only tried to interfere with a perfectly legitimate love affair, but you've got the town and the range against you for doing so. If you play square, you'll win 'em back in time. That's all."

Over and over again Crowell thought of this strange, one-sided interview as he rode back to the ranch. His power on the range was at stake; the fate of Ira was entirely in the hands of Lane and Berry. Ira had been uppish, hot-headed, and too dominant for his age—too certain sure of himself. And that was Adam's fault, too. At the ranch he ordered the hands not actually needed on the range to stand special guard duty in the bunkhouse. Yet he could not for the life of him understand why he did so.

When John Campbell recovered consciousness in the dark of early morning, the doctor was at his side in a moment. Jane and her daughter had been put to bed upstairs. After a glass of cold water, for which he asked, he spoke in a low thick voice to the doctor.

"Where are my wife and daughter?" he asked laboriously.

"They're here in the house," said the doctor. "You must be quiet."

The patient scowled a moment. "I only want to know one or two things. I'm much stronger. Where is Ricky Odell?"

"He's somewhere close, keeping watch, as he's anxious about your condition," said the doctor slowly.

"Good boy, that," muttered Campbell. "And Ira?"

"The sheriff took care of him. His father and mother were here to see how you were."

"Is it a bad crack I've got?" asked the sick man.

"A bullet wound on the forehead. Just knocked you out, like a blow on the chin. You'll be all right, but you've got to keep quiet and not talk any more just now."

"I'll have . . . plenty . . . to say later," said Campbell as he dropped off to sleep.

The doctor was delighted, for he saw immediate improvement in his charge. He dozed in any easy chair near the couch until daylight came.

Shortly after daylight, John Campbell was awake, his brain was clear, and, save from the bandages on his forehead, extending out around his head, none would have known he had been injured. He had a light breakfast with his wife and Hope, patting his daughter's hand from time to time. Several times he asked her: "Do you love him?" The answer was always in the affirmative, and Jane always smiled.

"Well, I had the low-down on him from the sheriff before he told you," Campbell boasted. "Fact is, the sheriff had a pretty good line on both of them before they left on that trip. But i he'd just been a common cowhand, I wouldn't have objected you really loved him."

After Mrs. Crowell had left to go home, the sheriff arrived a short inquiry. He went into no details. "You'll be all rig!

Lane said at parting, "and everything will be the same as usual, except, from what I hear, you're to have another man in the family. If you don't believe it, look there."

He pointed to Hope's rosy cheeks and chuckled as he went out.

"How about Vagle?" he asked.

"He's been around regularly," replied Jane. "He's looking after the horses, of course."

"Sure enough," said Campbell, "and we've got to think about getting back home. If I have to stay around town here, I will be sick."

"Don't forget I'm in charge here," warned the doctor. "I've got to take a look at those dressings this morning, too. Sorry one has to cover your right eye, but that'll be off soon enough."

"My eye!" said Campbell, startled. "Is . . . it gone, Doctor?"

"No, no, no," replied the doctor quickly, "but the wound is so close I have to cover it to secure the dressings properly. Your eye is all right. But it was a piece of luck."

Ricky and Slim kept in the background that day as much as possible. They moved Campbell to the hotel late in the afternoon, and arrangements were made to convey him in the buckboard to the ranch in the foothills the following day. Vagle was to drive, with Mrs. Campbell beside him. The doctor was to ride in the rear with Campbell. Hope was to ride Bismarck back to Prairie's End.

Campbell was inclined to rest a great deal and talked just enough to make sure they were going home. Ricky had met with no opposition when he had announced that he and Slim would ride up with them.

They started the next morning with Campbell's head pillowed against the doctor in the rear seat. Vagle and Mrs. Campbell were in the front seat, and Hope rode with Ricky, with Slim following a bit behind.

A mighty cheer went up from the townsfolk as they left, and Campbell managed to wave a hand. Vagle drove slowly to avoid jolting.

Ricky's face was somewhat stern and pale this day as he rode with Hope behind the buckboard. He was thinking of Ira's foolishness, partly blaming himself for it, and worrying about the condition of John Campbell.

"What makes you so terribly morose?" asked Hope, looking at him keenly.

"Oh. . . ." He smiled rather thinly. "It just seems of late that every turn I make I step into trouble. Not meaning you, sweetheart, because a man can't win such a prize just by wishing or something."

"You're worried about Ira," she accused. "Well, I'm not."

"I shouldn't think . . . ," Ricky began. "I mean I feel that I was part to blame. In the joy of the moment I sort of goaded him on. And then . . . I'm awfully worried about your dad, dear."

"I know the signs," said the girl convincingly. "He'll come around all right." She paused and then looked at him gravely. "Mother told me a few things," she said, lowering her voice, which immediately attracted his full attention. "Father still has an enemy he fears. He spoke his name the night he was hurt. Do you remember?"

"Yes," said Ricky, looking straight ahead.

"Then you know all about it?" she asked breathlessly.

"I know most of it," Ricky conceded. "But you must not ask me anything more because I cannot answer without breaking a promise. You just leave this business to me, sweet, and don't worry."

That was as much as Hope could get out of him, but she feared some dreadful climax was to come. She was glad Ricky was with them.

John Campbell stood the ride well and when home, resting on the comfortable, spacious lounge in his own living room, he seemed much better and greatly cheered. The doctor announced that he would stay the night, to watch the dressings, and then would ride up daily or every other day, as needed.

"Give the doc a glass of that prime chokecherry wine, Jane," he told his wife. "And I don't think a drop would hurt me. Doc, I've got wine made out of every kind of berries that's in these hills and it's all good."

Meanwhile Ricky and Slim had unsaddled, and Ricky had managed to slip a kiss to Hope as he took her horse before she went inside. Vagle looked after the team that had drawn the buckboard.

"Oh, here's a visitor who has maybe come too soon!" exclaimed Ricky. "I'll call Hope out to see."

He hurried to the porch as Adam Crowell was riding up the trail in the approaching sunset. But John Campbell overheard them talking excitedly. "Who is it?" he called. "Crowell? I want to see him, Doc. I want to see him."

"All right . . . for a short time," the doctor agreed. "I don't want anything to excite him," he told Jane, who came in with the wine. "I'll go out and warn Crowell."

The stockman removed his hat as he came in and bowed slightly to Jane. Then he looked a long time at the prostrate form of Campbell.

"Sit down, Adam, I can talk a little," Campbell invited.

Crowell's face was gray and his words came a bit unsteadily. "John, I'm downright knocked all cuckoo to see you this way, and Amy sent word that she's praying for you to get well quick," he said.

"Sure I will," responded Campbell cheerily. "I'm home already, you see, and drinking a glass of wine with the doctor. Jane, bring a glass for Adam. He looks a little pasty."

As Jane went for the wine, Campbell asked a straight question he had overlooked before. "How is Ira, Adam? I hope he doesn't feel too bad about all this."

"I dunno. He doesn't talk much . . . seems kinda stunned. He's in jail, you know."

Campbell half rose, but the doctor pushed him gently back.

"In jail?" said Campbell. "Why're they keeping him in jail? Didn't you offer bail if it's as bad as all that?"

"They won't bail him . . . not now, anyway," said Crowell, pressing his lips. "I don't see as it's doing any good to keep him in there when they know they can get him at home any time they want him. I was wondering, John, if you had made any complaint about him. I know he's headstrong and all that. I guess it's the way I brought him up. But he didn't mean. . . ."

"Never mind that," said Campbell sharply. "Of course I haven't made any complaint against him and don't intend to. Neither does my girl's man intend to make any complaint against him. I can speak for Ricky in that. Go tell Lane where to get off at and get him out of there."

"That's all right," soothed the doctor with a warning glance at Crowell. "We'll attend to that, all right. It was just a form."

Crowell said: "I'm glad to hear what you say, John, but I'm even gladder you're coming along all right. I mean that, John, and I speak for Amy, too."

He rose to go, and the doctor took his arm to lead him to the door. "No, I'm not going to bother you with a long visit at first, John," he said over his shoulder. "The doctor knows best what to do."

But Campbell fretted and tossed and complained until dusk, although the doctor gave him a strong sedative. Just before twilight, he told Hope to bring in Ricky Odell. "I know he's here and you bring him in," he demanded.

"Might as well let your father see him," said the doctor.

261

"Maybe it'll quiet him down."

When Ricky came in, John gave him his hand and got right down to business. "Ricky, I want you to ride right down and see Tom Lane and tell him not to hold Ira because of us. I'm coming along all right and the shooting was accidental. Tell him that and tell him that neither you nor me will make a complaint or appear as witnesses against Ira. Tell him so he'll understand, and tell him to let Ira go home." His hands were shaking and his lips twitching as he finished. "Will you do that right away?"

Ricky caught the doctor's nod. It was dangerous for Campbell to become excited like this.

"Of course I'll do it," Ricky replied immediately. "You'll hear my horse start in five minutes." He held out his hand and John Campbell took it.

"I believe you," he said. "Come back and tell me what he says."

When Ricky went out, the doctor gave his patient some more medicine, which Campbell took willingly. "Let's finish our wine," he told the physician as the latter seated himself comfortably.

Outside Ricky was talking with Slim and Hope. "It'll take that off his mind, and help old Crowell, whose heart is breaking," said Ricky in a determined voice. "And I don't think any of us want Ira to stay in jail. Besides . . . ," he hesitated. "Besides, I might get a line on things down there we might need to know. It won't take long, and, Slim, you can keep an eye out with Vagle."

Hope threw an arm about his neck and kissed him before he galloped away.

About an hour later, after they had eaten supper, Slim was dozing on the porch when hoof beats were heard on the uptrail. Vagle was out there somewhere and Hope came to the door and warned Slim to get out of sight quickly. "It can't be Ricky," she said. "Hide out until we see who it is."

In another moment a big form on a large horse hove in view, outlined by the starlight. The rider turned straight in.

A hoarse challenge came in Vagle's shrill voice. Then a gun to the right flashed and boomed sharply. The rider's own gun emitted two streaks of red and he rode on in as the reports echoed in the hills. He dismounted near the door where his bulk, his narrowed eyes, and the slant of the left one were clearly in view.

The rider swaggered to the porch and was clearly in the light. Slim's gun was trained on him, but he held his fire to be sure. The sheriff had said that—be sure. Hope appeared. "Did you want to see someone?"

"I just dropped in to see John Campbell," was the blunt reply.

The doctor pushed ahead of the girl. "You can't see him now, sir. He is a sick man . . . my patient. And I've just got him to sleep for a time with an opiate. I'm in charge here."

"Yeah? And who're you?" demanded the intruder.

"I'm Doctor Thomas from Pondera," replied the physician sternly.

"Then we'll sit down here on the porch a few minutes and find out a few things," said the rider. "What's happened to my old friend?"

Slim saw the white vision of the girl beside him as she took his arm. "Come, come at once!" she commanded in great excitement. "Bismarck is ready out here. I'll show you the cut-off trail through the trees. You must ride like mad and catch Ricky and bring him back. If that brute gets too bad, I'll shoot him down with my own gun. But the doctor is here, and Mother and me, and he won't get fresh soon. Come on, Slim, and go for Ricky and bring him back quickly. He's maybe killed poor Vagle, who fired first. Oh, Slim, get Ricky."

CHAPTER TWENTY-NINE

Brackett listened to the doctor with an ominous frown while the man of medicine explained something of what had happened and why it was necessary to keep Campbell quiet. Inside, in the living room, Jane Campbell, who had been joined by Hope, could barely catch snatches of the low conversation.

Suddenly the rider slapped his knee. "So the old boy has been playing his tricks up here, eh . . . and let a kid shoot him? By God, I can show him better territory. And him a dead shot . . . almost as good as me."

"Please don't talk so loud," said the doctor.

"I want to see him," insisted the gunman. "How do I know he isn't playing 'possum?"

"You have my word for it and that's sufficient," snapped the doctor. "I don't know what you are or who you are, but your appearance and manner do not impress me as favorable. I will let you see the patient to shut you up, but you're to keep your loud mouth closed while you're in the sick room."

Brackett was taken aback. "Why, you prescription scrimp, I've a notion. . . ." His hand dropped like lightning, but the old doctor's faithful Derringer slid out of his sleeve into his hand. It leveled instantly to aim on Brackett's heart. "I've had to protect a patient before, and I can do it again," he said sternly.

Brackett's keen mind took in the situation at a glance. He could foil the doctor, kill him if necessary. But he wanted no more shooting at present. Shots carried far and wide on a night wind.

"Cool your brain and watch your words, that's all." He scowled. "Now let's see your patient."

The doctor saw no alternative; the Derringer disappeared, and he led the way into the sick room. Brackett looked queerly at the motionless form of Campbell; he stooped and looked at him closer, then rose with a frown on his face. It lightened as he saw Jane Campbell.

"Why, hello, Jane," he said in a modulated tone. "So the old man got mixed up with the wrong end of a gun, eh? And this is the little panty girl?" He looked pleasantly at Hope, whose hands were behind her back, one clutching her ivory-handled pistol. "I knew you in a better country than this when you wore tiny blue overalls." Hope's eyes blazed. "Plenty of spunk, too," he said to Jane.

"Please," said Jane, "not at this time. I'm so worried about John now. Please go until he is better."

"Worried about Jack, eh?" sneered Brackett. "You'd have done better to have worried about me in the first place, back there in Zortman. Reckon you've lived on small pickings ever since. But I'll see to it that he gets a man's job that'll pay him real money and he won't have to play around with kids." There was a mean light in his eyes as he said this, and Hope's face went white. The girl felt sure she could kill him on the spot, but the very thought of it sent a chill of terror through her.

"I believe there's a man hurt out front," said the doctor softly. "Will you bring a lantern, Missus Campbell? This visitor and I will go out and take a look."

Brackett took a long glance at Campbell and another at the girl before he and the doctor went outside.

"Whoever he is, he fired on me first without cause," Brackett grumbled.

As the doctor flashed the light over the small form of Vagle on the ground, Brackett swore softly. "The weasel!" he exclaimed. "So that little rat has followed Jack Campbell all these years."

"Let's carry him to the bunkhouse so I can see what I can do," the doctor said.

"There's just about enough left of him to die," grunted Brackett. But, nevertheless, he showed interest in the proceedings that followed. He helped the doctor carry Vagle to the bunkhouse, where a lamp was lit. He helped the doctor undress his victim and watched the process of cleansing the two bullet wounds, the dressing and bandaging, and the administering of the hypodermic. He had never witnessed an attempt to bring one of his victims back to life before, and didn't believe it possible. He wore a half grin, half sneer on his pudgy lips.

"Why don't you tell the girl to come out and be nurse?" he asked the doctor sarcastically.

"He's doing as well as can be expected," said the doctor grimly. "You make a business of killing, do you?"

"You shut that candy mouth of yours and don't step in where you're not wanted!" flashed Brackett, bristling with antagonism.

At this moment the girl came with a pitcher of water, which she handed in to the doctor. "Wait a minute, miss!" Brackett called. But the girl ran for the house like a frightened deer. Brackett leered at the doctor. "She'll listen to me yet," he promised. "Got a drink of that water to spare?"

"I suppose so," grunted the doctor. He turned and took up the glass, his back to Brackett. Then he reluctantly handed the glass to Brackett, who drank thirstily. As he finished, he caught sight of a small pillbox in the doctor's hand. "What's that?" he asked suspiciously, putting down the glass.

"Oh, a little box," said the doctor, his eyes brightening. He opened it, disclosing three white tablets. Then, quick as a wink, he hurled box and tablets through the door into the night.

Brackett's gun was out and his eyes were spurting red. "Did you put some in my water?" he demanded.

"Be calm." The physician smiled. "I'm only a poor old doctor with a sugar mouth. But I know my trade. I put one tablet in your water . . . don't you get a bitter aftertaste?" Brackett instantly imagined he did. His face paled a bit.

"After Campbell has had his rest, I'll give you an antidote for the poison," the doctor said softly, with a cunning glance. "And no living person within miles and miles . . . and miles . . . of here can stop that dose from killing you in four hours or less, Mister Brackett. Now, you can have my gun if you wish. You can kill me and die as surely as the sun rises this morning . . . which it will . . . or you can be quiet and live."

Brackett's face had turned livid with fear. He raised his gun and swore a terrible oath. "By the heavens you give me the stuff to stop it now, or I'll shoot you while I can still pull the trigger!" he cried.

The doctor stood straight, his face pale. "Brackett, I'm an old man. I'm not afraid to go. As we're not going to the same place. I'm happy in the thought of never seeing you again, here or hereafter. Shoot, you coward, shoot!"

Every dark emotion ever experienced flitted across the killer's face and left stark terror burning in his eyes. He dropped limply upon a bunk. "I'll wait three hours," he managed to say tremblingly.

The doctor turned leisurely and went out.

Ricky had ridden away slowly. He was loath to leave the Campbell house, and, now that he thought of it, he could have contrived to have Slim go in his stead. Far down the trail three muffled echoes were brought to his ears on the wind. He pulled his horse up and listened. "I'd bet anything those were shots

. . . three of 'em," he muttered aloud, looking back over the way he had come. If they were shots, he could think of no place they would come from except the Campbell place. Three of them. He could imagine Brackett arriving there and the three shots coming from Vagle, Brackett, and Slim. But how could he have failed to miss Brackett on the trail if he had come that way? Had the man come from over the mountains, or by some other route? How could he know where Campbell lived? Why should the shooting start so quickly?

Thus he sat his horse and conjectured. Finally he became so uneasy that he turned back, thinking this time to send Slim on the errand. Slim was fast, but not fast enough with his gun to stand up against this Brackett, according to reports.

Ricky's turning back made it possible for Slim, riding hard on Bismarck, to meet him much sooner than he had expected. In a few short, breathless words, Slim explained what had happened.

"Go on to town and tell the sheriff the message and bring him back with you," Ricky commanded in a hard tone. "Leave the rest of it to me."

In another moment he was pushing Soldier hard on the back trail.

A short time after Brackett had drunk the water, the swift pound of Ricky's horse was heard on the uptrail. Hope and the doctor hurried to the porch as John Campbell roused, wide-awake. He heard the doctor's shout and it was enough. "My gun!" he cried. "Jane, my gun! I just had a dream. . . ." He pushed the bandage up from his eye, and swung from the couch.

Brackett also had heard. He forgot everything except here might be an enemy. He ran from the bunkhouse into the moonlit yard, just as Ricky flung himself from his horse. "It's Brackett!" he heard the girl cry. Then Brackett remembered. "Don't shoot!" he cried, elevating his hands. Then he saw the doctor at the end of the porch, laughing. He had been tricked. There had been nothing in the water!

His gun cracked on the early morning air as the doctor dropped to let the bullet whip over his head. Then appeared the weird, white form of John Campbell on the porch, gun in hand, the bandage pushed up from his right eye. Campbell shot the second he sighted Brackett. Then he dropped on a chair. "Jane! Jane!" he shrilled. "The bandage has dropped. Fix it quick, fix it . . . !"

The faltering words were drowned in Hope's wild cry. "Kill him, Ricky . . . kill him!"

Ricky had leaped forward and Brackett caught sight of his flying form and whirled on him.

"Go to it!" Ricky cried.

Brackett's gun came up like the snap of a whiplash and lunged in the act of firing from the hip as three bullets struck him in the chest as fast as a pencil could be tapped on paper. He went down firing his last shot aimlessly in the air.

Ricky dropped his gun to catch Hope in his arms and Jane was crying to her husband that Brackett had lost. The doctor led John Campbell, walking firmly, into the house, while Hope was hugging and kissing her gunman lover with the moon looking coldly down.

Sheriff Lane, Slim, and Crowell were there shortly after dawn. They talked briefly with Campbell, who was active and cheerful. The doctor came in with the word that he might have to stay another day. "I'm pulling him through," he said with a tired smile.

Then the sheriff said: "This ends it, John. You understand, Adam? We'll forget everything and you can come to town with me to get Ira. He feels plenty mean about it all, so don't ever throw it up at him."

Lane shook hands with Campbell, Jane, Hope, and the doctor. "Call Ricky and Slim," he ordered. When they came, he shook hands with Slim and turned to Ricky. "Everything's jake," he said, taking the youth's hand. "Everything, and it's lucky your dad taught you so well."

Then Lane and Crowell departed.

That afternoon, John Campbell gathered his wife, Hope, and Ricky about him. Over a glass of the mildly stimulating wine, he told them of the tempestuous years when he had been known as Terror Jack, under Brackett's banner, and of the job he had pulled with Pearlman. When he had finished, he took a sip at his glass and looked about him.

Jane's look was brave and admiring. Hope had edged away from Ricky at the first, but he had drawn her into his arms, stroking her hair and kissing her.

When Campbell had finished, Ricky rose and extended his hand, which Campbell gripped fiercely.

"Mister Campbell," said Ricky in a confiding voice, "I never like to hear bygones, so while you were talking I was thinking of Hope's future and mine so hard I didn't hear a word you said. That's final. If it's all right with you and Missus Campbell, Hope and I are going to be married in December. We'll all go down to my ranch, where it's a little warmer in the winter. What do I hear?"

Jane had gone to her daughter and taken her into her arms.

"I might have known it all along," said Campbell, his eyes quickening. "And we'll take that old wizard, Vagle, along. He told the doctor we'd have no more trouble 'cause the loons are dead."

Ricky and Hope went out, hand in hand, to view the glory of the sunset. Ricky pointed to the sky. "It's all rosy," he said, "just like our lives are going to be."

"Oh, Ricky,"—there was a sob in the girl's voice—"after all

this . . . this . . . everything. . . ."

"It came along just right to make us all the happier afterward," whispered Ricky in her ear. "Forever . . . just you and me . . . to live for each other and to love. . . ."

Their arms were about each other as they kissed.

"So long, folks!"

They separated to find Slim sitting his horse near them.

"Why . . . where you going?" Ricky asked

"I'm going to stop in Pondera tonight, and tomorrow I'm going over Fort Benton way to see if a certain girl has real red hair or if it's dyed. If it is dyed, I'll never have anything to do with girls again."

"You know a ranch girl wouldn't dye her hair, you bluffer," Ricky accused while Hope laughed happily. "Where would they get the stuff to begin with? Tell me that?"

"Where'd the Indians get their stuff to paint up with?" returned Slim, touching his horse with the spurs. "Think that over, you big stiff, and I'll see you both later. Of course, I throw you my congratulations."

He galloped away with a hand upflung, and Hope threw a kiss at him as she and Ricky walked out into the first purple mist of twilight.

ABOUT THE AUTHOR

Robert J. Horton was born in Coudersport, Pennsylvania in 1889. As a very young man he traveled extensively in the American West, working for newspapers. For several years he was sports editor for the Great Falls *Tribune* in Great Falls, Montana. He began writing Western fiction for Munsey's *All-Story Weekly* magazine before becoming a regular contributor to Street & Smith's *Western Story Magazine*. By the mid-1920s Horton was one of three authors to whom Street & Smith paid 5¢ a word—the other two being Frederick Faust, perhaps better known as Max Brand, and Robert Ormond Case. Some of Horton's serials for Street & Smith's *Western Story Magazine* were subsequently brought out as books by Chelsea House, Street & Smith's book publishing company. Although all of Horton's stories appeared under his byline in the magazine, for their book editions Chelsea House published them either as by Robert J. Horton or by James Roberts. Sometimes, as was the case with *Rovin' Redden* (Chelsea House, 1925) by James Roberts, a book would consist of three short novels that were editorially joined to form a "novel" and seriously abridged in the process. Other times the stories were magazine serials, also abridged to appear in book form, such as *Unwelcome Settlers* (Chelsea House, 1925) by James Roberts or *The Prairie Shrine* (Chelsea House, 1924) by Robert J. Horton. It may be obvious that Chelsea House, doing a number of books a year by the same author, thought it a prudent marketing strategy to give the author more than one name. Horton's Western stories are concerned most of all with character, and it is the characters that drive the plots rather than the other way around. Attended by his personal physician, he died of bronchial pneumonia in his Manhattan hotel room in 1934 at the relatively early age of forty-four. Several of his novels, after Street & Smith abandoned Chelsea House, were published only in British editions, and Robert J. Horton was not to appear at all in paperback books until quite recently.